BERT
BREEN'S
BARN

New York Classics
FRANK BERGMANN, SERIES EDITOR

BERT BREEN'S BARN

BY
WALTER D. EDMONDS

SYRACUSE UNIVERSITY PRESS

SYRACUSE UNIVERSITY PRESS EDITION 1991
91 92 93 94 95 96 97 98 99   6 5 4 3 2 1

Publication of this book is through arrangement
with Little, Brown and Co. Inc.

Illustrations from AN AGE OF BARNS by Eric Sloane. Copyright © 1966
by Eric Sloane. Reprinted by permission of HarperCollins Publishers.

This book is published with the assistance of a grant
from the John Ben Snow Foundation.

The paper used in this publication meets the minimum requirements
of American National Standard for Information Sciences—Permanence
of Paper for Printed Library Materials, ANSI Z39.48-1984.∞™

Library of Congress Cataloging-in-Publication Data
Edmonds, Walter Dumaux, 1903–
    Bert Breen's Barn/by Walter D. Edmonds.—Syracuse University
Press ed.
        p.   cm.—(New York classics)
    Illustrated by Eric Sloane.
    Summary: A young man attempts to claim ownership to an old
barn rumored to contain a hidden treasure.
    ISBN 0-8156-0255-3
    [1. Country life—Fiction.]   I. Sloane, Eric, ill.   II. Title.
III. Series.
PZ7.E247Be   1991
[Fic]—dc20   90-24308
                                                              CIP
                                                               AC

To my "English daughter"
Priscilla Owens
and, by extension, my "English granddaughters"
Philippa and Catherine
to whom I told Tom Dolan's story
some years ago

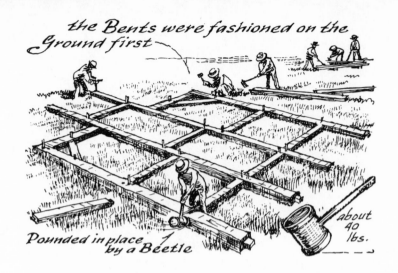

the Bents were fashioned on the Ground first

Pounded in place by a Beetle

about 40 lbs.

This is the way they built the barns

① *The* FOUNDATION

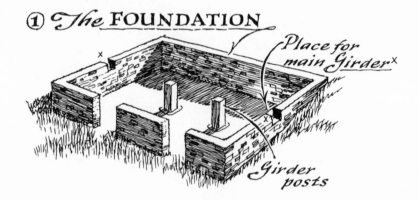

Place for main Girder ×

Girder posts

② *Laying* SILLS

over the Oak Main Girder

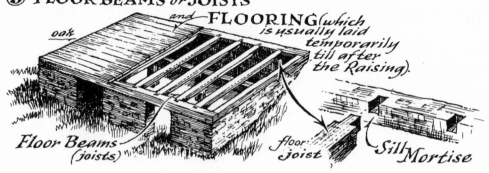

Laying the
③ FLOOR BEAMS or JOISTS
and FLOORING (which is usually laid temporarily till after the Raising).

oak

Floor Beams (joists)

floor joist

Sill Mortise

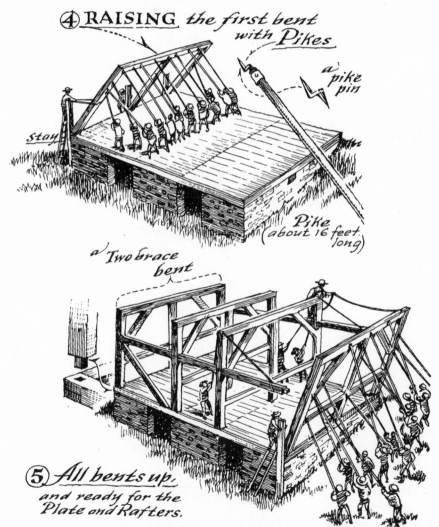

④ RAISING the first bent with Pikes

a pike pin

stay

Pike (about 16 feet long)

a Two brace bent

⑤ All bents up, and ready for the Plate and Rafters.

PART ONE

1

Bert Breen and his wife Amelie were among the first to settle in the sand-flat country across the Black River. They bought them a homestead lot and added some to it on the far side of the only hill you can see in that stretch of country. There are wooded rifts where the small brooks run down to the river valley and the richer bottom land. But the hill on their place was the only hill there was. After a time people came to call it Breen's Hill.

They started a farm. In the first years Bert put up a small barn. He cut spruce for the timbers, clear-grained spruce he felled in the swamp beyond his place and hauled to Hawkinsville to get sawed the size and length he wanted. The same with the board siding and roof boards. It was a plain-built barn and you could see light through the cracks in the siding but the roof was tight and the frame was as solid as any you could find in the country — fashioned in the old way with mortises and tenons and all pinned tight. When he had that finished he turned his time to putting up a frame house for himself and Amelie to replace the log shack they had used till then. He put it up on the side of the hill a bit above the barn, and from the front stoop you could see out east across the big swamp, gray and empty-looking in fall, so it seemed to some as if he had built his house on the outside edge of the world and looked off into nothingness. When they asked him why he hadn't built his house on the west side of the hill, where there was a view of the river valley beyond the wide belt of sand-flat country, he said that to a man his age it meant more to see the sun coming up than going down.

[2]

They lived in that house together for over thirty years. During that time half a dozen people bought land and put up houses along the road leading into Breen's. They started farms and worked the land for all it was worth. Sand land like that, when it was first opened, grew grand crops; but in a few years the forest loam began to give out, the sand came up through the crops, and you couldn't grow enough to feed a run-down rooster. People started moving out and by 1889 there were six empty houses along the road to Breen's. Now and then a family like Chick Hannaberry's would move into one. They'd stay there till the roof leaked too much for Chick to want to patch it, and then he'd pick out the best one left and move into it.

He and his family just scratched a living. His wife was dead, but he had five daughters and all summer he had them out picking berries or hunting ginseng while there was still a market for it. He raised some chickens, kept a stringy little cow that gave milk in small amounts for a few months whenever she happened to have a calf. None of them had much more clothes than those they carried on their backs, but Chick seemed a happy man. He was free to do whatever he fancied, which was mostly nothing, and there was no rent to pay on any of those tumbledown houses.

There wasn't because Bert Breen had bought them and the land with them. He got them for next to nothing. Once in a great while when he was in Boonville to trade for groceries, the bank president, Oscar Lambert, would tell him he was throwing away his money on that worn-out land. But Bert said he liked to have the road without no neighbors on it. The Hannaberrys, he said, weren't a bother, even when they came around begging salt or sugar

[3]

or something. If you didn't want them around, you told them, "Scat!" and they took off like little rabbits. Like quail, more like, maybe.

It bothered Oscar. He didn't know where Bert found the money even for that cheap land. Bert certainly didn't have an account with his bank, which was the only one; and Bert wasn't ever gone long enough to go to bank in Lowville or even Barneveld. It would have bothered Oscar even more if he had known Bert had been buying property here and there all around the county. He transacted through Billy-Bob Baxter, who had a small law office on Leyden Street and whom a lot of people didn't trust. The property was picked up under proxy names. Oscar Lambert would have been bothered a lot more if he had known of this going on, not because of Bert Breen buying up property, but because he did not know where Bert got his money from or where he banked it. Bert wasn't bothered by that because, naturally, he knew.

When Bert died in the spring of 1890, people wondered what his widow would plan to do. Except for the Hanna-berry family no one lived within a mile of her place. They expected she would have to move into town. But she fooled them. She went right on living in the house they'd built on the east slope of Breen's Hill. She came to town a few times, till Bert's will had been probated. It left all his property to her. That was all it did say; didn't mention another soul. It bothered Oscar Lambert more than ever. He didn't know a thing. But he had a nose for money. He knew it must be somewhere. He finally edged a question or two at Billy-Bob Baxter.

"I don't know no more than you," Billy-Bob said. "He always had the money when he needed it."

"He must have banked it somewhere," Oscar said.

[4]

"He never told me nothing," Billy-Bob said. "Except that he wouldn't trust no bank."

"Not even me? He was always friendly," Oscar said.

"Least of all you, I'd say," Billy-Bob told him.

"You see Amelie sometimes?" Oscar asked.

"Well, it's hard to say. Maybe once in a while."

Billy-Bob enjoyed seeing Oscar Lambert wriggling after answers and getting nowhere. Not that he could have told him much of anything anyway. Amelie went back to her house and stayed on alone. She kept chickens, but she sold off the four cows Bert had kept. She put in a small potato patch every spring and made a garden and she kept a large-size dog that had come out of the woods one evening nearly starved to death. Those few that went to her place to see her said it looked as much like a wolf as a dog.

Among those who did see her at home from time to time was the Hannaberry family. They still came to borrow as they always had, but sometimes Chick would stop by to leave a couple of trout, probably off one of his set lines in Armond's pond down in the valley. Sometimes he sold such trout to the Armonds themselves, but if they weren't home, he brought them back for his own use or to give to Amelie. It was a cheap way to repay her for the sugar.

There weren't so many Hannaberrys around any more. Four of the daughters had got themselves married and moved away. The one that lived nearest was Polly Ann. She had married Nob Dolan, who had a small farm down in the valley off the Moose River road, below Fisk Bridge. She was the prettiest of the sisters, a small girl with light-brown hair. Her head didn't come up even to Nob's shoulder, but people said she surely had bettered herself. Only it didn't turn out that way.

Nob Dolan proved to be as shiftless as her father had

[5]

been, and almost right away she was working to keep her new home together, just as she had tried to do in the Hannaberry family. As soon as Nob found out how well she could manage, finding food in the woods an ordinary person wouldn't dream was there, or wheedling eggs out of hens, or minding his small bunch of cows, he started leaving everything to her. He didn't just go off fishing or hunting rabbits the way her father had. He spent his time circulating among the bars and taverns, using up his money while his small buildings ran down. He turned out to be just about a total no-good.

Five years after their marriage he disappeared. Nobody knew where he'd gone or what had happened to him. Mostly nobody cared. But it was different for Polly Ann. Not that she wasn't as well or maybe better off without him. But there she was, a young woman not yet twenty-eight, living alone. In some ways having a man around, even if he is no good, is better than having none. And by then she had three children to look after as well as her rickety buildings. They were a boy and two younger girls who were twins.

2

She named the boy Tom, after her mother's brother, who had been the only successful member of the family she had ever heard about. She had never seen him because he lived out in the western part of the state, and naturally he never showed any interest in the Hannaberrys. But her mother liked to tell about him as long as she was alive. He had run a grocery store and had even risen to become a justice of the peace. Not many families could boast of a relation like that and Polly Ann hoped that naming her

[6]

son for this great-uncle might put the boy on the road to higher things.

Though she had never seen Great-Uncle Tom nor even a piece of paper with his writing on it, she would tell stories of his achievements to little Tom and describe his big house and the horses and carriages he had and the difficult legal decisions he had to make as a justice of the peace. It got in time so that she believed these stories she made up. Great-Uncle Tom became as real to her as her father, Chick, and a good deal more important in her thoughts. But whether the tales she told made any impression on Tom was hard to say.

He liked just as much the stories she told about herself when she was young and how Chick Hannaberry would take his five daughters back in the woods after blackberries, where the vines grew so tall and thick that the only way to get at the berries was to go along the tunnels the bears made. Doing that was easier for little girls than a grown man, so he sent them off each down a tunnel and told them to think nothing of the bears. One day Polly Ann smelled something sour up ahead in the shadowy green tunnel and when she turned the next corner came almost bump up against the rear end of an old boar bear. He had his head up and with one paw was raking the berries off into his mouth. And then he turned his head and looked at her. She felt her heart come up in her throat like a water-wet weasel. But the bear found the berries more interesting to him than a scared small girl and went back to his work. After a minute she started tiptoeing backwards and once she got around the corner she turned and ran.

But when she got out, Chick Hannaberry said of course the bear hadn't hurted her. It did no good her crying. He

[7]

made her go right back to picking. Berries was what they got cash money with, mostly. When they had their five-gallon pails full, Chick would take them home and hitch the old white horse to the spring wagon and they would drive across the sand flats and down into the valley to one or another house of the rich people, like the Armonds' or the Boyds' across the river. Chick wouldn't go up to the house himself. He always sent one of his daughters, with a five-gallon pail, which was about all she could manage to carry, and she would go up the back steps, barefoot, her clothes draggled from the berry vines tearing them, and ask if the lady wanted some berries. Mostly the lady would, because Chick knew where to find the long woods berries that were sweet and juicy when nobody else could — him and the bears.

Polly Ann said that if she had been Great-Uncle Tom's daughter instead of his niece she wouldn't ever have had to go to the back door of the Armond house looking that way, scratched and barefoot. Because she was the oldest it wasn't long before her sisters, one after another, took over this chore. Chick knew how difficult it was to say no to a little, ragged girl with a sweat-streaked face, lugging a five-gallon pail of berries. But it was almost as bad to watch your little sister go up to the back door and ask for the lady as to do it yourself. It wasn't that the berries they offered weren't the best anywhere in the woods. It was the way Chick made them do it. It felt like begging.

Her thin, birdlike voice hardened as she talked about these things, but Tom sometimes thought that it must have been a pretty good way to live, away off from other folks, picking berries if you had to, and poaching trout out of Armond's brook and pond, instead of sticking to the chores in the barn and around the fields and garden, small

[8]

as they were. From the time he was five Polly Ann expected him to hunt up the cows and bring them home. There were only four of them and they were small, too, like the place, being bred down from some little Swiss cows someone had brought over from Europe years ago because it was thought they could get along on less pasture. That turned out to be true, but walking along in back of them he couldn't help comparing them to Massey's big Holstein cows on the farm below them. One of Massey's cows put more milk in a pail night and morning than all four of their own cows put together.

He would drive them into the barn and stanchion them in the wooden stanchions that looked old-fashioned compared to the steel ones down at Massey's. Their barn wasn't much more than a shack, anyway, with a mow overhead that was hardly big enough to store what hay the cows and Drew, their horse, ate during the winter. But he liked being in it at milking time, especially in fall and winter. While Polly Ann milked he would wrestle down the small amount of hay that seemed to satisfy the cows and then get Drew's share. Drew was a rawboned sorrel with a white nose and a watch eye and he would stamp solemnly with his front feet until he had the hay in his manger. The twins, as soon as they were big enough, would climb up into the mow and hunt up the kittens. There were always kittens, it seemed, and the two little girls would cuddle and play with them. Cissie-Mae and Ellie were their names. The girls' names, not the kittens. If the kittens got names, only Cissie-Mae and Ellie knew what they were and they didn't tell. The haymow with the kittens in it was the best place in the world for those two small girls and they kept it to themselves.

When Tom was maybe eight, Polly Ann allowed that he

was big enough to do his share of the milking chore. It made him feel proud to sit on his own stool, yanking at the teats and after a while getting the milk to squirt tinnily against the side of the pail. He was still too small to hold the pail between his knees. He had to set it on the barn floor. But he would bore with his forehead into the soft side of the cow and feel as if he had taken a step towards being a man. Time came, though, he began thinking what it would be like to have real Holstein cows in a barn with a cement floor like Massey's. It started him thinking about how poor they were. He noticed the way his mother had to work to keep things going, even as thin as their way of living was.

One day a week she took in washing for the four unmarried farmhands that worked at Massey's, and when he saw her bent over her tub and rubbing on the washboard with someone else's clothes than theirs, her hands all red and the steam in her face and hair, it made him feel bad. Three other days a week she went up to Boonville washing or cleaning for people there. She made what she could, too, in other ways, peddling the few eggs their hens laid, when she had enough to make a basket, and she churned twice a week, selling the butter to the houses she worked for in town. And Sundays when there were berries she took Tom and his sisters into the woods to pick them, but she never told him or his sisters they had to take them up the back porch of any big house. She sold them herself.

He started doing jobs around the place he hadn't done before, but there wasn't such a lot he could do especially when there was school. The school they went to was about two miles down the valley and just the walking to get there and get home took a big piece out of his time. He couldn't see anyway that what he was learning there was going to be of help to him when he started out to turn around their lives.

3

He discussed it hesitantly that summer with Birdy Morris. Birdy was an old man who lived alone back beyond Buck's Corners on a bare little farm that just kept him and his few animals alive. Somewhere, though, he had got hold of an old mowing machine and managed to make it workable. It sounded like a couple of boys dragging sticks along a picket fence, but the grass fell down behind the cutter bar just the same. Every year he came to mow Mrs. Dolan's hay. It cost two dollars and was the biggest expense item in Polly Ann's budget.

When he was a baby his mother had dropped him over the rail of the front porch — "Didn't do it a-purpose," Birdy always said, "just she was absentminded and heard the string beans boiling over in the kitchen." His shoulder was out of joint when she thought to come back and pick him up, and he grew up with it histed up close to his ear. He didn't think anything of it, though. Said it made it easy to shoot rabbits running left of him.

He never was bothered about anything. He seemed a happy man to Tom, his eyes wrinkled up, and a look on him as if he was thinking up a joke inside of him. At first this used to make Tom think Birdy was laughing at him, but in a while he came to the conclusion that Birdy's joke generally was on himself. It was as if Birdy were two different people and one was always laughing at the other. Neither one of those two Birdys seemed to think there was anything out of the way in a boy going on nine wanting to better his way in life.

"With this little barn you folks have," Birdy pointed out, "there ain't much point thinking about getting any more cows."

"I know that," Tom said. "I guess it will take a lot of time before I can make enough money to put up a decent-sized barn. Unless maybe I could find timbers somewhere to frame it with."

"Yes, and if you did, you'd still have to do some growing," Birdy said, "before you'd have the heft and know enough to get the bents up."

"Well," Tom said, "I thought maybe a man could find some good timbers in those old houses on the sand-flat country where Ma used to live."

Birdy shook his head.

"Most of them have fell down," he told Tom. "Except Widow Breen's. There's her barn, though," he added thoughtfully. "It's a damn good barn. I helped to put it up."

"Maybe when I get a barn you could help me put it up, then," Tom said shyly.

"Mebbe I could," Birdy said. "Only that old Widow Breen ain't likely to sell. Not that she's kept anything in that barn since old Bert died. And if she did she'd ask four times what it's worth. That old woman would pinch the specs off a blind man, Tom."

It took some of the steam out of Tom's hopes. Maybe it showed, for Birdy went on. "Know what? Later on, when haying's done, you and me might take a day and ride up into that country and sort of look around."

"I'd like to do that," Tom said.

It was a long time, though, before they made the trip.

Birdy often suggested things, but then he would find reasons for doing something else. During the next two or three summers he would show up once in a while on a Sunday to fetch Tom, but every time it turned out he had something else in mind for them to do. It might be he had discovered a new springbank down the river and nothing would do except for them to try it out before somebody else got onto it. He showed Tom where to fish and how to get trout in different kinds of water, just as he showed him how to snare rabbits in winter. Tom learned a lot from the old man, but he was in his thirteenth summer when Birdy showed up one Sunday, with his ancient team hitched to a rickety buckboard and said, "How about us driving up to take a look at Widow Breen's barn today?"

After so long a time, Tom was more than ready. "I'll go ask Ma for some lunch," he said.

"No. I got lunch for both of us. Climb on."

4

They took the road back from the river to Buck's Corners and then turned south towards Hawkinsville. In those days it wasn't more than a track running through scrub pine. The mailman was the only person used it regularly; but being Sunday he wasn't on his route, and they didn't have to turn out for a soul all the way to Hawkinsville.

The village stood on the far side of the river, houses lining the main road as it mounted the steep hill beyond the bridge. To the left of the bridge the sawmill walls rose right from the stream bank, with great piles of new-sawed scantling shining silver-yellow in the sunlight. Upriver was the stone and timber dam and the flume feeding into the mill, and from the foot of the dam the water roared over rapids. They could hear the sound of it a long ways up the river road.

They passed three farms in the valley, then the road forked, one way heading down a slope to run along the river and the other leading uphill through woods. Birdy said the first one led to the Armond place and went on past it; he turned his team up the hill. It was a long, heavy drag for the old horses. The fellies of the wheels whispered as they dug in the sand, lifted it and spilled it back in little cataracts. The horses stopped once of their own accord and Birdy let them blow for a couple of minutes before starting them on. When they came out of the woods at the top of the hill they were lathered around their breechings. It was a relief to have a level road ahead.

"Sure is flat country," Birdy observed. "First people came here thought they had the world by the tail. They had the best crops anywhere about. Then the sand came up through. There wasn't anything would grow for them. They all got out. Some sold for what they could get. Fifty cents an acre, I heard. Others just packed up their turkey and quit."

Ahead on the left was the skeleton of a house. Beside it the barn had crumpled under snow, the ends leaning inward towards each other, like folding hands.

"Entwhistles lived there," Birdy continued. "Nice folks. They made out real good while the land lasted, but they went like the rest. Her pa lived by himself down that road." He pointed his whip to the right, but the road was now closed off by barbed wire. "He always chewed the same kind of tobacco. Warnick and Brown. He died. His house is gone too. Ain't nothing left but the cellar hole."

Tom thought he had never seen lonelier country. It stretched out ahead, mostly coarse grass, with a couple of maple groves and a small line of woods. Beyond the woods the land seemed higher and on the right was a round hill, maybe a hundred feet higher than the rest. It was the only break against the horizon.

"That's Widow Breen's hill," Birdy said.

It was maybe half a mile away, and they passed three more deserted broken-down houses before they came abreast of it. Birdy named the people to which each had belonged. He said something about each one, so you could almost see them the way they used to be living there, but Tom had a shivery sense that they were ghosts.

"That's the old Meyer place. Your ma lived there a spell, till the roof got leaking too bad. Then your gramp, he moved the family on up the road to Broom's house. It was from there your ma left to marry your pa."

The way he said it made Polly Ann seem to Tom like one of the other ghosts. He tried to picture how it was, whether she had just run away, or whether Nob Dolan had come to fetch her. He felt shy of asking Birdy about it. Maybe Birdy didn't know.

He brooded about it till he heard the old man saying, "I don't know where your folks lived before all that. They wasn't around when I helped Bert Breen put up his barn. You'll see it now when we get by this here line of choke-cherries."

5

Birdy turned the horses to the right through a gap in the chokecherries. It was hardly a road, just two lines leading through the silvery, dry June grass.

"Don't get used hardly any," Birdy explained.

Joe Hemphill, he said, came over once a month from the

livery stable in Boonville to take the Widow Breen to town to do her trading. "Excepting him, I don't think most anybody else ever gets back here. Nobody at all in winter. She must just hole up like a woodchuck."

The track through the June grass curved around a pair of maple trees and the Widow Breen's was just ahead. The house stood a way up the hill. Its clapboards, which had once been painted pumpkin yellow, had weathered to a dingy mustard color. The narrow porch across the front was bare except for a single decrepit rocking chair. Above the porch roof, a window light had broken and been replaced with brown paper. House and barn looked lifeless in the glaring sunlight.

The barn was at the foot of the hill, facing the house. If the mow doors had been open someone sitting on the porch could have looked straight through to the far end. Like most back country barns of the time, it had no clapboards and the unpainted siding showed daylight through the vertical cracks between the boards, which meant that there was no hay in the mow.

Birdy drove around the front of the barn to the far side, where there was some shade to leave the horses in. They got down from the wagon and came back to the front of the barn and Birdy rolled the wide door back along its track. Inside it was cool and empty, and Tom could tell there hadn't been any animals in it for a good many years. You couldn't smell cow, though there were eight stanchions — the old-fashioned wooden kind — on each side of the run. The run itself was made of timber, pieces of six-by-six fitted close, making a smooth walkway. At the far end were two horse stalls. All the stabling was made snug with an inside wall of matched boarding. He could see it had been a comfortable barn for beasts, comfortable for a man to work in.

He told Birdy that, which pleased the old man.

"You'd ought to come up in the mow, so you can see the way she's framed," he said.

They went up the open steps in the corner opposite the horse stalls and Tom looked up from the mow floor with its layer of dusty chaff. There was a lot more room than he had guessed, seeing the barn from the outside. There were two bents between the ends and he could tell that they had been built right. They stood plumb and square, the cross timbers tenoned and pinned and a top truss to carry the purlins. They had all been sawed on two sides. The rafters were round spruce poles, carefully matched; but he expected their top sides had been sawed, too, to accommodate the roof boards. It looked to him as sound as it must have been the day it was built, and he began thinking how it would be if he could buy it and move it down to their own place by the river below Fisk Bridge.

He knew, though, there wasn't any sense in thinking of it. He didn't have any money at all. None of his family had any. Just the same he knew exactly where he would set it up if he did have it. But that was crazy too. How was a kid going to move those timbers down seven miles of road? Let alone taking them apart or putting them up again if it came to that?

He walked over to the mow doors, so Birdy couldn't see how he was feeling and start asking questions. And being there he opened them, and a high harsh voice hollered at him, "Boy, what in hell are you doing in my barn?"

On the porch of the house just level with him stood an old woman in a faded gingham dress and a shiny canal-boater's black straw hat perched forward over her eyes. She was holding a double-barreled shotgun pointed about where his wishbone opened out above his belly and what impressed Tom most was that the muzzle never wavered a hair.

6

Tom didn't know what to say. But Birdy came up just then to stand beside him.

"Hello, Mis' Breen," he said placatingly. "It's just me showing young Tom Dolan the barn I helped Bert put up."

He smiled, showing his tobacco-stained teeth, and then thought to take his hat off, using his right hand, which, because of his hunched shoulder, made it necessary to turn his head to one side.

"We're just looking it over," he added.

She lowered the gun.

"Well," she said, "I don't like people nosing around my barn, or anywhere else here. But as long as I knows who is nosing I guess it's all right. Come up to the house and visit a while, Birdy, when you're done nosing."

"Yes, mam," he said, reaching out to close the mow door.

"I s'pose living alone the way she does makes her touchy," he told Tom. "We better get up to the house the way she says."

The Widow Breen watched them as they walked up the footpath from the barn with what might have been a smile tugging at her old and wrinkled lips. The youngster, already long in the leg, and the round-shouldered old man looked like a couple of boys who had been caught out. Pretty sheepish, she thought. She had always liked Birdy, though. He was the same simple honest person he'd been when he first showed up on their place.

"Come in and have some tea," she invited. "I made molasses cookies yesterday."

She opened the door and went in ahead. Stairs went up from the front hall and on the right there was a door open into the parlor. It was dusky in there, the window shades being down, but Tom saw a couple of fine settees with black horsehair covers, and a round stove with a polished nickel foot bar around its belly. He considered it a handsome room. But she led them to the kitchen at the back of the house, which was where she did her lonely living, and had them sit at the table.

The tea kettle was hissing on the stove and Mrs. Breen reached an old brown teapot off a shelf and stuffed a handful of green tea leaves into it. When the boiling water hit the leaves the bitter scent of them came out strong in the kitchen; but there was a big bowl of sugar and even on a hot day the tea tasted good. She put down a plate of the molasses cookies and said, "Well, Birdy. Who's this young friend of yours?"

Birdy Morris remembered he still had his hat on, so he took it off and put it on the floor behind his chair.

"It's Tom Dolan. His father, Nob, married Polly Ann Hannaberry. You'll remember her, no doubt, Amelie?"

"Yes, I do," said Mrs. Breen, "and I'm sorry she did not come along with the two of you."

"She wouldn't have wanted to," Birdy said. "She don't like to remember back to her early years."

The Widow Breen glanced at Tom, and he nodded.

"It's too bad," she said. "I'd have liked to see her. She was a small girl, but about the prettiest I ever saw."

Her thin eyelids dropped, and Tom thought maybe she was looking back into the years.

"Tom here," Birdy proclaimed, "aims to do better with their place when he grows up some more. Better than Nob, his pa, done with it. Nob's disappeared, Amelie."

"He never was no good," Mrs. Breen said with sudden tartness. "I saw it the last time I read the cards for Polly Ann. There was a man in them and he was no good. I told her, but she didn't listen."

Tom looked puzzled, and Birdy explained that the old lady could read the future in cards, or tea leaves, or sometimes by looking at your hand. "Used to be people around these parts used to say if you had anything you wanted to know you ought to tell it to the Widow Breen. But she was reading cards long before Bert died. Been doing it pretty near all your life, hain't you, Amelie?"

"Just about," she agreed, and almost absentmindedly she opened a drawer under the table and took out a pack of cards. She shuffled them in a quick arc from hand to hand. "If you like, I'll see if there's anything in 'em you'd like to know."

She put them down on the table in front of her, one by one, in an order that didn't make sense to Tom, keeping about half the pack in the bent fingers of her left hand. She studied the cards for a few minutes, her wrinkled lips pursed tight together, and told Tom, "Looks like your life *is* about to change. Looks like you're going to quit your schooling and make some money. Not a great lot of it," she added, to Tom's disappointment. She dealt out some more cards. "But there's quite a lot of money here later on. You ain't going to go around like a low-down Dolan any more."

She fell silent and Tom looked eagerly into her face.

"How long's that going to be, mam?" he asked.

"Long enough and not too long," she said. The corners of her mouth twitched and for a moment she smiled.

"It don't say where the money's coming from?" Tom asked.

"No," she said. But he had the idea she knew.

"Ain't there no girl in them cards for Tom?" Birdy asked.

"No," she replied. "He ain't going to be interested that way — anyway not before he gets his money."

She swept the cards together and poured herself another cup of tea. An old yellow cat came into the kitchen, from where Tom had no idea, and hopped up on the table beside her. When she held her teacup out to him he licked up a bit from it.

"Always had a notion for tea," she said.

"What's come of that big dog you had?" Birdy asked.

"Oh, he got old," she said. "Went off somewhere the way wild things do and didn't come back no more."

"You living all alone?"

"Me and Tabs here," she said. "But we keep company."

Birdy got up. Tom did the same. You could tell she was ready for them to go.

"Thanks for the tea," Birdy said. "Thanks for letting us see the barn and all."

"It's all right, boys. Come again if you've a mind to."

They went down to where they had left the wagon.

"Don't seem right to have your cards read and not get no notice in them about a girl," Birdy complained.

But Tom wasn't thinking of girls. He was thinking about money coming to him. "Quite a lot of money later on," the Widow Breen had said.

PART TWO

7

Tom didn't talk much about his trip up to the sand-flat country with Birdy Morris. He told Polly Ann that they had looked over the barn that Birdy had helped Bert Breen to build years ago, and he described how Mrs. Breen had asked them into the house to share a pot of tea and how the big dog had disappeared so she was living entirely by herself except for a cat named Tabs; but he didn't tell Polly Ann about her reading his cards and seeing money in them.

He didn't know what to think about that, but what the old woman had said about his quitting school and making money seemed sensible to him. He kept thinking about it through the last part of the summer. He always took time to think things over. If he quit school he would have to find work somewhere and he didn't know where a boy thirteen years old could get a job to pay him anything, even a boy who had grown as tall as he was.

Finally one evening when the chores were done and they had had their supper, he brought up the idea of quitting school. Cissie-Mae and Ellie had gone back out to the barn to prospect for a new litter of kittens, so Tom and Polly Ann had the kitchen to themselves. She looked levelly across the table at him, turning what he'd said in her mind.

"Where was you thinking of looking for work, Tom?"

He had thought about it a good deal. "If it was summer, I would try to get Joe Girton to take me on as a helper."

"Why him?" asked Polly Ann. "He works for the highway department most of the time."

"I know," Tom said. "He does their bridge and culvert

work. He knows how to lay stone and work with cement and putting up bridge trusses. I could learn a lot working with him, if he'd take me on."

"I don't see why you want to learn those kinds of things for," she said.

So he told her what he'd been thinking about pulling up their place into something better and how he believed if he could buy and move old Bert Breen's barn it would be a start to making a better farm. He told her the siding was warped and weathered, but the frame was still sound.

"Birdy says it's the frame counts," he told Polly Ann.

"That old man!" she exclaimed, half scornfully.

"I know, Ma. He likes shifting from one thing to another. But he did help build that barn. Birdy knows quite a lot."

"I guess, maybe," she admitted. "But where do you aim to get work if you don't go with Joe Girton?"

"I thought maybe I'd ask at Ackerman's mill," he said. "They're busy all the year. Winter don't make no difference to them."

"That's so," Polly Ann said. "But when you talk to Erlo Ackerman, you tell him Chick Hannaberry was your gramp. Him and Erlo used to go off fishing, and things." She grinned at Tom, and suddenly it came to him that she still looked like a young and pretty girl. "To tell the truth," she went on, "them two used to raise considerable hell one way or another when Erlo was young. But don't mention that to Erlo," she added. "Just tell him Chick was your gramp."

"I won't tell him," Tom said.

They were silent a while, and then she said, "You sure you want to quit school?"

"It ain't doing me any good right now that I can see. And I want to bring us some money."

She said a little stiffly, "Tom, I can make what we need for now."

"I know," he said. "I don't aim to give you all I make. I aim to save up maybe half of it. If I get a chance to buy Breen's barn, I want to have enough to make a down payment on to it."

8

Tom drove up to Boonville with Polly Ann next morning. It was one of her days for doing housework. Drew took his time on the long uphill grade between the river bridge and the canal, for he was getting to be an old horse. But he brisked up on the level going and came down to Mill Creek and on up the grade to the railroad crossing at a ringing trot. Coming into town, where there were other horses, to say nothing of dogs and people, seemed to put some ambition back in him.

Polly Ann pulled up beyond the depot. The mill was on the right, standing below the railroad embankment with Mill Creek running underneath. Four stories high, the first walled in limestone, the other three in clapboards weathered gray, it was almost as high as it was long. Enormous tall, it looked to Tom, thinking of Breen's barn, which had seemed big when he saw it with Birdy. Under the fourth-story window in the peak was a sign lettered white on a black ground:

ACKERMAN & HOOK
FLOUR AND FEED MILL
Est. 1831

He got down from the spring wagon and told Polly Ann that he would walk home, whether he got a job or not. She looked down at him a moment, her mouth working a minute before it got to smile. Then she touched Drew's rump with the whip and rattled off up the street to her day's work. Glancing up at the sign once more Tom turned down the narrow road to the mill.

A team and wagon was drawn up beside the loading platform and two men were dumping feed bags into the box.

"You looking for somebody, son?" one of them asked. His overalls were thick with grain dust and Tom figured he must be one of the mill hands.

"I'm looking for a job," he said. "If there is one."

"Well, sonny, you'll have to ask the boss. In the office."

The man tilted his head in the direction of a one-story projection at the front of the mill.

Tom looked and was embarrassed to see that there were steps leading up to a door which had "Office" painted on it; he had walked right by without even knowing it was there. He walked back, climbed the steps, lifted his hand to knock, and hesitated.

"Walk right in," the man yelled from the loading platform.

So Tom put his hand on the knob and with a kind of chill coming up his legs and the small of his back, turned it and stepped inside.

It was a smallish square room with plain board walls. A large round station stove stood against the left-hand wall with a door beside it leading into the mill. Opposite, two windows looked out against the green slope of the railroad embankment, but the sun was high enough now to shine down into them. At a table between them two men were playing checkers. Both turned to look at Tom when he came in and the younger one got out of his chair and came around to the counter where the high brass cash register was and pulled out a pad of order slips, asking, "What can we get for you today, my boy?"

That embarrassed Tom even more. He took his hat off, though both the men were wearing theirs. He started to clear his throat, but that turned out to be difficult, too, and when he did get his voice operating, it came out scratchy and high-pitched and he made himself repeat.

"I came to see if I could get a job here, mister."

He guessed that the older man with his white hair and bristly white beard must be Erlo Ackerman so the other would be George Hook, but he was afraid of misnaming them until he made sure.

"Well," said the man at the counter, "what would your name be?"

"Tom Dolan."

"How old are you, Tom?"

"Going on fourteen," Tom said, which was true enough and sounded better than thirteen.

"That's pretty young for a feed-mill job."

The old man's words came out with his breath. It gave them a rough, almost harsh sound, even though his voice was mellow.

"Now Erlo," the younger man said. "How old were you when you come to work here the first time?"

So now Tom was sure which man was Erlo Ackerman.

Erlo was looking up under his eyebrows at something on the wall back of Tom. Tom turned to look, too. It was a three-foot piece of polished dark walnut with letters which had been picked out with gold paint carved into it. They read:

> THIS MILL OPENED FOR BUSINESS
> THIS DAY
> *August 22, 1831*

His eyebrows, which were bushy and black, in contrast with his white beard, came down again, and Tom saw the shrewd eyes looking through them at him, like a badger's behind underbrush. But then he saw Erlo's mouth twitch a little underneath the beard.

"I was twelve, going on thirteen, George. As you well know. But there wasn't the business then there is now. Not enough to wear a boy down." He cleared his throat with a hawking sound and cast his eye towards the white china cuspidor in the corner, but he didn't use it. "But as you also know, George, I came out of a hardworking family." His eyes fastened on Tom's then. "If you're Tom Dolan, your pa must be Nob Dolan."

Tom saw the meaning behind that and felt the blood rush up into his head.

"Yes," he told Erlo, "Nob's my pa, but we ain't seen anything of him in eleven years. We get along without him. He wasn't much use afore he left, anyway." Then he straightened his back, facing both men. "And if it comes to that my grampa wasn't much for doing work, either. Ma's the only one who's ever worked hard in our family. I figure it's time I got a job, too."

"I didn't go for to rile you, son," Erlo Ackerman said. He rubbed his hand across the top of his brow, as if he was squeezing his memory. "Seems your gramp must have been Chick Hannaberry, Tom; but I don't remember which of his girls married Nob Dolan."

"Polly Ann," Tom said.

[29]

"Polly Ann," Erlo said, and nodded. "I remember her, now. Not much more than mouse high, George. Pretty girl, too."

His breath went in and out with a rough sound. Tom supposed old men might find breathing harder than when they were young. He didn't say anything; it didn't seem like a proper time to do so, with the old man rustling around with his thoughts and memories, mumbling to himself something about "a scalawag, that Chick was," half a-grin. And then he seemed to pull himself together. "Tell you what, Tom. We'll see what you can do for a week, eh? If it works out, then we'll keep you on."

He looked up at George Hook.

"Take him in and turn him over to Ox, George."

Tom stood still. He didn't know what to say, but he knew he had to ask anyway.

"What is it?" Erlo asked.

"I wondered what my pay would be," Tom said hesitantly.

"Twenty-five cents a day. I got ten cents when I started working here," Erlo said gruffly. "But twenty-five is what we pay a boy now, to start with."

Tom didn't know what to say, but Mr. Hook took him by the arm and led him through the door into the mill.

A maze, it looked like to Tom, with all the chutes coming down from the bins in the stories up above, the filled bags in ranks standing on end of the various meals, brans, flours, mixed feeds, and mashes, cracked and whole corn — some lettered in red, some in black, and some with no lettering at all — and the whole place choked with the smell of milled grain. It would take a long time, Tom thought, to learn his way around through all that.

At the far end a man was bagging bran. He worked in a

cloud of dust that puffed and thickened around him every time he opened the chute to fill a new bag. Tom had to admire the way he stopped the rush of bran at exactly the right instant with the bag filled out round and solid, then whipped a length of twine off a peg and closed the bag with a double hitch. He swung the bag to one side as easily as if it had been a pillow and stacked it in place. Then he turned as Mr. Hook spoke his name and stepped towards them out of his dust cloud.

"Ox," Mr. Hook said, "this here's Tom Dolan. He's going to work for us."

He was an old man, pretty near as old, Tom thought, as Erlo Ackerman, but a lot bigger, heavy-chested, with a bent-kneed way of walking that was like a bear's. When he put his hand out for Tom to shake, it was like taking hold of the butt end of a ham.

"Pleased to meet you, Tom," he said with a slow smile. And Tom felt more at ease than he had at any time since he had entered the mill.

Mr. Hook broke in to say, "All right, Ox. I'll leave him to you."

He walked back towards the office and the big man asked, "Ever worked in a feed mill, Tom?"

Tom said he hadn't.

"Well, the main thing is learning what's bagged where and which chute pours which kind of meal. Are them your good clothes?"

Tom said they were.

"Too bad to get them all dust," Ox said. "But I guess they'll shake out. I tell you what. I'll just finish bagging up this lot of bran and then you and me will go all over this mill."

9

That was how Tom Dolan went to work for Ackerman and Hook. The first day, going around with Ox, he found things confusing. It didn't seem he would ever learn which chute let down which meal or grain, and he wondered why they weren't labeled. He was too shy to ask, but then, before he knew it, he found that when Ox told him to pull a sack of laying mash or cracked corn, he went to the right chute instinctively. There was always a small identifying heap on the floor under the chute to check with, and before long he got so he could fill and tie off the bag almost as handy as Ox himself. Of course he didn't have the heft to handle the bag the way Ox could, but he could manage it all right with a hand truck.

Ox made it easy for him. He showed Tom clues to remember things by. When Tom got things wrong, Ox didn't raise his voice. He was slow and patient. Pretty soon Tom learned that his real name was Marvin Hubbard. He had two children, grown up and gone from home, and his wife was poorly. When he wasn't in the mill, he spent his time looking after her. Perhaps that was why he got to talking more and more with Tom and pretty soon having his lunch with him, when business didn't interfere.

Usually they went out on the loading platform if the weather was fine, sitting on the floor with their backs against the mill wall, shaded by the roof. The other two mill hands usually joined them. They were French-Canadian and brothers, Bancel and Louis Moucheaud, and they were inclined to be excitable, talking in loud voices and arguing with each other, or anybody else for that matter. They could never get Ox into a dispute, though. He only smiled at them and went on with his work, but one day he told Tom that in his opinion, if you translated their name into English, it would probably come out "much odd."

Sometimes their lunch would be interrupted by a customer driving down from the depot with an order. Generally Louis or Bancel would take care of that. Or it would be Mr. Hook coming from the office with an errand for Tom to run. The very first day he told Tom to go up to the pharmacy on Main Street for half a dozen Wheeling Stogies for Erlo Ackerman. But Herman Bondwin, the pharmacist, who didn't know Tom from Adam, was skeptical about a youngster coming to get stogie cigars like that and said Tom would have to have a note signed by Mr. Ackerman if he expected to be given any. Tom went back and told Erlo, and he got uneasy when the old man stared at him with hard and bulging eyes for almost a minute without saying a word. But then he heaved himself out of his chair and said, "All right, Tom. Come along and we'll go and have a little talk with Herman."

Erlo was slow and heavy in his walking but they got up to Main Street after a while and walked into the pharmacy. Tom could see Mr. Bondwin behind his dispensing counter, but apparently Erlo didn't because he went over to the tobacco counter on the other wall and brought his hand down three or four times on the desk bell standing on it, waiting there with his back to the store till Mr. Bondwin came around to wait on him.

"Yes, Erlo," he said. "Can I do anything for you?"

"You can," Erlo said, his breathing heavy. "You can give Tom Dolan here the six Wheeling Stogie ceegars I asked him to get me half an hour ago. You can charge them to my account, Herman. Or do I still have an account here?"

[33]

Mr. Bondwin put on a smile which Tom thought didn't fit his face too well.

"You sure do, Erlo," he said.

"Well, then," Erlo said, "if you'll put them in a twist of paper, and give them to Tom Dolan, here, I'll be obliged."

He waited, his breathing sounding through the store till Mr. Bondwin had done so.

"Herman," he said then, "now you know Tom Dolan works for me. If he works for me, he can be trusted. I knew his grandpa, Chick Hannaberry. I used to go fishing with him. And I knew his ma, Polly Ann, while she was growing up and the prettiest girl on the other side of Black River, and the prettiest on this side too, if it comes to that. And if I send Tom to you for six Wheeling Stogie ceegars that smoke pink and lilac, I want you to let him have them. You understand?"

He put his hand on Tom's shoulder and turned him towards the street door. They went out and they walked back down to the mill, just as slow as they had come up, and Erlo Ackerman didn't say a word more till they got to the office steps.

"You can hand me those stogie ceegars now," he told Tom then and went inside.

It seemed to Tom a strange way to take care of the matter, but just the same he felt good inside.

He felt as if he belonged there at Ackerman and Hook's mill. He had never had the feeling of belonging in a place with grown men before.

10

Tom was late getting home that first evening. The mill didn't close till six-thirty and the three-mile walk back to his own place seemed a lot longer than he had expected it would. But he went up on the kitchen stoop with the good feeling still inside him. Polly Ann came to the door with a kitchen spoon in her hand and her face flushed from the stove. When she saw the white dust all over his good clothes her jaw fell, but she didn't say anything. He could tell by the smell she had made corned beef hash for supper. It smelled fine.

"Hello, Ma," he said. "I'm back. I got the job. It's for one week, though. For trial."

She smiled. "Then you'll keep it, for sure, Tom."

He washed his hands and face at the basin on the porch shelf while she took his jacket and shook what dust she could from it.

"I'll wear my old overalls after this," he said. "But Mr. Ackerman thought I ought to start right in today."

She nodded. "Best not to think about it, Tom."

In the kitchen Cissie-Mae and Ellie were already seated at the table with a coloring book. They wanted to know what Tom had been doing up in town to make him so late, but he didn't tell them much. It was only when he and Polly Ann had the kitchen to themselves that he started to tell her how his day had been. When he got to the part about going up with Erlo Ackerman to see the pharmacist and how Erlo had said she was his mother and he had known her growing up and how pretty she was, Polly Ann turned pink. She said that was just nonsense and Erlo's noddle must be overaged. But Tom could see she liked it.

He told her he would get twenty-five cents a day to start with and she thought it was fair enough.

"They'll pay more in a while," she told him firmly.

After the supper things were cleared away, they went down to the barn to shut the doors, though Drew was the only creature in it — unless a new batch of kittens had arrived. It was dark and when they got back to the kitchen, Tom sat down at the table with a paper block and started to do some figuring.

It seemed to him he ought to put half his pay into Polly Ann's keeping for the family, and at twenty-five cents a day that meant that he could save $39 a year for himself, and most of that could go for buying the Breen barn — if Mrs. Breen was willing to sell.

Then he tried how it would go if he got thirty cents a day. It came all the way to $93.60 a year, out of which he could keep $46.80. At that rate the barn seemed a lot closer in reach. Then he wondered what forty cents a day would do, and by his figuring it gave him $124.80 a year. He stopped right there. He might never get to earn that much money in his whole life. It was too much money even to think about now. He was afraid doing so would make him softheaded. Still, he tore the sheet of paper off the block and took it up to bed with him. He put it in the drawer of the table that served him for a bureau. He didn't have to look at it, only to know that it was there. Next morning, when he got up, he didn't even think about it.

It was quarter to five, because he had to be at the mill at half past seven and before then he had to get the cows and help with milking, eat his breakfast, and walk the three miles to the mill. They would be slower than the miles coming home, being mostly uphill. Later on, when the nights got so cold they would keep the cows in, he would save some time, but then the walking would be harder, especially when there was snow. The town road crew didn't do snow plowing. Each farmer broke road with his sleigh from his place to the next and Tom wouldn't always be able to count on the road being plowed all the way to town.

But the fall stayed open well into December. With early dark Ackerman's closed earlier, and by that time Tom had got used to his job there. He felt easy with the men. Louis and Bancel Moucheaud every now and then would play a practical joke on him, but that didn't bother him; and Ox said they wouldn't do that kind of thing if they hadn't taken a liking to him. They never tried a joke on Ox. One man had, they said, a young fellow, six feet tall and muscle-proud. He had found Ox on the second floor of the mill and taken a measure of bran out of a hopper and poured it over Ox's head. They said it took a minute for Ox to clean his eyeglasses and get his eyes free of the bran. But then with a sudden move he had come up behind the smart aleck and taken him by the collar of his shirt and the seat of his pants and swung him up over his head. Louis and Bancel said that Ox carried the big squirt that way back to the bran hopper and with kind of a flip tossed him head first into it. It took the squirt quite a while to get himself upright in the bin and scramble out. He had nothing to say, either, to Ox; but he took his trade to Bisbee's feedstore on Main Street after that. Neither Erlo nor George Hook seemed to mind, though, when they heard the story.

The customers coming in from farms all over the township, and even from the neighboring ones over the county line, generally passed more or less time talking with the mill people, sometimes about the feed they were buying and more often about what was going on on neighbor farms as well as their own. In this way Tom now and then heard about the Widow Breen.

People wondered how she could go on living way off there all by herself. She didn't do anything except not die, they said. Some of their women thought it was cruel awful for a body to be left that way. But Joe Hemphill from the livery, who fetched her into town once a month to trade for groceries and such, said that was how she liked it. She was real chirpy for so old a body, he said, and talked quite a lot on their rides into town and back, but she wasn't interested a bit in what became of other people. She talked about the wild animals that came around her place or her cat, Tabs; only she was getting kind of worried about him now, him being so old.

Tom always tried to get to fill Joe Hemphill's order so he could listen to him talk about the Widow Breen. He wanted to ask how her barn was holding up, but he didn't want other people knowing he was interested in it. And every day something else turned up in the talk at the mill to run his mind from the old woman, at least until Joe Hemphill came again with his spring wagon for oats and mash for the livery horses.

The days spun out and kept getting shorter as December turned towards Christmas. His walk home now was in the dark and it was getting a lot colder. One night after eating, he looked in the box he kept his savings in and found he had thirteen dollars and a quarter saved. It was more money than he had ever had of his own. More than he had ever seen in Polly Ann's possession, at least that didn't have to be spent next day for groceries or to pay off some-

[38]

thing she owed on. It kept him awake for close to half an hour, wondering whether he should take some of it out and maybe buy some Christmas gifts for Polly Ann and his sisters.

He had no idea how much that would be, but just before dropping off to sleep he thought two dollars and a quarter might do it. It seemed a lot, but he had never had money to buy presents with before and he figured he could afford it. Next morning, though, it seemed an awful big fraction of his total savings. He tried putting a dollar back in the box, but a dollar and a quarter hardly seemed enough. Then he put the quarter back, but somehow it seemed better to leave the round sum of eleven dollars. Even so he didn't know whether the two dollars and a quarter would be enough to take care of the girls as well as Polly Ann. In the end he put the two dollars and a quarter in his pocket the way he'd planned and came downstairs.

It was biting cold when he went to the barn and still pitch-dark. His breath fogged against the light when he hung the lantern over the run between the cows. He had begun milking when Polly Ann came in, her cheeks bright from the cold, and he saw suddenly that she was a pretty woman, as Erlo Ackerman had remembered her being as a girl. Right then he knew that taking out the full two dollars and a quarter had been the right thing to do. He didn't know what he would find to get her. Something to wear, most likely; something pretty.

Thinking what he might buy for her helped to shorten his long walk, but as he came up the steep pitch to the canal bridge, it started to snow, a few scattered flakes whirling on the beginning of a northeast wind, and a long way before he reached the mill the cold had eaten in through his clothes. Ox took one look at him and hustled him right into the office where a big fire roared in the stove. Mr. Hook was there, sitting with his boots against the stove rail, but Erlo Ackerman hadn't showed up yet.

He came in, though, a minute later, pausing inside the door to knock the snow from his hat and shake out his overcoat.

Ox said, "I brought Tom in here to get warmed up."

Erlo nodded. "It's a long walk," he said. "And it looks to me it's going to get worse. Like winter's really got here now."

It seemed he must be right. The snow mounted up all morning and not many customers turned up. Bancel said you had to expect it. Beginning snow made it a time between rolling and sliding; there wasn't yet enough snow for a pung and a farmer didn't like to come with his lumber wagon for fear the snow would get too deep. They hung around in the mill with the doors closed onto the loading platform, occasionally going into the office to warm up, and towards noon Tom asked Ox if he could go up to Main Street in his lunch hour to do his Christmas shopping.

"Why, yes," Ox said. "I'd forgot it's only three days to Christmas. I better do my own, but you get along now. We won't need you here the way things are going."

11

There were three inches of snow on the sidewalk. The elm trees on the village green, which was shaped like a triangle, were white with it and the bandstand underneath them looked like a cake, sugar-frosted. He walked down Main Street under the storekeepers' signs looking for Baker's

Millinery. It was the first time he had ever walked along the storefronts with money to spend in his pocket, and he felt a bit strange and self-conscious. But he made up his mind he wouldn't let that stop him from going straight into the store.

Only it didn't work out that way. When he got to the store window there was a sheet that looked as if it had come out of a newspaper stuck to the inside of the glass. It said, SPECIAL PRE-CHRISTMAS OFFERINGS. There was a series of money figures and underneath the goods offered at that figure. The first was *10¢*, but it didn't include anything that looked suitable for Polly Ann. The next one was *17¢*. He couldn't find anything there, either, though it did list Hair ribbons, Silk, that might do for Cissie-Mae and Ellie. He stayed there, reading down the list with the snow thickening on his cap and shoulders, through *75¢*, where it said, *Here are goods worth $1.00 to $1.25, and the buyer saves the price of a dinner*, which Tom thought a tempting offer except there was nothing in it he fancied for Polly Ann.

The next group was headed *1.00: Items good enough for a Queen; cheap enough at $2.00*, which raised his hopes, but it seemed to include nothing but ladies' underwear, and he didn't think that was quite the thing a boy ought to buy for his mother.

So it came down to the final category, listed at *$2.00–$2.50*, and underneath it said, *Choicest Millinery Offerings this side of New York City. Even in the Great Metropolis you will not find Many Items duplicating These*. It surely did sound interesting, and then Tom spotted in the listed items Ladies' Fine Shirtwaists; and it seemed as if that might be just the thing to give to Polly Ann. A new shirtwaist, which she could put right on for Christmas Day itself. He drew a deep breath and with his hand clutching the money in his pants pocket walked into the store.

Inside the store there were a lot of counters, with salesladies behind some of them and a lot of female customers looking over the goods. They all seemed to be talking to each other, their voices high-pitched and excited, kind of like chicken voices in a yard, when one hen or another had scratched up something special. Tom felt a kind of wildness in his eye as he looked around. There wasn't another man or boy in the whole enduring store. It would have been easier if he had had any idea where they had the shirtwaists laid out, but he didn't, and all of a sudden he found that he was plain scared of asking.

But then a saleslady turned up beside him and asked if she could help him in any way, and he gulped and said maybe she could. But then his voice drew abruptly to a close, so she had to ask was there anything special he was looking for? And he said he was looking for a present to give someone at Christmas.

She asked, did he have any idea what kind of thing?

And he said, his voice back where it ought to be, a shirtwaist, maybe. So she took him over to a counter on the far side and asked if he had any particular sort in mind.

"It has got to be one of the two-dollar ones," he told her, looking up at her for the first time. To his surprise she was quite young, maybe younger than his mother herself.

"Well," she said, "we have some real nice ones. Do you know the size?"

That was something Tom hadn't even thought about, and he got to feeling desperate. The saleslady saw from the way he looked that he didn't have the remotest idea.

[42]

"Maybe we can figure it out," she said. "How tall is your friend compared to you?"

"It's for my mother," he blurted. "And she's small, not much over the top of my shoulder. I mean the top of her head's not much more than that."

"I see," the saleslady said. "Is she stout-built?"

"Oh no!" he exclaimed. "She's made real small."

"I see," the saleslady said again. "I should think that might be a thirty-four. You don't see too many ladies that size around here. I wonder if I might know her."

"She's Polly Ann Dolan," Tom told her.

She smiled. What seemed to him a very nice smile.

"Why, I know who she is," she said, "and I'm sure a thirty-two would be just right."

She reached into the counter and brought out several shirtwaists of that size and laid them out on top for Tom to take his pick. It took him a while. Costing two dollars, he wanted to make sure it would be one that suited Polly Ann's looks. In the end he picked one with a bit of ruffling around the neck and down the front where it buttoned.

The saleslady seemed to approve.

"I'm sure she's going to like it," she said.

He was mightily relieved, but he had another anxious moment when she took his money and the shirtwaist somewhere to the back of the store. However, in a few minutes she was back, handing him a done-up package, and the strange thing to him was that she said thank you after taking so much pains to help him. So he thanked her, which seemed more reasonable, and got out of the store as quickly as he could.

The snow was still coming down, heavier than before, and standing on the sidewalk, his hat all whitened with it, was Mr. Hook. He looked surprised to see Tom coming out of Baker's Millinery.

"Christmas shopping, Tom?"

Tom allowed he was. And then suddenly remembered that he hadn't got the hair ribbons he'd been thinking of for Cissie-Mae and Ellie. He grinned a little sheepishly at Mr. Hook, admitting he'd forgotten part of his errand.

"Well, go back in," Mr. Hook told him. "If you're quick we can walk back down to the mill together."

So Tom ducked back through the door. It was easier this second time and besides, he had seen where the hair ribbons were displayed and could go right over to them. A saleslady was standing there. She was older than the first one and got the transaction over in jig time. He bought a blue one for Ellie and a red one for Cissie-Mae, and paid her the quarter. When she came back with the ribbons in a package, she gave him his change, which meant that he had eight cents left over from his Christmas buying. More than he had expected.

12

Mr. Hook was still on the sidewalk when Tom came out. They turned up Main Street together, not hurrying, but making better time than Tom had with Erlo Ackerman.

"Got your shopping all done?" asked Mr. Hook.

Tom said he had.

"It's a good thing, giving presents for Christmas," Mr. Hook went on; but he sounded as if for him there wasn't much to it any more. Tom recalled hearing Ox say that Mr. Hook lived alone. His wife, Ox said, had gone off with another man not long after they were married. No one knew what lay behind it, but George Hook hadn't married again, though there were plenty of young women who would have been glad to oblige him if he had ever asked. He lived by himself on upper Schuyler Street, in a house which a Mrs. Conroy, an elderly, respectable person, took care of for him.

He and Tom didn't have a great deal to say to each other on the walk back to the mill. Whether because of his broken marriage or because it was his nature, Mr. Hook was not a man to talk a lot; and Tom's mind was full of the presents he had bought and what he was going to do with them when he got home that night, so Polly Ann and the girls wouldn't guess what he had been up to. They went on through the falling snow, which was a good bit deeper than it had been. A strong blue line of smoke was going up from the mill chimney.

"Must have put on fresh wood," observed Mr. Hook, and Tom allowed he must be right.

They walked down the road to the office door, but before Mr. Hook went in he said, "Any time it gets too snowy, Tom, you could spend the night in my house. I'd be glad to have you."

It took Tom by surprise. He wouldn't have thought of Mr. Hook's making an offer like that. But he had wits enough to say his thanks and added that tonight, at least, he'd go home even if it did get stormier.

"If I didn't show up, Ma would think something had happened to me and would probably come out looking," he explained.

"Well," Mr. Hook said, "if she knew you had a place to stay in town in a bad storm, then she wouldn't worry."

Tom said he would tell her, and Mr. Hook turned the doorknob and they went in.

Ox and the Moucheaud brothers were in the office with

[45]

Erlo Ackerman, and it was evident that some sort of argument had been going on. Erlo's breathing was heavy and Tom could see that, though he wasn't mad, he wasn't going to have any more discussion.

"This mill's stayed open until six o'clock in the winter," he said, "ever since I came to work here, and it's going to stay open till then, snow or no snow, as long as I'm running it. You can't decently shut a business like this earlier unless you advertise beforehand in the newspaper. How would you like turning up here with your lumber wagon if you was a farmer from way the backside of Jackson Hill, and finding this mill closed? You wouldn't like it a damn bit, and you know it. So we're open till six o'clock and that's that. Now, I agree there's probably not going to be many people coming, or any at all. So when you get the mill ready for bed, why don't you come in here and we'll have a pinochle game? But we'll be here, if anybody does show up."

They went off sheepishly. There wasn't much to do, and when things got shipshape they went back into the office, which was almost furnace-hot with the new fire in the stove, and they settled down with the cards. Tom had never played pinochle, so he settled down to watch. He would have liked to start home early, on account of the snow, but he wasn't going to ask after what Erlo said. He had to admit the old man was right, and he thought if he ever had the chance to run a mill, he would do it the same way. But it didn't seem likely that running a mill was something he would ever do. You had to have money to own one.

By quarter to four it was getting too dark to see the cards, though sunset was yet a half hour off, and Ox got up to light the office lamps. There were three of them, brass yellow-shaded affairs, that pulled down from the ceiling and pushed up again. One was over the counter, lighting the cash register; one was over Erlo's checkers table; and the third hung from just about the middle of the ceiling. When they were all lighted the office became a changed place, as comfortable and close, Tom thought, as their own kitchen at home. You didn't think of the snowstorm outside.

Inside the men went on playing pinochle, with Erlo Ackerman doing most of the winning. Louis Moucheaud said the boss kept them playing so they would be too poor to think of going any other place, but Erlo only gave a snort and shuffled for a new deal. To Tom it was amazing what his stiff-fingered hands could do in shuffling cards.

After a while he looked up at the old wooden clock on the wall at the end of the counter, and saw it was quarter to six. Mr. Hook looked up too, and said it was time to think of closing up. Not a customer had showed up in all that time, but no one mentioned the fact. Erlo got up and looked at his watch to check it with the clock and said the clock was five minutes slow. Ox went out into the mill with Bancel to lock the doors, and Mr. Hook suggested that Tom get going, considering the long walk home he had ahead of him.

Erlo agreed. "Yes, boy, you get started right now," he growled. "If you think you can make it all right."

Tom said he could, but he was anxious to lose no more time. He got his coat from the mill and put it on. He wound his scarf around his neck and pulled down the earmuffs of his cap. He buttoned his presents inside his coat and put on the red mittens Polly Ann had knitted for him last Christmas. Then he said good night and went out through the office door.

13

Outside it was black-dark, except for the lighted office windows. He could see the snow against them driving almost level with the force of the wind. It was going to be a heavy snow. It was close to four inches already, and he found it hard going up the road to the railroad embankment. There were more lights there, from the depot windows, and the down-track semaphore showed a tiny glittering point of green, for the midnight train from Ogdensburg and Watertown, he supposed, though it was five and a half hours till it was due, and if the snow kept on at this rate, it would be late, for sure.

He crossed the tracks and went down the steep grade of lower Schuyler which, when it stopped being a street, became the Fisk Bridge road, his way home. The wind did not reach down into the hollow. The lighted windows of the houses he passed showed the snow falling hard, but not driving almost level the way it had been up by the depot. The wind was still blowing. He could hear the tearing roar of it up above the rim of the hollow and he knew that when he came up towards the first canal bridge the storm would leap at him again. Luckily, however, the wind would be at his back almost all the rest of his way.

The wind was a different thing when he came up into it again. It seemed to have doubled in force. It took hold of him and he had to squeeze his arm around the packages under his coat to hold them safe. For a minute he doubted if he was going to be able to make it home, and he thought maybe he ought to turn back into town and look for Mr. Hook's house. But the instinct to get home, with his presents, was stronger. He went ahead, telling himself not to think of going back.

There were no lighted windows up here. There were no houses anywhere along the road till after it crossed the second bridge and had got down into the river valley. In the dark, with the driving flakes, there were no landmarks to follow. He couldn't even see the road edges. He would have to find his way by feeling with his feet, and the snow was getting deeper, packing into the ruts.

He felt near helpless. The storm now had him all to itself, the way a cat has its mouse. Whichever way he moved the wind had hold of him. The thing was not to stop moving. If he could keep moving through the upland stretch to the second canal bridge and down the grade into the valley, then the wind would no longer be able to grip him so tight. It was only three quarters of a mile between the bridges, he told himself. But he hadn't yet felt the planks of the first bridge under his feet. Maybe he couldn't with so much snow on the road. Maybe he couldn't even see the bridge trusses on either side. They were white-painted, the same as the white, howling dark.

He kept moving ahead, lifting his feet in turn out of the snow and stamping forward. Suddenly, not so much by feeling, and certainly not by sound inside that roar of wind, he knew he was crossing the first of the bridges.

Beyond the bridge the road curved slightly to the left, but after that it ran straight all the way to the next bridge and from there down into the valley. That wouldn't make it easier to find his way. He'd have to guess at what was straight ahead and every time he put his foot down wonder if he was still in one rut or the other. If he did go off the road entirely, there was a snake fence on his left to warn him back. There was nothing on his right except open land, not even a tree, so he'd have to keep favoring his left whenever he had any doubt of his direction.

This reassured him, but it did not make the going easier. Where the snow had begun drifting it was nearly knee-deep. He couldn't see a drift until he got into it and started floundering through, which made it hard to hold the packages safe up under his coat. Each time it happened he became more upset and angry. He wanted to punish the drift, kick it, hurt it some way, but there wasn't any way to hurt snow unless maybe by melting it. The notion of having to melt his way all the way from town to home was absurd enough almost to start him laughing. He felt better, and for a while it was easier to plow ahead.

He had no idea how long he had been walking since leaving the mill. It wouldn't have done him any good, either, if he had had a watch. He couldn't have seen it to tell time, with the wind and snow driving like a river around him. But only a little farther on he felt the ground pitch up under his feet. Then after a few feet it leveled off again, and his heart skipped a beat, thinking he must be on the second canal bridge. To find out he edged carefully to the left and presently he felt the bridge truss sure enough. In front of him the night seemed darker and he realized that he was looking straight out against the sky. At his next step the road slanted downward. He was on his way into the river valley.

Everything seemed easier now, though he still had half a mile to go. The snow fell just as thick, but the force of the wind eased more and more as he went down the hill. And all at once he saw a light ahead on his right, and then a second to one side of it. Before he could get opposite, the second light went out, and then another, small and dim and low to the ground, creeping through the falling snow towards the first — Mr. Quarry, he guessed, was coming back to his house after closing up his barn.

A larger light bloomed, sending a strong beam out towards him, and he saw Mr. Quarry mounting the kitchen steps and entering his kitchen. Then the door closed, but he knew what the kitchen looked like. Close to three times the size of their own, with a great black iron stove, dried herbs and onions hanging in bunches from the ceiling hooks, and the sink with running water in it. Mrs. Quarry had given him cocoa there a couple of times when he'd gone on an errand for Polly Ann; and he thought if he went to the door and knocked, the Quarrys would ask him in and she would give him cocoa as she had the other times. But he put the notion away. The thing was to get home with his packages and he began wondering how he would get them into the house without his mother or sisters knowing.

The light from the Quarry house was behind him now, but he found the walking harder. The snow was deeper and his legs had got tired and their muscles ached. He felt tired all over. The cold had worked in through his clothes for some time, and he kept thinking about getting into bed until it seemed the most important thing in his mind. He recollected hearing Birdy once talk about how a man got sleepier and sleepier before he froze, and he wondered if that was what was happening to him. He couldn't beat his arms to start his blood moving through his body for fear of letting his parcels drop, so he kept on going until, after a while, he found himself on Fisk Bridge with the river running under him. He imagined he could see the black slide of water to the rapids farther down. But it didn't matter now he was across with only a hundred yards to go before the fork where their own road turned off to the left.

It ran narrow, through close-grown spruce to begin with, with sharp curves, but the minute he came under the trees he felt at home. He didn't need to see to find his way. When he was seven he had boasted to Polly Ann that he could get home along the road blindfold on a pitch-black night. Now it was easier, for the snow made the road white under the dark spruces, as black as sorrow Birdy had once said of them. There was no wind, not even the sound of it, and the snow that came to ground dropped as light as flour sifted through a sieve.

Then the trees opened. The clearing of the small home meadow lay ahead, the lighted kitchen window in the middle of it, and the shadow of the barn beyond. He went on to the barn, opening the door carefully to make no noise, and went in, bumping at once against a wagon. He felt his way past and found a pair of horses hitched to it, standing placidly on the run between the cows — Birdy Morris's old team. The barn felt nearly as warm as a house with the extra animals and when he opened his coat to take the parcels out to hide them in the feed bin until morning, he began feeling warmer himself almost at once.

He closed the barn door as carefully as he had opened it and made his way across the yard. No footprints showed in the snow except his own, so Birdy must have come early and been persuaded to stay for supper. As he went up the porch steps, his tiredness took hold of his whole body. It was an effort to turn the doorknob. Cissie-Mae saw him first and let out a little screech. Looking down at himself he saw that he was plastered white with snow all over. Cissie-Mae said afterwards she had been sure he was a hant.

They were all sitting around the table, Birdy Morris with them, and Tom's own place empty at the end. Polly Ann whirled up out of her chair crying, "Tom! You poor frozen boy!"

She made Birdy grin. "Not quite," he said, around his humped shoulder, "or he wouldn't have got up them steps onto the porch."

"It felt pretty near that way," Tom said, enjoying all the fuss Polly Ann made over him, taking off his coat, shaking it, getting down on her knees in front of him to slap the snow from his pants and then unlacing his boots. He looked down on the top of her head with the wide rounded parting of brown hair, and grinned back at Birdy as if to ask him did he ever see anyone get as much attention as he was. His heart filled towards Polly Ann, and his sisters too, both watching their mother with round eyes. Looking down again at her smooth, pretty head, it came to him that he was now in truth the man of his family, and he was glad he had chosen such a fine gift for his mother.

14

They had finished their supper, but they all sat around the table to watch him eat, a huge plate of johnny cake with thick brown gravy saved from the Sunday roast of pork and cold white baked beans with vinegar on the side. He hadn't known he was hungry till he started eating, but there wasn't anything better to line a hungry man than johnny cake and gravy. Polly Ann brought him and Birdy and herself cups of tea from the teapot on the back of the stove, and the girls got themselves more milk, which they sipped until Tom had done eating. Only then did Birdy ask about his walk home through the storm.

He told them how it was, the hardest part finding his way across the stretch between the canal bridges. Birdy said he'd done well not to get confused or lost and Polly Ann cried that he shouldn't have left town at all, or at least stopped when he got to Quarry's. Tom said that Mr. Hook had offered to put him up in his house, but he didn't want Polly Ann worrying or maybe even coming out herself to look for him. Another time he would stay if it got really bad. Birdy told Polly Ann not to fuss. Tom, he said, had Hannaberry blood in him, and you might as well try to drown a mink as to expect a Hannaberry not to turn up, no matter what.

He went on to say, in a wry lopsided way, almost, Tom thought, like a raccoon peering sideways through the slats of a chicken coop, that while he didn't think this storm would last more than through the night, it did look like a big snow winter, with the black-and-white wasps hanging their nests so high, and the foxes' tails out thick as early as November. It wasn't a good idea to tackle that walk in heavy snow on foot. Polly Ann agreed and Tom had to admit Birdy made sense with his own walk home fresh in his mind, in the whole of his body for that matter. But he didn't like the idea of not getting back home nights, either. Birdy said, well, it applied just as much *getting to* the mill, too. He added that he would think about Tom's problem, but now it was time he was getting home, and thank you kindly, Polly Ann, for supper.

He put his coat on and they all went to the door and out on the porch to look at the snow. It was coming down wilder than ever. Tom's footprints going to and coming from the barn had been completely covered over. Polly Ann protested it was no time for Birdy to be heading home, and to her and everyone's surprise Birdy agreed. He would spend the night, he said, and in the morning he would take Tom up to the mill. His horses were old but snow didn't bother them and if the road wasn't open, they would break through, though it would be pretty slow going.

It proved to be. The snow was knee-deep in the yard when Tom went down to the barn before breakfast to start milking. He had to edge past Birdy's team, which had stood all night in their harness, to get his brush and shovel. He swept the square-timber floor of the run back of them and cleaned up the gutters behind the cows and took care of Drew in his stall at the far end. He shook down hay for the cows and horses and got his pail and stool and nudged the end cow, placed the stool and sat on it, and began milking in the warm barn smell and the soft crunching sound of the animals eating hay. He kept wondering how he was going to get his presents up to the house. For a while he could figure no way at all of doing it.

Then Polly Ann came in to milk with Birdy traipsing along and Birdy backed his wagon out by hand into the snow in the yard, giving it a good run inside the barn to have momentum enough to shove it well back in the deep snow. The barn got a darn sight cooler while he was doing that, but when he came back and shut the doors it warmed up soon enough. He offered to do the rest of Polly Ann's milking for her, and she thanked him and gave him her pail gladly, saying she would go and get breakfast started. It was then Tom saw how to handle his problem with the presents. He had just finished his last cow so he set the pail down and got the package for the girls out of the feed bin and asked Polly Ann to smuggle it into the house and hide it without either one of them seeing it. He said the best way to do that would be for her to tell Cissie-Mae and Ellie to come down to the barn to carry back her milk pail when Birdy got done milking.

His plan worked out fine. The girls came down, acting a little sulky to be sent down to the barn before breakfast, especially both of them having to come for just one pail of milk; but when he got the package for Polly Ann out and they saw the pretty way it was wrapped and found they were to be part of a secret, they got excited. They didn't see though, how they could get anything so nice and pretty-looking past Polly Ann who, they said, could see behind her back. So Tom suggested that Birdy go up with them. He would finish milking and bring both pails himself.

Birdy fitted right in with the scheme. He told the girls to wait on the porch till they heard a kettle drop to the floor. He went in and asked Polly Ann's pardon to wash his hands in the sink and took the saucepan of heating water from the stove and hit it against the edge of the sink and let her go, and the steaming water ran on the floor and across his shoes and he pretended to have a hotfoot, which got Polly Ann all concerned for him and with mopping up, and the girls got through the kitchen without her so much as noticing a thing. They sat down to breakfast feeling just fine, each in his or her own way.

There wasn't any school that day for the girls, and as Polly Ann didn't have housework in Boonville either, she said they would plan to find a Christmas tree in the woods. The girls had been making chains and cones and snow-flakes out of paper and intended to make more. They waved from the porch when Birdy had hitched his team to the wagon and Tom got up on the seat beside him and they turned out of the yard.

The old horses were accustomed to dealing with heavy snow. Their place back beyond Buck's Corners on the

Moose River road was, as you might say, the end of the line as far as farms were concerned, so they were always breaking road if they went out at all. Now they plowed on, methodically, a step at a time, and when they wanted to blow a little, they stopped. Birdy paid them no mind at all. The sun shone bright, without much warmth, out of a pale sky. There was no wind. He said he would lay in a load of winter provisions and get back to his place soon as he could. He didn't figure it would snow today or maybe tomorrow, but it surely would again on Christmas. Maybe he would stop by then snow or no snow.

That made Tom think he ought to get something in the way of a present for Birdy, too. That was the difficulty. You started giving some people presents and it turned out there were more besides you ought to give to. Birdy had seen the presents for Polly Ann and the girls. If he came by Christmas and saw gifts all over the house, it wouldn't seem kind if he had none for himself. He didn't know what in the world he could get for Birdy, though. And to distract his mind, he asked Birdy if he had seen Widow Breen this fall.

"I was up that way commencement of November," Birdy said. "Follered a seven-point buck half a day and came out at her place about four o'clock. The tracks led right plumb up to her house and when I got near I seen her setting out on the porch wrapped around in a whole mess of blankets. I told her hello, and asked her if she'd seen anything of a seven-point buck.

" 'Yes, I have,' she said. 'Only he wasn't seven points. He's a six-pointer. I know because I called him to the porch and told him where to go to shake loose of you.' "

Birdy glanced sidewise at Tom. He held the reins loose and paid no attention to his old team.

"Widow Breen told me she wouldn't have nobody hunting deer across her land so I might as well come into the house and have a cup of tea, and I did so. If she said she had told that six-point deer where to go to shake loose of me, there wasn't no point in keeping on after him. She can talk to animals, Tom, and they understand what she tells them, wild as well as tame. Some people think she's a witch because of it. I don't. I just think she talks to critters, that's all, and they understand her."

"Did she say anything about keeping on in her house?" Tom asked.

"No, she didn't. She talked some about that deer. Said she'd known him since two years back. And then she talked about me and Bert, and building the barn together."

"Did you look at the barn?" Tom asked.

"Sure I did, and it looked as good as ever to me," Birdy said. "Stands good and square just the way it has right along. She asked some about you, too. Wanted to know what you was doing. How you was getting on. She was kind of pleased to know you'd quit school and gone to work. Said the cards had told her that would be so."

Tom was surprised she should have asked after him. It made him think about the other thing she had told him from the cards — about his getting a lot of money later on. He wondered what she had meant when she said the time he'd have to wait before it came would be long enough but not too long. Half a year of that time had gone by already, but it worried him that someone else might come along to buy the barn, or that she might die and leave the place to some relation.

He asked Birdy how she seemed.

"She seemed well," Birdy answered. "Oh, she was slow and kind of cricky-moving, like any real old person. But she keeps her house neat as ever, and that old yeller cat lives with her still."

"Tabs," Tom said.

"Think of you recalling that old cat's name!" Birdy said admiringly.

But Tom found it easy to remember every detail of that visiting with the Widow Breen; and he thought now how lonesome it must be, looking out from the hillside at the white snow, the old woman peering from her window, the house at the end of the unplowed road. He didn't see how a person could stand it.

15

Mr. Quarry had broken road with a plow shoe and wing on the right rear runner of his big lumber sleigh, and the going was much easier. Birdy's old team didn't increase their pace any, however, they just didn't stop to blow so often. The trip from home to the depot took a full hour, but Tom was grateful he hadn't had to walk it. He thanked Birdy and got down from the wagon and walked down to the mill. The road had been plowed out and the turnaround by the platform shoveled clear. It gave the mill a new look: grayer, gaunter, and a lot taller than it had been.

What seemed to be a general discussion was in progress in the office when Tom entered, but for a moment all faces turned towards him and Erlo growled, "Glad you are back all right, boy. That was a worse storm than we realized."

Mr. Hook and Ox smiled and the Moucheauds nodded, good. That was that; Erlo went back to the subject, which was whether the mill office ought to install a telephone.

"This mill's operated since 1831 without a telephone,"

the old man said. "Now you tell me what we need a telephone for anyway."

"It would save time for Tom, here, running errands," Mr. Hook said. "Like going to the pharmacy and things like that."

"I don't see how he's going to get ceegars out through a telephone box hung back of the counter, there," Erlo said. "And it never hurt a young boy any to stretch his legs running errands."

"Well," Mr. Hook said, good-humoredly. "Suppose you'd forgot what Aggie wanted you to pick up for her at Baker's Millinery or Goodall's Grocery Store? You wouldn't want to lose Tom's time going all that way up to your house when all you'd have to do was leave your checkers for a minute and walk behind the counter there and turn the one long turn and three shorts, that is if your house is on the same line as the mill."

"You mean to tell me that we would have a mess of people hooked in on our line? Listening in to what I say? Or you say, for that matter, George?"

"No, that's when you have a party line. You don't have to call the operator to get someone else on your line. With us it would be better maybe, to have our own line."

"Then how do you get ahold of someone else?" Erlo demanded.

"You turn the crank one ring," George explained. "That gets the operator on your line. She says, 'Number please.' You give her the number of the person you want to call. There's nothing to it."

"Now look," Erlo grumbled. "How do I know what that number is? My memory's getting worse and worse."

"All the more reason why you need a telephone," Mr.

Hook interrupted. "Keep you out of trouble with Aggie, for one thing."

Erlo Ackerman thumped his fist on the table so all the checkermen jumped up.

"I see *that*," he said. "But how am I going to remember Aggie's number? Tell me that."

"Well," George Hook said in a reasonable voice. "Every telephone subscriber gets a telephone book of the neighborhood he lives in. It's got all the numbers."

"What do you mean, 'subscriber'?" asked Erlo.

"I mean you get your telephone put in and then you pay so much a month for the service you get. More, if you call any long-distance number. That's charged separately."

"You mean the mill has to pay *money every month* for a damn wooden box on the wall? You mean I have to pay for any telephone I have in my house, as well?"

"Yes," said Mr. Hook.

"And then I make a call long distance I got to pay even more?"

"It depends how far away the place is."

"You mean like Remsen? Like Lyons Falls? Maybe even Lowville?"

"Oh, those places, or even farther away."

"Utica?" asked Erlo.

"Sure," said Mr. Hook. "Albany or Rochester, maybe. Or even farther on, like New York City or Chicago."

"Well then," Erlo wanted to know, "I don't have books for all those places, do I?"

"Naturally you don't, Erlo. So you call the operator. She says, 'Number, please . . .' "

"Is that all that dumb girl knows what to say?" asked Erlo.

Mr. Hook ignored him. "You ask her for Long Distance, and she gives you the Long Distance operator, and then you say you are calling someone in Chicago or Des Moines, as the case may be . . ."

"I've never wanted to talk to anyone in Des Moines all my life," growled Erlo.

"I know. But if you did and didn't know the number in Des Moines, she would give you Information in Des Moines, and Information would tell you the number of the person you wanted to talk to and then you'd tell the Des Moines operator the number and she would ring the party."

"Turning her damn little crank," grumbled Erlo. Then another idea struck him. "*She. She. She.* Nothing but *she.* What is it anyway? A kind of suffragism? Ain't there any telephone *men?*"

"Oh, yes," George Hook said. "They run the business and take care of the wires."

"Wires?" shouted Erlo. "You mean if I call Des Moines — I ain't ever going to want to, but if I did — my voice would have to go running all that way along a damn wire?"

"Yes," Mr. Hook said. "Time will come when the telephone will reach into every corner of the United States, just the way it's doing right here in Boonville."

"You mean to say people here are putting in telephones?"

"Pretty near every businessman is doing so," George Hook assured him. "Bondwin's Pharmacy. Baker's Millinery. Goodall's Grocery. Both the banks are too. And Billy-Bob Baxter and Dr. Shoe. And Bisbee's Feeds."

"Bisbee! That chiseler. Cutting into our business,

which had done Boonville all right by itself near seventy years! He's got a telephone, you say, George?"

"Yes, I do."

"Why didn't you tell me that? No question about it. If that squirt has got one, we aren't going to be behind him. Order it in right away, George. Call the company and tell them I want to be hooked up by two o'clock this afternoon."

Mr. Hook smiled. "We haven't got it yet, Erlo. I'll have to walk up to the office and give the order. And then it takes about a week before they can put it in."

"Week!" roared Erlo. "*Week!* Who's the manager up there? I'm going up to see him myself."

"It won't make any difference. They've got so many orders for telephones they have to put them in by turn. Only fair way," Mr. Hook said.

"That so?" Erlo Ackerman suddenly relaxed. "If that's how it is, do you know something, George? It might be a good thing to invest some of our capital in this telephone company."

Mr. Hook thought it might not be a bad idea at all, and Ox observed sententiously, "In for a penny, in for a pound."

16

To everyone's surprise, except Erlo Ackerman's, the telephone wagon came down the mill drive early two mornings later, even though it was Christmas Eve. Behind the wagon was a two-wheel trailer, rather like a sulky, Tom thought, that had two or three telephone poles on it. Part of the crew took one of the poles off halfway down the grade and began digging a hole to stand it in. The ground was frozen, but not as deep as it would be later on. Another man unloaded two coils of wire, which he unrolled along the side of the road, first one, and then the other, and Tom realized, though he had never noticed before, that there were telephone lines at the top of the hill with a pole there serving the depot. Meanwhile a couple of more men came into the office, one of them carrying the telephone itself. He asked where it should go.

"In the corner, back of the counter, there," Erlo told him.

The man hesitated. "It's kind of dark there," he pointed out.

"Yes," Erlo said. "It won't show up as bad there. Anyway, you don't need light to talk, do you?"

"No," the telephone man said. "But light makes it easier looking up a number in your telephone book."

Tom could see that Erlo hadn't taken that idea into consideration. He hunched his head down in his shoulders and growled something sinister, like a bull grumbling between the bars of a bullpen.

"Look," the telephone man said. "If I hang it here next the window, it will be light enough to read the book. Easy for a customer to use if he has to, too, without his having to go back behind the counter, getting in the way and all. And close enough to the counter to be handy for your folks, Erlo."

He held it in place against the wall. "Goes good with the window casing," he said.

Erlo growled again. "Put it there," he said, as if that was where he'd planned to have it all along. He looked over at Tom, Ox, and the Moucheauds from under his brows.

[64]

"Seems to me I see Chris Oakum coming down outside, so you boys better get out in the mill and go to work."

They trooped out into the cold mill and Tom said to Ox that he hadn't supposed the telephone would be put in so soon.

"When Erlo makes up his mind something has got to be done," Ox said with his slow smile, "people around here get busy and it generally gets done right away. Maybe that's because," he added thoughtfully, "Erlo's done more for this town than most."

They took care of Chris Oakum's order while he stayed in the office, surveying the work going on there. But then other customers began driving down from the depot and his sleigh had to give room. For a while it seemed the news that Ackerman and Hook were putting in a telephone had got around the whole town, reminding farmers that they better check their feed bins, and all of them decided to stock up before Christmas. The mill crew were kept on the hop till near noon. Then when Tom looked out he saw that the telephone wires, shining new like silver in the frosty sunlight, stretched from the pole at the depot to their own pole and came sliding on from there into the outside corner of the office wall. The telephone wagon, which had been parked up near the depot, had gone.

In the office they found Erlo Ackerman and George Hook seated at the checkers table, but they kept raising their eyes to look at the telephone on the wall. It hung there, a box of shiny oak with two bells in line at the top edge, the mouthpiece jutting out and slightly upward, and the listening part slung from a cradle on the left side with its thick brown cord hanging in a loose loop. On the other side was the crank that started all the business. It surely looked impressive.

Erlo Ackerman pushed his chair back and hauled out his thick gold watch.

"Want to break off for lunch, Erlo?" Mr. Hook asked.

"Yes. But I got to make a telephone call first. Promised Aggie I'd give her a ring at noon."

"You got a telephone put into your home, Erlo?" Ox asked incredulously.

"I did. Why shouldn't I? What'd be the use, me having a phone in the office and Aggie not having one? I got it put in yesterday."

He pulled out a wallet from his hip pocket and went shuffling through a wad of paper slips he took out of it.

"Can't already remember our number," he grumbled. "And it won't be in the book until the new edition comes out the end of January. So I wrote it down somewhere here. I got it, now."

He heaved himself out of his chair and stood a moment, the slip of paper in his hand.

"By the way, Erlo," asked Mr. Hook, "what's our ring?"

"One long and three short," Erlo answered.

And then, in the moment's pause, the telephone bell came to life. It echoed shrilly in the utter silence. It rang once and paused; and then it rang three times quickly.

"Our number," said Erlo with satisfaction. He moved heavily across the room and reached for the receiver. He was a bit awkward fitting it against his ear.

"Hello," he said.

All of them could hear the voice coming in over the wire. "Erlo!" it said. "You was going to call me at noon."

"Now Aggie," Erlo said, hauling his watch out for the second time. "I couldn't put my hand on our number. And anyways, it's only four minutes after noon."

[66]

"You said you would call me at noon. You ought to do it at noon. I started getting worried."

"Well, I'm all right. I just couldn't find the number."

"You better start right home for dinner," the voice said. "And stop at the pharmacy for a bottle of Mr. Bondwin's Celery Compound. And we need some calomel, too."

"All right, Aggie," Erlo said, breathing heavily into the telephone. "I'll get them."

"You feel all right?" the voice demanded. "You sound as though you was blowing bad."

"I feel fine, Aggie," Erlo assured the mouthpiece.

"Well, you come right home, or you'll be late to dinner."

All of them heard the click at the other end of the line, and after a moment in which he looked a bit bewildered, Erlo hung up himself.

"It's a great thing," he said admiringly.

Ox looked as if he wasn't too sure about it; but Tom couldn't help thinking how wonderful it would be to have one in their own house so as to be able to let Polly Ann know if he couldn't get home from the mill.

17

Business in the afternoon wasn't as brisk as it had been during the morning, but everyone was kept busy until about half past five. It was already dark then. The lanterns hanging from the ceiling hooks made pools of light here and there, out of which the grain chutes rose like tree trunks. The mill after dark had always seemed mysterious and spooky to Tom. The ranked bags of grain were like herding beasts. When Mr. Hook suddenly appeared in their midst, Tom almost jumped out of his skin; but all

Mr. Hook said was, "Erlo would like you boys in the office now."

The faces of Louis and Bancel Moucheaud lit up, as if they had been waiting for the message for quite a while. They headed straight for the office door, barging through even ahead of Mr. Hook. Ox was more deliberate. He finished tying off the bag of barley he had just pulled and told Tom to finish his.

"Erlo likes to have a little party Christmas Eve," he explained to Tom. "After he figures we'll get no more business."

They walked through the dimly lighted mill and went into the office together.

Erlo Ackerman stood behind the counter, which he had arranged as a bar, with two quart bottles of whiskey and six glasses and a pitcher of water that had been chilling outside in the snow. The bottles were bourbon and Scotch, identified by their labels as Belle of Nelson and Usher's Green Stripe. Ox and the Moucheauds asked for the bourbon; Mr. Hook asked for the Usher's. Erlo looked at Tom for a moment and cleared his throat.

"You're kind of young to have hard liquor, Tom, but you've worked real well here, and I guess a mite of whiskey's not going to hurt you any."

He poured maybe half an inch into the glass and added a more liberal amount of water. Then he helped himself and raised his own glass.

"Merry Christmas, all," he said. The men raised their glasses, echoing him, and Tom did the same.

He didn't think much of the way whiskey tasted. He would a lot sooner have had a glass of Polly Ann's birch beer or raspberry vinegar, but he drank it down and put the glass back on the counter. Just in time as it seemed. For a minute things blurred for him, and Erlo's face suddenly consisted entirely of eyebrows. But things came back to round and square after a small spell, and it seemed that Erlo had something else on his mind.

"Anybody wishing another drink, help themselves. Though you, Tom, I guess had better stick with one. Meanwhile I want to pass out these envelopes same as I've always done, with our appreciation here at Ackerman and Hook. You make this a good place and for a man as old as me that means a lot. Ox."

Ox, who hadn't taken more whiskey, went up to the counter and accepted an envelope. Then Louis and Bancel, who had taken more drink, went up and got theirs. After which Erlo said, "Tom, though you came to work with us less'n four months ago, George Hook and me have decided you belong in our family now. So this is for you." And he gave Tom his envelope.

Tom didn't know whether he should open it, but then he noticed that Ox and the Moucheauds had put theirs in their pockets so he thanked Erlo and did the same with his. By then it was time to close up the mill and he followed the men back into it to tend to doors and lanterns. As soon as they had left the office, Louis and Bancel opened their envelopes and extracted a new five-dollar bill from each, Louis kissing his in an elaborate way. But Ox didn't open his, so Tom left his own envelope in his pocket until they had put the mill to bed and walked up to the depot in the dark, parting there to go their separate ways.

Standing by himself in the light from the depot windows, Tom took the envelope out of his pocket and opened it. Even before he had done so, he could tell that it did not contain paper money. What rolled out in his hand was a shining new half-dollar piece. He felt disappointed. He didn't exactly know what he had expected, but Louis kissing the five-dollar bill stuck in his mind. Five dollars that hadn't been earned. But perhaps it had in a way; he had been with Ackerman and Hook only a little less than a third of the year. So that, it seemed to him, might be worth a dollar.

Ox must have looked around and seen Tom standing rigid in the light from the depot, for he suddenly drifted up beside him. For a minute he stood that way, not talking. Then he asked, "Worrying about something, Tom?"

"No," Tom said.

"Well, you sure look like someone who's got something on his mind. And maybe I can guess what it is."

Tom had nothing to say.

"What did you get in your Christmas envelope?" Ox asked gently.

Tom opened his hand. Both of them looked down at the new silver half-dollar shining on his palm.

"It don't look much to you, against those five-dollar bills Bancel and Louis got, does it?"

Tom shook his head. For some reason he felt teary. He didn't want to talk.

"Well," Ox said, "when I come to work for Ackerman and Hook, it was October. I knowed as much about milling grist as they did and a good deal more than the rest in the mill; but when Erlo handed out his Christmas envelopes, I got a dollar where the others got five. I hadn't been here quite as long as you have, Tom, but I got more pay than you. You've got to take that into account, you see. Right now you're at the bottom of the ladder. A lot of people mightn't have give you anything at all."

[70]

He waited a while for Tom to take that in, and after a bit Tom could see how it was and what Erlo's thinking was. The half-dollar still seemed small compared to five dollars, but it was a gift.

He put it in his pocket and grinned at Ox, and Ox said, "Merry Christmas, Tom," and walked slowly off up Schuyler Street.

18

Tom waited till he was out of sight. He didn't feel as bad as he had a short time before. He knew Ox was right, saying he was at the bottom of the ladder; but in a way he wasn't, for it had occurred to him that things in his life had come to a changing point. He and Polly Ann and the girls were better off than they had been last summer. He might still be at the bottom, he thought, but he had his foot on the first rung.

He remembered that he had meant to get a gift for Birdy Morris, to give him when he came to their house for Christmas dinner, and now he had a half-dollar in his pocket to buy it with. He took the alley past the depot hotel to get to Main Street, hurrying because the stores must be closing up.

All but the pharmacy and one or two others like Tharratt's Clothing were shut. He couldn't think of anything he could buy for Birdy at Tharratt's for fifty cents, so he went into the pharmacy and looked over the tobacco counter. It occurred to him he might get five ten-cent cigars, but then he couldn't recall ever having seen Birdy with one in his mouth. Birdy generally chewed his tobacco or now and then smoked it in a well-charred corncob pipe. So Tom decided to get him two packages of Warnick and

Brown's tobacco, which was good for either, and putting one in each pocket of his coat, started out for home.

Not having any presents to hide he went straight up on the kitchen porch. Polly Ann and the girls were through with their supper and the girls were excited. They had found a tree, they told Tom, and wanted him to come and see it right away. Polly Ann said they ought to let him eat his supper first, but he was anxious to see the tree too, and with the girls leading they all went into the parlor, Polly Ann holding a carrying lamp, and admired the tree.

Tom could tell it was a sweet balsam from the smell even before he went in. It stood in the middle of the room with little paper cones of different colors hanging on it, paper chains the girls had made, and about a dozen packages stuck safely back on the branches. He could see the one he had bought for Polly Ann and he guessed two of the others were the ribbons he had got for the girls wrapped up in tissue. He took the packages of Warnick and Brown tobacco out of his pockets to put on the tree too, but Polly Ann protested.

"Aren't you going to wrap them, Tom?"

He explained they were just for Birdy and he didn't have any paper for them anyway.

"Give them to me," Polly Ann said. "It might hurt his feelings if his presents wasn't wrapped like ours."

He didn't think it would matter to Birdy but he was glad on Christmas day when Birdy opened them with his brown stubby fingers, taking pains not to tear the paper or break the pieces of colored wool Polly Ann had used for ribbons. He folded the paper carefully and put it to one side for Polly Ann to use again if she was so minded, but the wool he wound in little circles just as carefully and put them in his pocket. Tom wondered what he planned to do

[72]

with them but didn't want to ask. Early in March when he went to visit with Birdy one Sunday, he found that Birdy had made decorative knots out of each one and hung one in each of his two kitchen windows. There didn't seem any point in saying anything about them then, either.

Snowflakes had begun to fall that Christmas morning when he saw Birdy coming through the back door. He must have been to the barn for some reason, but he didn't tell what. He shook the flakes off his hat and said hello to all of them in turn. It was past noon then and Polly Ann was getting ready to dish up their dinner.

She had been fussing over it all morning, since day before yesterday if it came to that. When she put it on the table, her face all flushed with the heat of the stove and her hair ends curling from the steam, they could see why.

There was a big baked fresh ham with a dish of apple-sauce and hash-fried potatoes and corn Polly Ann had put up from the garden and carrots. They had tea to drink and a big deep-dish apple pie for dessert, and Birdy said it was the best dinner he had sat down to in his life or got up from, either.

Then they went into the parlor and admired the tree again and sat down to open their presents. Cissie-Mae and Ellie were to hand the presents off the tree and they were just getting ready to when Birdy asked to be excused and went out through the kitchen. They heard him going down the steps and then the hinges of the barn door squeaked and his feet came back up the steps and a strong breath of cold air came in as he opened the kitchen door. He set something down outside the parlor door and came in, looking sheepish.

"Just something I forgot," he mumbled and sat down.

Cissie-Mae and Ellie got going with the handing out of

the presents once more. They brought Polly Ann hers from Tom first, because they were dreadfully curious about it and also had a sort of part in getting it too, considering the way they and Birdy had smuggled it into the house.

Polly Ann just sat with it on her lap a minute, till Ellie asked, "Ain't you going to open it, Ma?" And then she took hold of the red and silver ribbon ends and untied the bow. When she had the paper open she gave a little gasp.

"Why, Tom!" she said. "Why, Tom! It's lovely." She held it up against herself. "It's going to fit just perfect," she said, and then nothing would do for the girls unless she went out and put it on.

Birdy agreed. So she went in the kitchen and changed into it. She came back pink-cheeked and shining-eyed. "It's beautiful, Tom! No one *ever* bought me anything like this before."

Even Tom could see it did become her. When she sat down again on the black horsehair granny chair she looked to him hardly older than his sisters.

But Ellie and Cissie-Mae took over the proceedings once more. First they got their own presents from Tom and like their mother had to put them on; but after that things went along smoothly. Tom got a pair of wool-lined mittens from Polly Ann; Cissie-Mae had knit him wristers and Ellie a scarf of matching wool and they had pooled their savings to buy Polly Ann a muff. It seemed, Birdy said, as if everybody had been thinking about winter weather, which reminded him he had brought something over for Tom.

He went back into the kitchen and returned with a pair of snowshoes.

[74]

"Old Broken-Crow Redner made them," he said. "Made good snowshoes all his life. I come on them in a dinky little crossroads store over back of Gray. He marked all his shoes with a double notch on the main crossbar, so I knew who had made these. Just about like new when I found them, but I've varnished the frames so you might say they're just as good as."

They looked fine to Tom and he said so. Birdy showed his brown teeth, grinning.

"I've fixed them with a toe strap and rawhide thongs. It's the way Indians use them. I'll show you the hitch. It leaves your feet a lot more free than a harness does."

"I won't have to worry how the roads are," Tom said, still admiring them. "I can just take off across country."

Polly Ann and the girls exclaimed what a wonderful present it was for Tom, and that was when the girls remembered to hand Birdy his gifts from Tom, and he began to open them.

"Warnick and Brown," he said. "Ain't no better tobacco in the world."

19

Deep snow came to stay six days after New Year's with a blizzard that dumped two feet of it over the valley. From that time on Tom used his snowshoes to go to and from work. At first he went around by the road and used Fisk Bridge to get across the river, but after it froze over late in January, he headed straight for it through the spruce woods, crossing on the ice and taking a beeline along Mill Creek.

Christmas afternoon, after the last present had been

opened, Birdy had taken Tom out into the barnyard and shown him how to fasten on his snowshoes, bringing the thongs around back of his heel and then crossing them around themselves over his instep and tying them in a bow. That way there was enough tension to hold his foot snug in the toe strap.

"Better practice on them some before you start out for Boonville. They'll make your legs lame for a while, but you'll soon get used to them," Birdy said. "And another thing, on steady route-going the way you'll be doing, it's best to always follow the same line. That way you'll build up a hard-packed path underneath new snow, which makes the going a lot easier."

Tom soon found that it was so. He discovered, too, that after he had been using them a while, he traveled a lot faster. With snowshoes you had to match your stride to the length of the shoe and once you stopped being lame you could move your legs as fast as in plain walking. It freed him from worry about making it to work or getting home at night. He felt it would take an almighty howling blizzard to keep him from making the trip.

He found that Birdy was right, also, about keeping to the same track. Following it, especially after a new fall of snow, was a lot easier than going at random. He found that out when once in a while he would stray from his track and hit unpacked snow. When the weather stayed fair for several days, crossing the meadows on his beaten path was as easy as traveling on a boulevard, even after the snow had mounted to four feet on the level. After the snow thawed he could see why this had been so. His winter track remained on the bare meadow, a white icy wall more than a foot high snaking over the new pale grass.

It seemed strange, looking back, that that snow track was the only traveling he did all winter, except for one trip he made one Sunday up on the sand-flat country the end of February. Coming home one Saturday evening he had a notion to go up there to see how the Widow Breen's barn was holding up, and next morning, after chores were done, he got Polly Ann to put him up some lunch.

The thermometer advertising Ackerman and Hook, which Ox had let him take, showed about three degrees above zero, but the sun was out and there was no wind and Tom figured to get to the Breen place in two hours or a little under. The going wasn't as easy as following his track to the mill, but there was a crust on the snow which a lot of the way his snowshoes didn't break through. He followed the road he and Birdy had taken in the summer, first to Hawkinsville and then up the river to where the road forked, one way leading on along the river to Armond's, the other going up the hill.

The hill road hadn't been broken out like the river road. No tracks went up it. The snow lay as it had fallen. Tom wondered if anybody had passed along it since late fall. It didn't seem so. Near the top of the hill a deer had crossed it, and farther on he came on two rabbit tracks, also crossing it. But nothing had gone along the road.

The flat upland country under deep snow looked larger and lonelier than Tom remembered. The bare frame of the Entwhistle house looked about the way it had, though the beams were capped with snow; but the ends of the barn had collapsed. When he got beyond the thin line of woods he found that two of the three deserted houses had also given way, a few studs and broken rafters poking up out of the snow like the end of a game of jackstraws. In the third Tom could see that a porcupine had made a home. His tracks went in and out the sagging door and he had bedded, to judge from the deep pile of droppings, under a table with two legs gone that made a kind of shanty for him. Tom thought that porcupine must be the nearest thing to a neighbor that the Widow Breen had.

Her hill was ahead of him now and pretty soon as he went forward he saw the roof of her house rising beyond the shoulder of it. Then the whole house came in view, looking grayer than it had seemed in summer, with a few more shingles missing from the roof. But the barn looked just the same. The roof line showed no sag, the corners stood square and plumb. Birdy was right in saying it was a well-built barn. He snowshoed up to it, thinking as he had so many times how it would look on their own place.

He went around the back of it and came along the far side towards the house. Mrs. Breen wasn't on the porch, which was not surprising seeing it was so cold and also that he'd made no noise at all coming out from the road. He expected that during the winter she didn't find much call to look out the windows towards the road. And he saw, too, that there weren't any tracks coming from the house. No tracks anywhere around it, for that matter. He stared up at the windows, but they showed only the blue-white blankness of reflected sky. It occurred to him that maybe she had left late in fall, though Joe Hemphill hadn't mentioned it. Maybe someone else had come to fetch her away. Then another thought occurred to him.

But as he stood there looking up at the house he saw a line of smoke stealing up from the chimney. It was thread-thin, but it showed his thought was wrong, because wood had been put on a fire. He had been planning to look

[78]

inside the barn again. Now he put that idea aside and snow-shoed up to the front porch. The snow was deep enough so he could walk up onto the porch floor without unfastening his snowshoes. They clattered on the boards as he walked over to look in the parlor windows. There was nothing to see. The door leading into the hall was closed. He crossed the porch and knocked on the front door, but could hear no stirring in the house. So he stepped down off the porch and went around the house to look through the kitchen windows.

20

The snow had drifted against the back almost to the windowsills. He had to bend down to look inside. At first he couldn't see anybody. After a minute, however, he made out what looked like a big cocoon in the far corner of the kitchen beyond the stove. While he stared at it, it began to move. Very slowly, a bit at a time, the outside wrapping unpeeled. A small thin hand appeared, then the other, and then he could make out the face of Mrs. Breen staring back at him out of her thick pile of quilts and blankets.

Even more slowly she got herself on her feet and dropped some of the blankets behind her, but she kept a pink and blue and yellow quilt worked in a star pattern wrapped around her and began the long journey to the kitchen door. When Tom saw she recognized him and was going to let him in, he kneeled down and took his snowshoes off. Using one for a shovel he cleared the snow away from the door so when she opened it he wouldn't drag a lot in with him. He stuck his snowshoes upright in the snow beside the place he had cleared and waited for Mrs. Breen to open the door. He must have waited four or five minutes before he saw the handle start to turn.

He would have turned it himself and opened the door, but he was afraid she might get struck by it, so he waited some more for her to do it at her own pace, and pretty soon the door did open slowly. It gave him a strange feeling that everything in the Widow Breen's house moved at the same infinitely slow pace, as if life itself had slowed down to a mere creeping.

She talked slowly, too, in a voice it was hard for him to hear, silent as the white world was outside.

"I know you," she said. "You was here with Birdy last summer. But I can't recollect your name."

Tom told her, and she nodded.

"Yes, I recall it, Tom. Knowed your mother, Polly Ann. She and her family lived down the road a spell. Those were livelier days than now. I'm glad to see you, Tom. Set down. I'd give you tea but I've just about run out of wood."

She sat down carefully in the chair at the end of the table, where she had sat last summer. When she was settled, Tom asked, "You haven't got any wood at all, mam?"

He was appalled at the idea, wondering how in the little time he had he could cut enough wood nearby and fetch it to the house. But she shook her head.

"There's plenty in the barn. Joe Hemphill got the Tatum boys to cut me four cords last fall, and I had them stack it there. But now, with all this snow, and the way I've got stiffened up, I can't get down to get it, Tom."

She gave a little smile that hardly showed in her wrinkled lips. In his relief he said he would fetch in enough to fill her woodbox and stack a good supply on the front porch. She told him she would take that kindly. There was a shovel in the front hall he could shovel out the barn door with, so it would roll back along its track, and inside there was a handsled Bert had made when they first came here, close to sixty years ago.

She started to get up to show him, but he told her to stay where she was, he could find things easy. He worked for a couple of hours, first filling the woodbox and stoking up the fire, and filling the kettle from the pump beside her kitchen sink. He wondered how anyone so frail-seeming could work a pump but he didn't like to ask. She smiled as he looked around and answered his thought.

"Oh, I can work the pump, Tom. Only a good deal slower than you."

It embarrassed him, though there were other things that puzzled him, like how she had got that black settee into the kitchen from the parlor. When she saw him looking at it, she said she had got the Tatum boys to move it for her, before she paid them off for cutting her wood. She might have had them bring in her bed, but being old she found it easier to sleep propped up. He had heard that said about some old people. For that matter he had heard that some horses getting old would go to sleep standing. When once in a while they would fall in their sleep they seemed to get in a hopeless tangle with their legs and would have to be lifted back on their feet. With a heavy horse it sometimes took a block and sling to do it. The thought of Widow Breen sitting always in the same position on that black settee made him realize how alone she was more than anything else had — no neighbor closer than that porcupine in the sagging house back down the road. He couldn't see any sign of her old cat, Tabs, either; but he didn't want to ask about him.

He felt troubled about the whole situation, but when he

[81]

asked if she didn't want someone to come out and bring her into town, though she didn't exactly get snappy with him, she made it clear that she wanted nobody bothering about her.

"I been in this house nearly my whole life, Tom, and I'm going to stay in it. It seems sort of lonesome to you, I guess. But I've got things to think about. There ain't such a thing as an empty room here any more."

He asked if she had edibles enough, if she didn't want him to bring out some for her next Sunday.

She said, no thank you. Her larder was well stocked. And then she gave her small, almost secret smile.

"It don't take much to feed a body as old as mine is, Tom."

She had made tea over the fire he had set roaring in her stove. They sat a while over their cups at the kitchen table. Tom remembered how her yellow cat had sat on the table beside her cup and sipped a little tea when she offered him some. Perhaps that was a thing she remembered there, too; and suddenly to Tom it seemed the cat actually was there.

He got up then and told her he must be heading home. It was near four o'clock. He would be late helping with the chores.

She watched from her place on the settee while he fastened his snowshoes. Then he rose and said good-bye and clattered out through the kitchen door. He heard her small voice say good-bye. She didn't wave when he looked back in through the window.

He went across to the road and started down it, feeling sudden loneliness overwhelming him. It had begun to snow. It was a snow without wind, drifting straight and softly to the earth, but there was a lot of it. As he came down the hill to join the river road he knew that his snow-shoe track would be all dusted over back on the flats.

There would be nothing to show he had visited the Widow Breen.

PART THREE

21

Nobody saw the Widow Breen alive again. Now and then Tom thought about going back to see her, but it seemed something else always turned up on Sundays. He thought of telling Mr. Hook about the way she was, living so far from anybody else with not even the road broken out. But each time he stopped himself, as if her whispery voice said again how she had lived in her house so long and was going to stay there. After a time he stopped thinking about her.

Then one day at the start of April, Joe Hemphill drove down to the mill with his feed order and the news that the Widow Breen was dead.

Yesterday he had gone up to the flats to call for her as he had always done the first of April, if the snow was gone, to drive her in to Boonville to do her spring trading. He had gone earlier than he did other times, because on her first trip after the winter she always had a great deal more to buy. Here and there he found the last traces of snowdrifts on the road, but none deep enough to make breaking through hard for his horses. Up there across the sand flats there was no mud to contend with. It was all smooth going, his wheels making the first tracks along it since last fall. The horses felt brisk, and turning off the road towards the Breen house they broke into a smart trot. He thought that the Widow Breen would be sure to hear him coming; but there was no sign of her at the front windows when he pulled up the buckboard at the front steps.

He called a couple of times, but there was no answer. He didn't want to leave the horses just standing while he went up on the porch; feeling so brisk they might have taken it into their heads to start home and it was too long a walk to suit him. There was nothing to hitch them to, so he led them down to the barn and rolled the door open and left them standing inside.

Then he went back up on the porch. There was a stack of stove wood on it and it looked to Joe as if maybe a half of what had been there originally had been used, but there was a good amount left. He couldn't see anything through the parlor windows, so he tried the front door. It wasn't locked, and he walked in. He said there was a kind of thin stale smell, sort of musty, in the hall, but it was hardly enough to notice.

It didn't occur to him to look upstairs in the bedroom; he had never seen Mrs. Breen anywhere in the house except the kitchen or on the front porch. As he walked on down the hall towards the kitchen door, he said, his footsteps sounded like pistol shots, the house was so still, even though he tried to walk soft; and when he stopped to open the door he could hear his own heart beating on the inside of his chest.

He saw her the minute he opened the door. She was sitting up on the horsehair settee that used to be in the parlor, all wrapped around in a nest of blankets, just showing her face. It didn't look but a mite grayer than it had the last time he saw her, but her eyes were shut.

He said, "Mrs. Breen," though he usually called her by her first name, Amelie. He didn't know yet why he had done that. He supposed he knew then that she was dead.

He touched her face with a finger. She was so nested in the blankets she did not move. He stood looking around the kitchen, but he couldn't see any sign anything had happened there. Nobody had broken in. So he backed out and left her, walking down the hall to the front door. He took the key out and locked the door after him from the outside and then he got his team from the barn and drove right back into Boonville.

He went to see Billy-Bob Baxter first thing he did, and Billy-Bob told him that when a dead person was found that way the Coroner and the Sheriff had to see them. So Billy-Bob got onto the telephone and got hold of the men one after another at Utica Court House and told them if they came up by train he would hire Joe Hemphill to drive them up to the Widow Breen's place to show them how he'd found her; and then he told Joe that if he got into any kind of trouble, like suspicion of murder, he — Billy-Bob — would be glad to act as his attorney.

Which made Joe Hemphill mad.

"Why would I want to kill that old woman?" he demanded. "She was a steady customer of mine. I liked her fine, even if she did talk a lot, driving back and forth between her house and town. Why, if I'd wanted to do that I could have blowed her up her own chimney with one breath!"

No one at the mill knew what blowing her up her chimney had to do with it, but they made no comments. Tom, however, felt concerned. He wanted to know how big the pile of wood Joe had seen on the front porch was.

"Oh, about four foot high and four foot long if you was to square it up. Why?"

Tom hadn't expected a question, and it took him a minute to answer. Then he said he'd heard the Tatum boys had cut her stove wood in the fall and there had been plenty.

"I seen some more in the barn," Joe said. But he lost interest right away. He was due to meet the 10:25 train tomorrow morning and drive the Sheriff and the Coroner up to the Breen place.

[88]

"Got the door key in my pants pocket," he said. He brought it out for them to look at. Then he started in to tell everybody all over how it was going into the house.

Tom didn't want to hear any more. He looked away from the key and found Ox watching him. He was deeply troubled, though he didn't quite know why. She had wood enough and food enough when he left her; but maybe he ought to have gone back once more. Yet he felt sure if he had done that, she wouldn't have changed her mind about staying in her house.

He left the men still listening to Joe Hemphill's story about the way it was and went through the office door into the mill.

22

He was standing in the door to the loading platform that looked over where Mill Creek came from between the houses in its steep and narrow valley and burrowed under the mill. It disappeared after that until it came out on the far side of the railroad embankment. It was running bank high from melting snow, boiling and eddying, and coffee-brown.

Tom's eyes didn't see the creek. They were preoccupied with the image of the old woman sitting in her kitchen when he had gone away. As Joe Hemphill described the amount of wood left on the porch she must have been using it about two weeks. That meant she must have lived until about the middle of March. And then the time had come to die. He wondered if she had been afraid. He wondered if it had happened during the day or in the dark. He wondered if she had known it was coming. He had the feeling that she would have known it, and got herself settled in her wraps on the settee, and waited with her eyes open to it. But he didn't know.

Then Ox's slow voice said behind him, "Tom, we better put Joe Hemphill's feed order on his wagon and start the team up the hill, or he'll go on telling about himself all day."

Ox had the order slip in his hand and they got the bags of bran and whole oats and a small one of oil meal out on the loading platform. Then Tom got in the wagon and Ox heaved the heavy bags over into the wagon and Tom piled them. By that time another team was turning down from the depot, so Ox went into the office and told Joe he would have to make room for other customers and if he didn't right away Tom Dolan had orders to wrap the lines around the whip butt and start the team off on their own.

That took care of Joe Hemphill, which Erlo Ackerman declared was better than a mercy for them all, and the day went on like any other day, right up to closing time. The Moucheauds had left a couple of minutes early, leaving Ox and Tom to lock up, and as they made the rounds, Ox asked quietly, "Did you know the Widow Breen, Tom?"

It took Tom by surprise and for some reason it frightened him.

"I thought maybe, the way you looked at her door key, you might have seen her some time lately," Ox said.

Tom nodded.

Then he started telling how he had gone up on the sand-flat country the end of February. The words tumbled out of him. He hadn't realized how much he wanted to tell somebody about the old woman, her loneliness, and how he had left her with so much doubt on his mind.

Ox listened without comment until he had done, but

before Tom could go on with the speculation that haunted him of how the Widow Breen had died, Ox said, "I think it would be a good idea if we went into the office and you told this to George Hook."

Erlo Ackerman had already left, after calling his wife on the telephone to say he was heading home and getting instructions to do an errand for her on the way, and George Hook was sitting alone at the checkers table going over notices and flyers from feed companies out west. Ox closed the door to the mill behind them and waited for Mr. Hook to look up.

"Tom here, has been telling me about the Widow Breen. I think it would be a good idea if you heard him, too."

So Tom once more told how he had snowshoed up the end of February and found the old woman with no more wood in the house and no way of getting any more in from the barn, feeble as she had become. Mr. Hook listened carefully. When Tom stopped, he asked, "Did you go up there just to see Mrs. Breen?"

Tom hesitated. He hadn't wanted to tell anybody about his plan of moving the Breen barn down to their place. Telling them about wanting to buy it when they knew he had next to no money, let alone tearing it down and moving it and putting it up again when he was still not more than just a kid, he didn't know what they would think. But he couldn't see any way to not tell them, either. So he did.

He told how Birdy had taken him up there because Birdy had helped Bert Breen put up the barn, and seeing it, he got his idea of owning it himself. He told them how good the barn still was, and then he told them about their visit with the Widow Breen in her kitchen, though he

[91]

didn't say anything about her reading cards for him, and about him coming into money, sometime. So he kept his story just to the barn and having tea.

Mr. Hook looked at him a good long minute after he had finished.

"I suppose it would have been better if you'd told someone about her, the way she was living, after that last time, Tom. But I don't know if it would have done any good. And maybe she died pretty soon after you'd been there."

Tom shook his head.

"I figure she must have stayed alive about two weeks."

"How do you figure that?" Mr. Hook asked.

"From how much wood there was left on the porch," Tom told him.

"Well," Mr. Hook said, "I think you'll have to tell the Coroner and the Sheriff about your last visit, Tom. They'll want to talk to the last person who saw Mrs. Breen alive. Not much question that means you."

"I couldn't tell them no more than I told you," Tom said, alarmed at the idea of being questioned by officers of the law.

"There's nothing to worry about, Tom. I'll go with you if you like."

It relieved Tom to know he would have Mr. Hook with him.

23

Next morning Tom heard the whistle of the 10:25 from Utica coming into the Main Street crossing down below and a couple of minutes later the grinding of brakes made him look out the back window and he could see Engine 1099 up above him on the embankment panting like a dog. Pretty soon, she tooted one blow on her whistle and the drivers spun on the rails while a blast came out of her smokestack and the next thing he knew the cars were passing by above, heeled over with the cant of the curve, and in a minute the train had chugged out of sight and then out of hearing. Ten minutes later Mr. Hook came in from the office.

"Tom," he called. "I think we better go up to the Hulbert House."

Tom dusted off his clothes and followed Mr. Hook back into the office. It occurred to him, now it was too late, that he ought to have brought his good clothes, and he said as much to Mr. Hook. Mr. Hook said not to think about it, and Erlo Ackerman growled from his chair at the checkers table, "Better go looking natural, Tom. There's nothing to be scared of with Considine and Purley. They wouldn't have sense enough to keep from swallowing if a fly flew in their mouths," a remark that Tom didn't find especially reassuring.

The Hulbert House was the biggest hotel in Boonville, where political visitors or sportsmen on their way into the woods put up. It had always looked very impressive to Tom, with its walls of gray limestone and a six-pillared portico, three stories high, with fancy railed balconies between them at the second and third floors. It had never occurred to Tom to look inside the building. It looked far too costly for a boy like him. But going into it didn't faze Mr. Hook a bit.

He walked through the front door and looked to his left into the lounge. When he saw no sign of the Sheriff and the Coroner there, he crossed the hall into the bar where Jerry Pastor was polishing glasses and exchanging a few words with his first customer of the day, a seedy-looking man who looked to Tom as if he might be uncertain whether this morning was yesterday or not.

"Morning, Jerry. Know where the Coroner is?"

Jerry jerked his head towards the back of the barroom.

"In the private dining room. Him and Sheriff Purley has Joe Hemphill in there. Putting him through the wringer, I guess."

Tom admired the way Mr. Hook nodded, crossed the barroom to the indicated door, knocked, and walked right in. Joe Hemphill was sitting at one end of the dining table and opposite were the Coroner and the Sheriff. Tom could tell which was which because the Sheriff wore a gray flannel shirt and had his badge pinned to a breast pocket of it. Only it seemed to Tom as if a small, ordinary man like him ought to have changed jobs with the big fat man beside him. Dr. Considine had gray hair and red cheeks and wore a dark-blue suit with a heavy watch chain that barely made it from one pocket of his waistcoat to the other. If he wasn't the biggest man Tom had ever seen, he was the fattest.

He stared out over his swollen front with a scowl. "What do you want?" he demanded roughly.

"I'm George Hook, from Ackerman and Hook's Feed Mill, and I've brought this boy because he has some evidence to give you about Mrs. Breen. Tom Dolan works for us, and we can vouch for him and anything he says."

Dr. Considine turned his scowl on Tom. "What is the purport of this boy's testimony?" he asked.

"He saw Mrs. Breen the end of February," Mr. Hook replied. "I suppose that means he was the last person to see her while she was alive."

Sheriff Purley grinned at Joe Hemphill. "Well, Joe. If that's true, it means she was alive when you left her up there last fall and we don't need to ask you no more questions about it."

Joe Hemphill's face was a mixture of relief and exasperation. The way the questions had been going he had been fearful of maybe having to have Billy-Bob Baxter defend him in a trial, the way Billy-Bob had offered to do, and that would have cost him money. On the other hand he hated seeing a young snot like Tom Dolan taking the luster from his story. But then his face brightened once more. After all Tom hadn't seen the old woman dead, and he had. Nobody could take that away from him, no matter what.

Dr. Considine cleared his throat. It sounded like five empty barrels rolling down a chute into an empty cellar. He pressed his front against the table edge and reached for a pad of yellow ruled paper and a pencil that were lying in front of him and pulled them towards him as close as his stomach would allow him to see. He got the pad adjusted after two or three tries, looked up, and said, "Give me your name, boy."

"Tom Dolan."

Dr. Considine looked up again. "Tom for Thomas, I suppose."

"I don't know," Tom said. "Nobody has ever called me Thomas."

Dr. Considine wrote down Thomas Dolan.

"Your address."

"We live about a quarter mile off Moose River road, below Fisk Bridge," Tom told him.

"What mail route is that on?" the Coroner asked testily.

Tom looked puzzled. He couldn't recollect. Mail meant almost nothing in the Dolan family. There was nobody who wrote them letters; they didn't get catalogues; the mailman went by every weekday in his buggy, driving his old sorrel mare; if they saw him they waved and if he saw them he waved back. They didn't have a mailbox.

He didn't see how he was going to make that clear to a person like Dr. Considine and he looked worriedly towards Mr. Hook, who said, "I think it's on Route Five, Coroner."

"Let the boy do his own answering," Dr. Considine said. But he wrote down the route number anyway.

"How old are you?"

"Fourteen," Tom said, and Dr. Considine wrote that down too. Then he pushed his chair back enough to relieve the pressure on his forward bulge and said, "Now, Dolan, give us your testimony."

Tom had never heard the word "testimony" before, but Sheriff Purley put him right.

"All Doc wants is for you to tell him about you seeing the Widow Breen," he explained.

So Tom had to tell his story over again and when he had finished, the only question Doc Considine asked was, "What day of February did you say you went there?"

"It was the last Sunday," Tom said. "I don't remember which day of the month it was."

Mr. Hook pulled a small calendar from his wallet. It was February 25th, he reported; and Doc Considine wrote that down, too.

"I guess that winds us up down here. We'd better go up to look the place over and get the body. You made arrangements for that, Fred?"

Sheriff Purley said he had instructed Undertaker Vance to follow behind their buckboard. Mr. Vance had declared it impossible to risk a hearse on those back roads, so he was coming with a spring wagon which had rings to fasten the collection box to. They were going to leave as soon as Joe

Hemphill could bring his rig around to the Hulbert House door.

Joe Hemphill said it was already there. He had ordered his hired man to bring the team and buckboard and tell Ed Vance to get there the same time he did. They could start as soon as they put their hats on.

"All right," Doc said. "Let's go right now."

"I want Tom Dolan to come with us," Sheriff Purley said. "Seems he might know more about that place than the rest of us."

Tom looked questioningly at Mr. Hook.

"You go along," Mr. Hook said. "Take the day off. The mill can get along without you for one day."

24

It was past noon before they did get started. Doc Considine held out for a while for having lunch at the hotel, to which Sheriff Purley objected that they didn't have the time if they were going to finish up and get back to Utica by the late afternoon train. He had already ordered sandwich lunches for them to eat on the road. Doc finally consented, but he had to have a mug of draught beer to carry him through the trip into the back country.

While he was sucking this into himself, the bartender came through from the kitchen with five packs of sandwiches wrapped in newspaper. He handed them to Sheriff Purley, who took them out to the wagons. He put three packs under the front seat of Joe Hemphill's livery buckboard, and gave Tom the other two.

"Will it be all right if Tom Dolan here rides with you, . Mr. Vance?"

The undertaker was sitting on the seat of his spring

wagon behind Joe Hemphill's rig, and Tom looked at him with interest. He wore a derby hat and a black coat, but otherwise he seemed to Tom like any other person. He even smiled when he saw that Tom had a packet of sandwiches for him, too, and said, "Hop aboard, son."

As soon as Doc Considine came out, Tom saw why Fred Purley had asked him to ride with Mr. Vance. The whole buckboard leaned heavily to the left when Doc got his weight on the back-seat step and once he was in, the rear springs looked squashed down. He filled the entire seat all by himself, and with Joe Hemphill and the Sheriff on the front seat the buckboard was hogged down all around. The horses had a surprised look when they took up the traces and started off down Main Street. Mr. Vance touched his horse with the tip of his whip and they followed. Tom looked back at the hotel and saw Mr. Hook watching them off, so he raised his hand and Mr. Hook raised his in acknowledgment, and then the house at the corner of Main and Schuyler streets closed the view. That was the first time he noticed the collection box fastened with four rope hitches to the bed of the spring wagon behind them. It gave Tom a queer feeling to think old Mrs. Breen would be riding back with them inside the box, leaving her house and place for the last time, and he wondered if even when dead she would know and resent what was happening to her.

People along Main Street paused to look at the two wagons, knowing Mr. Vance even if they didn't recognize Doc Considine and the Sheriff, and they looked at Tom, too, wondering what a boy like him was doing on such business. But as soon as the wagons went up on the canal bridge and down the other side, there was hardly anyone to notice them and still fewer when they turned off the main highway on the road to White Lake Corners. They crossed the canal again at Hawkinsville and came down the steep hill through the village to the river, turning right on the far side of the bridge; and after that the way was all familiar to Tom.

He got out the sandwiches then, unwrapped both packs, handing one to Mr. Vance. Mr. Vance was not talkative. He took big bites from his sandwich and was done with the first before Tom was halfway through his own, and finishing his fourth when Tom was only starting in on his third. He looked so hard at Tom's last sandwich that after a minute Tom felt obliged to offer it. Mr. Vance just about snatched it out of his hand, and Tom thought that dealing so much with dead persons must cause a man to have an appetite for food.

They were well across the sand flats by the time they had done eating and not long after that the gable of the Widow Breen's house came into view around the shoulder of the hill. Joe Hemphill touched up his horses and both rigs drove up to the front steps at a smart trot. The two buildings looked just the same as when Tom had last seen them, only there was no snow; and it didn't seem as lonely with all of them climbing down from the wagons and clustering on the porch.

Joe Hemphill said he wanted to put his team in the barn, but Sheriff Purley told him to wait a minute.

"Give me that door key, Joe," he said.

Tom could see that Joe Hemphill didn't like handing it over. He wanted to be the man who let them into the house and showed them what was what.

"Come on, Joe," Fred Purley said. "We've got no time to waste."

So Joe handed the key over and Purley opened the door

and the rest of them went in. Things looked just as Joe Hemphill had said they were. The parlor looked as if nobody had been into it for a long long time. They went down the hall to the kitchen and opened the door and went inside. That didn't look any different, either; nor did the Widow Breen when Tom nerved himself to look at her. Only the small face looking out of the nest of covers was a little grayer. Tom, searching his mind for how she looked different, decided that somehow her face looked very far away, and a little as if she were watching them all from that distant spot, wherever it might be.

Sheriff Purley looked around the kitchen. There was no sign of anything being disturbed. Doc Considine asked Tom if the room was the same as when he had been there in February. It was. When he had left, Mrs. Breen was sitting just the way she did now, peering out of quilts and blankets. But of course she must have been up and down after that or the stove wood wouldn't have got burned.

Doc and the Sheriff agreed.

"Anything different from the time you was here with your friend last summer?" the Coroner asked.

"Just the settee. It was in the parlor then. She got the Tatums to move it in here when they was cutting wood for her."

"Yes, you told us that," Sheriff Purley said. "Well, Mr. Vance, I guess here's where you start your undertaking job."

Mr. Vance agreed. Joe Hemphill had put his horses in the barn so Vance asked him to help bring in the box. Joe began talking a stream, about how it had been, coming into the house by himself, how he had found the old woman sitting just the way she was now, how it had come to him to lock the front door as he went out. In his own mind it was clear Joe Hemphill considered himself the most important person there, and he looked annoyed when Sheriff Purley said he wanted to check around upstairs and invited Tom to come with him.

25

The stairway was steep and narrow and at the top there was a narrow landing running back beside the stairwell with two doors opening off it into two bedrooms. The one at the front had been the one that Bert and Amelie had shared in their married time. It had a big walnut double bed with clustered fruit carved at the peak of the tall head-piece; and there was a chest of drawers, the handles of which were carved to look like tree roots, and a dressing table with a tall mirror and marble top to its low base, and finally a commode matching the other pieces to hold a hand basin and pitcher, with a door underneath where the night china pot was kept. All the pieces were there and made a matching set with a pattern of wild roses and for-get-me-nots, which seemed to Tom the prettiest he had ever seen. That chinaware gave the entire room a feeling of delicacy and a picture entered his mind of Mrs. Breen moving about in it when she was a young wife just come there, and looking at herself in the tall looking glass.

But at the same time there was a wrong feeling to the room. Sheriff Purley felt that also for he went quickly to the chest of drawers and pulled one out. Everything in it had been disturbed; handkerchiefs and shirts were all mixed up, as if someone had pawed through them in a hurry. The Sheriff pulled out the other drawers and they were in the same state.

"What kind of a person was Mrs. Breen, Tom?"

"Everything was tidy downstairs when I was here," Tom said. "And Birdy told me she was the neatest housekeeper he ever knew."

"Well, somebody sure has been messing with this chest of drawers," the Sheriff said. It was the same with every other drawer he looked into and also the closet. The clothes were off the hooks and lay on the floor in a jumble.

"Let's look into the other room," Purley said.

The back room was a little smaller. It had a bed and a washstand and a small chest of drawers, but no dressing table. In place of that was a small desk with a hinged front that let down so a person could use it for writing on. This was where the Sheriff considered it likely that Mr. Breen had kept accounts and written letters and seed orders and done work of that sort. But this room too had been gone over by someone. Papers were scattered over the floor, the desk drawers hadn't even been closed. There was no sign of such a thing as a ledger or account books either, though there were a lot of old seed catalogues and others from mail-order houses and a whole mess of old almanacs, all of them dumped in a heap in one corner.

"Tom," Sheriff Purley said soberly, "you sure you didn't come up here when you came to the house in February?"

"No," Tom said, "I didn't. When I wasn't talking to Mrs. Breen I was busy the whole time fetching her wood up on the porch. I never been up here before."

"I believe you," Sheriff Purley said. "But somebody was sure anxious to find something." He rubbed the back of his head, shoving his hat forward over his eyes. "Would you have any notion what it might be?"

Tom didn't but he made a suggestion that Birdy Morris might have an idea. He knew the Widow Breen better than anyone else.

"I'll ask him," Sheriff Purley said. He looked thoughtful. "I wonder when whoever it was, was up here. It must have been before Joe Hemphill came and locked the front door, because there's no windows broken or anything like that. Unless, of course, Joe himself came up here looking for it."

"I don't think Joe did that," Tom said. "I think he got real nervous when he found she was dead. I think what he wanted then was to get out of the house soon as he could."

Sheriff Purley smiled.

"*I* think you're right, Tom. Better get back downstairs now, I guess. We can't learn anything up here."

By the time they'd got downstairs, Mr. Vance and Joe Hemphill had taken the collection box out of the house and tied it down on the spring wagon. Doc Considine told Purley there was no sign of violence.

"She just died," he said, "and there was so little to her it was like she had just dried up."

"Well," Purley said, "something has been going on upstairs." He briefly described what he and Tom had found. "Think you ought to have a look, Doc?"

Considine looked up the stairs, considering their steepness and narrowness. He shook his head. "You've seen everything there was to see, Fred. I think we ought to get started back."

They went out the front door and Sheriff Purley locked it behind them, putting the key in his pocket, an action that nettled Joe Hemphill considerably. He had valued showing the key to people. But at least he could say that he had helped put the old woman in the box. "Hardly weighed a thing. Like lifting a milkweed pod, it was."

He got his team from the barn and the two rigs started on the return trip. Mr. Vance was a bit more talkative. He speculated for a good piece of the way where money for the burial might come from. It seemed to be considerably on his mind.

"She have any children?" he wanted to know. "Or any relatives?"

Tom couldn't tell him. He had gathered from Birdy that the Breens hadn't had any children. He didn't know about relatives, but he hadn't heard anybody mention any. It made her seem lonelier than ever, driving away from the one place she had loved, alone in the collection box.

26

The inquest turned out to be a simple matter. Amelie Breen, of the town of Boonville, widow, had died of natural causes. Tom had to give his testimony, but by now he was accustomed to it. Joe Hemphill, also, had to give his, which he relished doing. No one came forward to claim any relationship with the Widow Breen. Mr. Oscar Lambert, president of the bank, testified that neither the deceased widow nor her previously deceased husband had ever had an account in his bank, a matter he found regrettable. Nor did any other bank around about, in Oneida or Lewis counties, report having any transactions with Mr. or Mrs. Breen. Mr. Vance had had grounds for his speculations. No money was forthcoming for her burial so she was buried on the town, in a corner of the cemetery.

Tom asked for time off to go to the burial. No one was there except the gravedigger, Birdy Morris, himself, and Father Devaney, for it was presumed from her name that if she had ever belonged to any church it must have been the Catholic. The Father murmured quickly what he had to say, of which Tom heard almost nothing and understood less; even so, it gave him a comfortable feeling to have the Father there. Polly Ann might have come except for it being her day to work at the Grieves' house, and she thought it best not to ask for the time off, because the Grieves had no patience with the poor.

But hearing the earth begin to fall on her funeral box didn't mean for Tom that he had done with the Widow Breen. He began to wonder what would happen to the place, and especially to the barn. There was nothing he could do about the barn now; maybe in a couple of years.

Stories began going around how a man, fishing Cold Brook that ran along two sides of Breen's Hill, had seen the house in the twilight with a light moving from one window to the other. It began to be said the house was haunted. People said it was old Bert come back looking for his money. And then people started remembering how he had transacted in real estate and never banked anything that anybody ever knew of. Neighbors reported wagon tracks going up to the road across the sand flats. Those weren't ghosts, you could bet, Birdy Morris said. He had come by the house hunting that fall and had left the trail he had been following to walk over to it. The door had been smashed open, there were windows broke too. Inside it was a shambles. People had been in there tearing the plaster off the walls to get a look at the studding, knocking it down from the ceilings, ripping up the floorboards. There wasn't a whole wall left anywhere in the house. In the cellar the earth floor had all been dug up and turned over. Even the potato cellar old Bert had dug in the sandy side of the hill up above where the house stood had had its plank lining thrown out and been all caved in by someone digging there. Birdy said it was a shame to see a good place torn to ruin like that. It wasn't ghosts did things like that, it was people looking for old Bert's pile of money.

When Tom asked him about the barn, Birdy said they hadn't done much there except rip out the mangers in the two horse stalls, tear out most of the inside matched boarding on the wall of the critter-space, and knock down the feed bin. All they hadn't touched was that box inside the main door.

"You recollect it Tom? Stood just by the door, about three foot square? Bert always had it half full of sand and chaff. I don't know what for, unless he fed it to his hens in winter."

Tom recalled the box because it had puzzled him some, but he didn't think sand and chaff was anything you gave to chickens.

Otherwise, Birdy went on, they had left the barn alone. There wasn't many places in it you could hide something like a chest of money. A barn built like that one was honest, anyways, he said. It didn't hide nothing from you.

Tom agreed. "Was it in good shape, except for what they done to it?" he asked.

"It looked fine," Birdy said. "It will stand the way it is for fifty years, I bet. You still hankering to buy it, Tom?"

Tom admitted he was. "But I won't have money to buy it with for two, three years."

He knew he wasn't likely to have the money in three, let alone two, years, but he had to say it. It kept the barn somehow more in his reach.

He asked, "Do you think somebody's likely to buy her place?"

"I doubt it," Birdy said. "It never was much of a piece

of land. Not more'n twenty acres. Too small to make a farm on. But Bert Breen wasn't interested in farming. All he wanted was dealing in land lots, buying and then selling. So he found him that place back there, way off from almost everybody. It would be too lonesome for anyone to live on now."

"What will come of it, then?" Tom wanted to know.

"Oh, I guess the County will put it up for taxes."

Birdy had to explain, the best he knew, that when a piece of land got abandoned like the Breen place and no taxes got paid on it, the County would put it up for sale. The person who bought it had to pay at least the taxes due on it. Then he held it for two years, paying the taxes as they came due, and after that, if no claim was made on the land by someone else, the place became his property. He had a clear deed to it.

Tom asked what the taxes would be on a place like Breen's.

"They don't amount to a great lot on back-country land like that, Tom."

But Tom had to know how much.

"Well, I don't know. Maybe eight or ten dollars. Maybe a bit more. Maybe less."

All of a sudden Tom realized that it might be possible for him to buy the Breen place. Three years of taxes wouldn't amount to over thirty dollars. He didn't want that land, but if he had to buy the land to get hold of his barn, he would do it.

Depending, of course, on no one else turning up with a claim to it.

"Birdy," he asked, "if I bought the place for taxes, could I take the barn off of it in the first year?"

"I don't know about that," Birdy replied. "You'd have to ask somebody who knows about law. Billy-Bob Baxter could tell you that."

27

A year, when you are fourteen years old, seems a lot longer time to get through than it does later on in life. Tom wasn't worried about finding money to pay the tax on Breen's, especially after his pay was raised to thirty cents a day in September. It didn't seem likely, either, that anyone would get interested in buying land so far off and lonesome. From any point of view it seemed as if the barn was just about as good as his, but he wanted to feel sure of it.

Thinking about just where he would set it and how it was going to look when he had the frame up and the siding on made him take a new look at their house, and he saw for the first time how shabby and run-down looking it was, with shingles missing from the roof, and here and there split clapboards, the front steps sagging, and the paint so nearly weathered away it was hard to tell what color the house had been in the first place. He made his mind up that before he put up the barn he would have to get the house in shape, and that was what he worked at during that summer, outside of his hours at Ackerman and Hook's.

The job hadn't seemed any great thing when he made up his mind it ought to be done; but he found it was more complicated than just getting paint and a couple of brushes and maybe a bundle of shingles. Nob Dolan hadn't ever fixed up his house all the time he was around after marrying Polly Ann, so there was nothing on the place like a putty knife or a paint scraper, not to mention a paint-brush. There wasn't even a ladder. Polly Ann told Tom that the once or twice his father had ever had to have a ladder he borrowed it from someone. He hadn't even bothered to return it, knowing the lending party would come after it after a while.

Tom didn't want to borrow a ladder because he intended using it through the summer, but when he priced them at Rymer's Hardware the cost of a new one was a shock. He told Birdy Morris about it and Birdy said it was a bigger cost than he would want to get into himself. If he had had a good ladder of his own Tom would have been welcome to use it, but the one he had had lost some of its rungs and even if they were replaced the ladder wouldn't be safe. But he said he would look around to see if he could pick one up somewhere secondhand. He told Tom he ought to get one in good shape to use in putting up the barn after he got done painting the house. He ought to have two of them for the barn job.

Tom hadn't thought of that. One ladder was all he needed for now. But a few days later Birdy came back with a grin on his face. He said he had heard of a man who had done painting for a living, lived beyond Talcotville, and was named Wemple. He had developed a heart condition and had to quit outside work. So Birdy had gone out there yesterday and the old man had a couple of good sound ladders, both of them twenty-four feet, and when Birdy said he had a customer might take the two of them, Mr. Wemple offered them for fourteen dollars cash and said he would throw in a light ten-foot single ladder along with them. Birdy had given him a dollar to hold the deal and said he would be back next Sunday.

Seeing all the trouble Birdy had gone to there wasn't

much Tom could do but say he would buy the ladders. He could see that they were a good value, taking the barn into consideration in addition to the house job. But when he got his savings box out after supper and saw the hole fourteen dollars was going to make in it, his nerve was shaken. During the winter he had had to help Polly Ann with medicine for the two girls when they got sick for near a month with some kind of chest complaint. He had also had to buy two work shirts and new overalls for himself, having outgrown his old clothes. At the time he had enjoyed that, and the money had seemed well spent; but now he wished he had stayed small and kept his money. Fourteen out of the thirty-one dollars in the box would leave only seventeen dollars, out of which he would have to buy a couple of paintbrushes and the paint. You couldn't buy paint secondhand, either, the way you could a ladder.

It wasn't till Sunday, when he and Birdy were driving up to Talcotville to collect the ladders, that Tom realized that he would still have to buy shingles to patch the roof and maybe a dozen clapboards. It looked likely after all these expenses that the only money he would have to put up for the Breen place would be his salary for the rest of the year. But he didn't see how he could back out of fixing the house over now.

Mr. Wemple was a short, stout, red-faced man with some white hair left, who sounded as if he were talking under water, the words coming out of him like mumbled bubbles that burst into recognizable sounds some time after they had left his mouth. He helped them put the ladders on Birdy's wagon and accepted Tom's money. Tom never met him again, but it was from then on, as he came to look back on it, that the pattern of his life began to speed up.

Not just at once. The whole of Sunday was spent discussing the color he should paint the house. Everybody had a favorite color. It didn't matter what it was because there was not enough of the original paint to make any difference. In the end they decided on white, which was Polly Ann's choice, with a red trim, because Cissie-Mae wanted the house red. Ellie had been for light blue, but she was accustomed to giving in to her sister, and Birdy and Tom had no particular ideas.

Next day Tom drove up with Polly Ann to town and at noon he got old Drew out of the barn behind the house Polly Ann was working for and went to Garfield's Lumber Mill to buy a bundle of shingles and a dozen new clapboards. That same evening after he got home he began patching the roof. He had never done any work of that sort and at first he made mistakes and split the old shingles. But then he recalled Birdy's telling him, "Just go easy and slow, Tom. You'll get along faster in the long run doing it that way."

Tom found it was true. Pretty soon, taking his time, he found he was getting more done faster. In two weeks he was ready to buy his paint. After he had paid for it he found he'd used up all his savings and two weeks of wages besides. But when he had the front of the house painted and the red trim done and drawn the window sashes in white with their frames red, the house looked changed so much he had to feel proud. He stopped worrying about money for the Breen place. It seemed to him he was bound to get it when the time came. And then in September when the house was done, all four sides of it painted, the mill gave him his raise to thirty cents a day, which meant he could save close to fifty dollars a year, which was more than enough to meet taxes on the Breen place.

28

He didn't know where to go to put in his bid with the County, or how to go about doing it, so he took Birdy Morris's advice and went to see Billy-Bob Baxter.

The office was in the same little house on Leyden Street that Bert Breen used to go to when he needed some law work done on one or other of his land transactions. Beside the door there was a brass plate which had the name William Roberts Baxter, Attorney-at-Law, on it in black letters. It looked as polished up as it had in Bert Breen's time, but Billy-Bob Baxter himself showed the amount of time that had gone by since then. His coat was a little shiny, like the top of his head. He bent over a good deal when he got out of his chair, and there was a gray trail down his waistcoat where his cigar ashes had tumbled down him. The black leather chairs looked rusty and one had a small split that had been carefully stitched up. But Billy-Bob's smile, when he heard who Tom was, had the old crafty fox look to it.

"Sure, I remember your grandpa, Tom. Him and me we used to go bird shooting back in those days. Like as not we had Erlo Ackerman along with us with his old orange-spot setter dog. Erlo was quite a sport till his bottom half widened out on him and he grew his pomposity so big."

He had Tom sit in the black leather chair with the sewed-up split in it and sat down himself in the cane-seated, walnut desk chair on the other side of his desk, stuck his hand in a drawer and brought it out with a couple of stogies, one of which he offered Tom, and when Tom refused he put it in his waistcoat pocket and lit the other up.

"Now, what did you come to see me about, Tom?" he asked, tossing his match at the big white spittoon in the corner. Tom watched the match go through the air and when it went into the spittoon, he looked back at Billy-Bob, who was watching him sort of slantwise, with his ears almost pricked up. For some reason Tom trusted him and so he told him about wanting a barn and seeing the one Birdy Morris had helped build on the Widow Breen's place and planning to take it down and move it to their own small farm if he could only get to buy it. He told Billy-Bob what Birdy Morris had told him about a place being put up by the County for taxes. Billy-Bob said Birdy had it near enough right. He blew smoke from his cigar in Tom's direction and said, "I guess you'd like me to find out what the cost will amount to, and so on."

Tom said that was so, if it wasn't going to be too much trouble.

"That's no problem," Billy-Bob said. "I've got business in the Court House next week and I'll check on the Breen farm. Of course, some relative might yet show up claiming it, but I don't think it's likely, and I don't think any Breen would be dumb enough to claim a place like that. Of course, it's different with you, Tom. Wanting the barn and so forth."

Tom asked him then if he could take the barn off the place the first year, before the redeem period, and Billy-Bob said he'd have to look into that. But it wouldn't hurt Tom to wait two years, nor the barn either if it was in fair shape.

Tom said it was, and then he told Billy-Bob how people had been ripping out the inside of the house.

"I heard that," the old lawyer said. "Trying to find old Bert's money. You know, Tom, he never told me he kept it up there, but if he did, you can bet none of those wild rummies is likely to find it. He knew a thing or two about where dumb people like them, the kind that always try making it on someone else's money, would spend their time hunting and you can bet he found some other place to put his."

He wasn't surprised the money-hunters had turned their attention to the barn.

"You know," he went on, "I wouldn't want to go up there at night myself. Bert Breen must be stomping up out of his grave by now, and I wouldn't want to meet him."

He asked Tom how much pay he was drawing from the mill, but made no comment when Tom told him. He came around his desk to walk Tom to the front door and shook hands.

"I'll look into this for you, Tom," he said. "Come to that, I've an idea Bert Breen would be pleased about you wanting his barn. He set a lot of store by it — more than he did his house."

29

Tom didn't see Billy-Bob Baxter again for quite a while. But he was kept too busy to think of much of anything. There were more people moving up into the northern districts, and Boonville got its share, a lot of them Polish people, who not only worked hard on their farms but believed in well-fed stock, which meant more business for Ackerman and Hook's. Mr. Hook talked some of taking on an additional mill hand, but Erlo Ackerman vetoed the idea and after a time things settled down. The mill was busy all day every day, but Tom and the other three had become accustomed to the extra work.

Then on the Monday after Thanksgiving, when Tom was in the office picking up the slips on the next order, the telephone rang, and Mr. Hook answered it, listened a minute, and said into the instrument, "You want to speak to him, Billy-Bob?"

Apparently the answer was no, because Mr. Hook hung up the receiver piece, and turned to the counter.

"That was for you, Tom. Billy-Bob Baxter wondered if you would stop at his office some time before too long. Have you got a business deal with him?"

Since Mr. Hook knew all about Tom's hopes and plans anyway, Tom told him how he had gone to see Billy-Bob at Birdy Morris's suggestion, and how Billy-Bob had promised to find out when the Breen place was coming up on the County list.

"I'd have done that for you, Tom, and not charged you a fee, either," Mr. Hook said.

"He didn't say anything about money for himself," Tom said. "I didn't ask him, either."

"Well, we'll see what he does. Billy-Bob goes his own way."

Tom hadn't taken into account the possibility of a lawyer fee. It was much on his mind when he went up to Billy-Bob's office after closing that evening. Lights were on in house windows and in the brick Episcopal Church, where he could hear somebody playing the organ. He thought it sounded melancholy and it increased his uneasiness when he went into the lawyer's office. He caught a faint smell of whiskey, as if Billy-Bob had been treating himself to a drink before supper, but he could see no sign of it anywhere, and Billy-Bob seemed friendlier than he had the first time.

He sat Tom down in the same chair, went around to his

own side of the desk, and picked up his stogie cigar from a blue saucer. He told Tom that he had looked into the matter of the Breen place coming up on the County list, and it seemed as if it might be next April, or it might be a year from then, depending on one thing or another. He advised Tom to go about his regular doings and not worry about it and he himself would keep his eye on things and let Tom know if they were coming up to scratch.

Tom thanked him and said it would be better for him if it didn't come on the list next April but the year after. Then he asked Billy-Bob if he owed him any money for the trouble he'd been put to.

"Don't worry about that, either, Tom. It only took a few minutes, and the traveling time I spent would come onto my other business, anyway. I'll let you know if you owe me anything when you get your barn. That fair?"

Tom had to say it was. He didn't know what else he could say. He liked Billy-Bob, but the way Mr. Hook had talked had made him uncertain. It bothered him off and on through the rest of that fall. It was still on his mind when Christmas came, which may have been partly why Christmas that year didn't seem the same as the one before. He was worried about the money he had spent fixing up the house, for one thing. He hadn't felt entitled to spend as much money on presents. He got Birdy tobacco again, and more ribbons for Cissie-Mae and Ellie, but he couldn't afford another shirtwaist for Polly Ann. He had hunted through all the stores without finding anything that seemed right for her. In the end he had picked out a white and gold teapot that he came upon in the Trading Post and paid a dollar for. It looked handsome to him, but he was troubled at the idea of giving Polly Ann anything that had belonged to someone else, that wasn't new, that had cost him only a dollar. He didn't feel right about it, even when she kept saying what a beautiful teapot it was.

Birdy also admired it, taking the lid off and putting it back on again and again. He seemed much more at home with them than he had the year before, as if he had become one of the family. He had brought Tom a handsaw. It was old and thin-bladed, more flexible than modern saws came, but Tom could see that it was very good and had been well cared for. Birdy had set and filed the teeth himself. When Tom came to try it, he found that it cut faster than any saw he had used. It was easy to follow a mark with it; like any good tool, it seemed to guide itself. He knew that Birdy had thought of it helping put up the barn.

It turned out later in the day that someone else had been thinking about Tom and his barn. Just before sunset sleigh bells rang out down their road. The silver ripple of notes grew loud so fast that they hurried to the front windows to see the rig go by. It didn't, drawing up instead at the steps to their front porch, a tall, gray roan horse hitched to a new cutter with travois runners and its top folded back. One glance at the driver told Tom who it was, but he couldn't imagine what had brought Mr. Hook their way.

He looked taller than usual, getting out, maybe because of the long, gray greatcoat he wore. It had a broad black astrakan collar to match his cap. He fetched a hitching weight from under the seat, which he snapped to one ring of the horse's bit, and then reached back under the lap-robe and brought out a parcel. He said, "Merry Christmas," as Tom opened the door, and held out the parcel. "This isn't exactly a Christmas present, Tom. But I thought you might like it."

Tom didn't know what to say, but Polly Ann came out

on the porch then and said, "Won't you come inside, Mr. Hook? It's cold out here."

George Hook took off his cap as she spoke and smiled at her, and then quickly at Cissie-Mae and Ellie, who had come out behind her.

"Just for a minute, Mrs. Dolan. My horse is pretty warm."

"You'll stay for a cup of tea, surely," she said. "I want to use my new Christmas teapot. Tom can put your horse in the barn."

"I couldn't say no. To such a nice invitation," he said, smiling once more at her and the girls, and she colored a little, turning ahead of him into the house.

"Oh," she said, "I forgot to introduce Birdy Morris to you. Mr. Hook. Mr. Morris. Birdy's had Christmas dinner with us."

Mr. Hook shook hands. But Birdy was shy and embarrassed.

"I'll be starting home, Polly Ann," he said. "Best to get back afore dark."

She tried to keep him, but he wouldn't stay. He went out to the barn with Tom and the gray horse to get his own old team. They spent a few minutes admiring the gray horse, and Tom tried to persuade Birdy to stay to supper, but again he wouldn't. He'd had a fine dinner, but he wanted to get back. Tom knew he was uneasy in front of Mr. Hook and let him go, but he felt sorry as the old man drove off.

When he himself returned to the house, Polly Ann was carrying the tea into the parlor. The girls had evidently got over their first frozen shyness. Ellie was taking Mr. Hook's coat and cap into the hall to hang them on the deer horns that served for a hat rack, and in the parlor Cissie-

Mae was telling Mr. Hook how well she got on with her arithmetic.

Polly Ann put down the tray and poured them tea from her Christmas teapot. Tom picked up the package Mr. Hook had brought and opened it. It was a book, a large one, as large and heavy as the Bible that had belonged to Polly Ann's mother and as long as Tom had lived had been the only printed book in the house. It was bound in heavy black cloth and had gilt lettering that said *Encyclopedia of Practical Carpentry*, Mark Foster, Editor. It wasn't really an encyclopedia but a series of chapters, beginning with "Basic Rules," going on with "Proper Use and Care of Tools," to more elaborate descriptions, like "Framing the House," "Framing the Barn," and a chapter called "Trusses: For Large Buildings, Bridges, etc." Almost every page had a diagram or drawing. Tom saw that he could learn a lot, even though he found reading a slow and difficult business.

Mr. Hook said he hoped it might be helpful. It was an old book. His father had had a copy of it that had somehow disappeared. He had found this one in a secondhand bookstore in Syracuse.

Tom looked up. Cissie-Mae and Ellie were leaning over his arms and Polly Ann was looking over his shoulder. They were all admiring the book, Cissie-Mae offering to help him with the figures in it and Ellie saying she would help him in reading the harder parts and Polly Ann just admiring. The funny thing was that he wasn't thinking about carpentry or even the barn. It had come to him that if Mr. Hook could buy him a present in a second hand bookstore it must be all right for him to buy Polly Ann a teapot in the Trading Post. He hadn't felt so happy the whole of Christmas.

30

During the winter he spent a good part of his evenings studying in the big carpentry book. He bought himself a carpenter's square and learned from the pictures how to use it, not only for squaring off a board but to make various angles by holding different figures against the edge of the board. He practiced making mortises, and tenons to fit them, and by the end of the winter he had made a box for Polly Ann's sewing things, with the corners dovetailed. The diagrams and drawings seemed to make reading come easier for him, and sometimes he did the lessons the girls brought home from school, while they made a game of being his room teacher.

The winter went by faster than any he could remember. By the time the roads opened and he could hang his snowshoes on the woodshed wall, he had got some money back in his savings box. It didn't amount to but a bit over twelve dollars, but he figured if the Breen place came up for sale he would find enough money somewhere to bid it in.

Just the same, he was relieved when Billy-Bob Baxter told him that the place wasn't among those on the April list. A year more of saving and he would have likely fifty dollars to bid in on the place with. He went up one Sunday with a six-foot rule to measure out the barn foundation. He wrote the figures down in a small notebook Cissie-Mae had given him on his birthday. While he was doing it, he heard the house door slam. He looked that way and saw a man standing on the porch, looking down at him.

"What you think you're doing there, boy?" the man asked.

Tom said he was getting the floor dimensions of the barn.

"What you want them for?" the man demanded harshly.

"I'm going to put up a barn on my own place," Tom said. "If I get a chance I want to buy this one and move it down."

The man came down off the porch and moved on till he was about a foot away from Tom. He was thin and tall. His eyes watered a little. They were a kind of lightless gray. His nose bent a small bit leftward. There were tobacco stains at the corners of his mouth, which also had a smell of whiskey. But he wasn't drunk. Tom could see that. He was whiskey-mean. His hand flashed out like a snakehead and caught Tom's wrist, squeezing it till Tom's fingers had to open and the notebook fell to the grass.

The man bent down to pick it up, but he kept his head turned so the watery eyes never lost sight of Tom. When he had the book he moved back a pace or two and looked through the pages. He threw it back on the grass and said, "Seems that's what you was doing. But I don't like people nosing around this place."

"It ain't yours, is it?" Tom said.

"That don't matter. I don't want people nosing around. So you git, boy. And don't come back."

Tom said, "If I get to buy the barn, I'll be back."

The man said, "If I'm done here, you can have it. If I ain't you better stay off."

Tom could see he meant it. He wasn't a man who would take someone crossing him easy. He was one to be afraid of. As he turned back to the house, Tom saw a couple of men staring at him from the broken upstairs windows. They had the same look as the first man, who had gone up on the porch now. He was looking back at Tom with the sunlight striking his face. In it his eyes looked close to being white. Tom felt a chill and knew it was a good time to vamoose. He got in the wagon, turned Drew around, and headed for the road.

As he started back towards Hawkinsville it came to him who the man must be. His name was Yantis Flancher. Birdy Morris had told about him and his brothers, Newman and Enders. They lived back beyond Highmarket and if you came on any one of them you could know the other two were somewhere not far off. They lived the way they liked to. If they wanted beef, they would help themselves to a cow or young steer from anybody's herd. People who had tried to pin the killing on them had had bad luck. A barn burned down. A water trough got poisoned. The linchpin of their wagon was filed nearly through to break coming home with a load of feed. Or else the Flanchers would get hold of the man himself. That had happened twice. After that people said it didn't pay to truckle with the Flanchers.

The one who planned things was Yantis; he was the oldest and the brainiest, Birdy said. Newman and Enders were slow-minded, but just as mean. It would be a good thing for Tom to stay away from Breen's, he said. The Flanchers were obviously on the hunt for Widow Breen's money. Yantis probably had got a new idea about where it might be hidden, and he and his brothers would be worse than mean to anybody they thought might be trying to get in ahead of them.

They would have to give up looking in time, though. That would be soon enough to think of taking down the barn.

31

Tom and Birdy took time the first Sunday in May to survey where they would put the barn, once they had moved the timbers to the Dolan place. Using the figures in Tom's notebook they staked out first one outline and then another behind the house. In the end Tom decided that the best location would be where their present barn stood, except that there wouldn't be room for the larger Breen barn, the ground rising as it did almost eight feet right at the back. Then Birdy said there wasn't anything to stop them in that. They could dig into the knoll, turning the end of the building into a sidehill barn. It would be warmer for the horses that way, and besides there would be no need of a ramp to draw a hay load up to the mow floor, as there was at Breen's. The back mow doors would be just level with the knoll, which would become a natural ramp for hay wagons.

Tom could see the barn as if it was already standing in place. Then suddenly it seemed foolish to him to plan it that way, supposing for some reason he couldn't get it. But Birdy said stoutly that if they couldn't get the Breen barn they'd build another like it out of other timbers. Built into the knoll as they had planned it now, it would be a different kind of barn anyhow. The sills would carry only as far as the knoll and from there the stable walls would not be wood. They would have to be stone, rising to the mow floor clear around the horse stable. That would mean getting a lot of stone together. But he knew of four or five abandoned farms in the flat country beyond his own place which had stone both for the barn and the house-cellar walls.

So during the summer, evenings and on Sundays, Tom would hitch up Drew and drive back to Birdy's place. Sometimes he picked the old man up. Sometimes, mainly Sundays, Birdy brought his own team and wagon too, and they would pry down a cellar wall and load the wagons and drive home to the Dolans, feeling good about their loads. Birdy insisted on stacking the stone in a neat square. He said you couldn't tell how much you had if you tumbled the stones in a heap, any old way. September was about done before he figured they had laid up enough for the barn wall.

Then on a Sunday soon after, he suggested that they drive up to the Breen place together to see what might be going on. It was warm and bright, the sun hotter than you expected in October, and Birdy had his shotgun under the wagon seat.

"I haven't ever truckled with Flanchers," he explained. "And I don't aim to now. But if it turns out that way, I want things so I can answer back."

Perhaps because it was Sunday, they saw nobody at the Breen place as they drove up, though Birdy said he didn't expect that was because the Flanchers had gone to church. If they had, he said, pulling the shotgun out from under the seat, it wouldn't be to say any prayers but more likely to make off with the collection boxes.

The house was forlorn and empty. There wasn't a window left with glass in it. Inside it looked as if the Flanchers had been determined to leave no cranny unopened. Outside the ground had been dug up systematically for fifty yards around the house.

"This ain't the kind of work those Flanchers are used to doing," Birdy said. "Beating up somebody or killing cows is more their line. Must be Yantis thinks he knows something about the money."

They went down to the barn and let themselves in. Tom wanted to figure out where the ground sills would have to be cut to accommodate the knoll and how to tie into the high stone wall inside it. Now he realized how much he had learned from his carpentry book. He told Birdy he thought they ought to put in a heavy post for the stone wall to butt on, a timber maybe fourteen inches square, to connect the ground sill with the second sill carrying the mow floor, and brace it two ways. Birdy agreed. He didn't know where he could find a timber that size, but he had a spruce stand in his own back lot with a few real big trees in it, and he said he could surely find one he could get the two posts out of. They would fell it right away so it would have plenty of time to season, and Birdy would square it himself. He had his father's broadax, which he had used some in his time. He couldn't do the kind of job his father did, he told Tom diffidently, but he could make it square enough. They could put the best-looking face inside where it would show, with the wood wall joining on one side and the stone butting on the other, so it wouldn't seem too bad. Tom said whatever Birdy did would look fine, and the two of them went up on the mow floor to look at the framing once more. It seemed a pity they couldn't start taking it down right away. But there was no way they could get to do that till the place was listed.

They left, driving through the stand of chokecherry and turning down the Hawkinsville road. The Meyer house, in which Tom had seen the porcupine signs two winters before, was the first on their right, and as they came close to it, three men walked out and stood beside the road. Birdy brought the old shotgun out from under the seat with a motion so quick and easy Tom realized the men hadn't even seen it. Or perhaps they weren't looking for anybody to take up a gun in front of them. He didn't need anyone to tell him who they were, but Birdy said, "Flanchers," as if he was naming some kind of snake.

"Where you fellers been?" Yantis asked for himself and the other two.

Birdy worked on his chewing tobacco a minute and when he had it oily enough he spit out over the wheel, a calculated spit that lit about just halfway between him and Yantis.

"Up to Breen's," he said. "You mind?"

Yantis moved his eyes slowly to look at Tom. Tom had the notion that looking at them was like seeing the inside of ice.

"I told you, boy, to stay clear of there, didn't I?"

"You've got no claim on it," Birdy said. "It don't belong to you or anybody until it's bought in for taxes. We got as much right there as you have, Yantis. We'll go there when we like."

Tom saw Enders and Newman edge closer to the road. They were about ten feet away from the front wheel of the wagon. Yantis paid no heed.

"What you want there, Morris?"

"None of your business that I can see," Birdy said. "But we was studying the barn to see how we could fit it into Tom's place."

"Maybe that's so," Yantis said. "But stay off of there till we're through. And that boy needs a lesson. Take him down, boys."

The brothers stepped forward and the muzzle of Birdy's shotgun pointed straight at Yantis's face.

"You step right back, Enders, Newman," he said. "Or else your big brother's face is going to get altered."

Yantis's lip lifted.

"That old gun! I don't believe cartridges is made for it any more. I doubt if it's loaded anyway."

"Then it won't matter if I pull the trigger and find out," Birdy said, tipping the muzzle up a fraction. The gun roared, belching smoke. Newman and Enders jumped like a pair of rabbits, but Yantis, though his face showed sweat, held his ground.

"Truth is," Birdy said, "I don't recollect putting that cartridge in myself. Maybe didn't put one in the other barrel, either. You boys want to find out?"

Yantis's mouth stretched to show his teeth, a kind of dog's grin.

"We'll believe you, Morris. But I'm telling Dolan there to quit messing around the Breen place. I told him once already and I'm not telling him again."

"If he comes to take the barn down, I'll come with him," Birdy said. "And if we need more fellers we'll bring them, Yantis."

Yantis didn't move when Birdy told Tom to drive on. His face remained blank, like his eyes. But Newman and Enders looked put out and angry.

Birdy said, "They didn't expect I'd have my gun along. They was planning to haul us off the wagon and give us a beating or maybe worse than that. But they get rough only when they know you can't fight 'em back. Don't go up to Breen's alone, ever, Tom. But we'll take the barn down all right, no matter what they think they're going to do, when you get title to it."

32

Tom didn't get title to the Breen place. Things had to work out differently. A couple of weeks after he and Birdy had had their encounter with the Flanchers he found a telephone message from Billy-Bob Baxter waiting for him when he got to the mill. Billy-Bob would like for him to come to the office as soon as was convenient. He used his lunch hour that same day to go up to the little house on Leyden Street.

The lawyer was in his office, and his housekeeper, an elderly woman with a seamed brown face like an Indian's, was just carrying in his lunch on a tray which she put on his desk.

"Come in, Tom, and set down," he said. "Had your lunch?"

Tom said he hadn't. He had left it at the mill but would eat it as time served when orders slacked off. Billy-Bob examined his plate and said, "Liver," approvingly.

"There's nothing beats liver to thicken your blood when you get old," he remarked. "Calves' liver, that is. I don't hold with pork or beef liver." He cut off a piece and chewed it up deliberately. Watching him, Tom became anxious, and the lawyer, looking up to meet his eyes, nodded.

"I'm afraid I've got a piece of news you won't like to hear, Tom. Someone's bought up the Breen place."

For a minute Tom couldn't answer. It felt as if the bottom had dropped out of the world. He could only stare at Billy-Bob, a freeze clamping onto his heart. Finally he managed to say, "I thought it was going to get auctioned."

Billy-Bob nodded. "That's how it generally happens.

But if somebody offers a good price for the land, the County usually lets it go."

He went on eating his lunch with Tom just staring at him. Finally he wiped his mouth and put the napkin down and reached into the desk drawer for one of his stogie cigars.

"I know this meant a lot to you, Tom. But don't let it get you down. Not too far, anyway."

"Who bought it, Mr. Baxter? Do you know who?"

"Yes, I found out. Ab Lambert. He lives way up the White Lake Corners road. Cousin of Oscar Lambert at the bank. But he's not in banking. Not in much of anything, I'd say."

"What would he want the place for?" Tom asked.

"Don't expect he does want it, Tom." Billy-Bob got his stogie drawing and blew some smoke down on the desk top between them. "He's most likely acting as a front, buying it for somebody else."

"Why would anybody want to do that?" Tom asked.

"Well, if a man wants to buy up land, he doesn't want people to know it, to buy it first and then hold him up for a bigger price. Ab Lambert's done this before, and I guess I know who he's acting for this time. But I'll make sure, and then I'll tell you. When we know for sure who's bought the land maybe you can make him an offer for your barn."

It seemed to be the only thing Tom could do, but it didn't seem to promise much. He felt bitter about it. All the planning he had done, he and Birdy too for that matter; the stone they'd gathered for the foundation; even his idea of getting two or three nice heifers, maybe persuading Mr. Massey to let them go at a price he could afford: all of it seemed to have gone for nothing. He knew Billy-Bob's eyes were watching him so he tried not to let his face show the way he felt, but he couldn't stop swallowing, so he guessed Billy-Bob knew pretty well.

"I shouldn't wonder," the lawyer said, "if it wasn't better for you not to own that land. It ain't worth anything, Tom. All it's worth is the barn that stands on it. And *that's* what you want, not twenty sandy acres. You'll be better off having just that. Soon as I find out for sure who the place really belongs to, I'll let you know."

The rest of the day at the mill didn't mean anything. Afterwards he couldn't remember who had come in or what anybody had said, and when it came time to start home he found he hadn't eaten his lunch. He tossed the sandwiches into the river when he was crossing Fisk Bridge so Polly Ann wouldn't know, but he did not have appetite for supper either. He sat there picking at his plate and hardly talking at all, though he knew the girls and Polly Ann were watching him. He sat there the same glum way all the time the girls were doing their homework. When their bedtime came he said he was going up himself, but Polly Ann said, "Not yet, Tom. I want to talk to you."

She made him sit down at the kitchen table and poured them each another cup of tea.

"Has something gone wrong for you, Tom? *Something's* on your mind."

She looked steadily at him, her eyes big and full of kindness, so he felt he wanted to cry.

"The Breen place has been bought out," he blurted.

She waited a minute, seeing how bad he felt, to let him pull himself together.

"Why," she said, "did you want to buy it yourself?"

He nodded.

"But what for?"

He realized then that he hadn't told any of his family about his plan to get the barn for the price of the unpaid taxes. He had wanted to be able to tell them the barn was his, so they would wonder how he had managed it after spending so much money at fixing up the house. He had been counting on the way they would admire him. Now it wasn't possible, he had to tell Polly Ann about his no-good plan.

She said sympathetically, "It's too bad, Tom. I'm sorry." She looked down to stir her tea, showing the white part in her hair that was shaped by the round of her head. Then she lifted her eyes to his. When she spoke to him again her small voice had hardened, the way it used to when she told him about having to sell berries at the kitchen doors of the big houses up the valley. "It's not as if it was bad news, Tom. Like, for instance, you losing your job with Ackerman and Hook. That's a real thing and your idea about the barn and getting it for taxes was a dream you'd worked out. I'm not saying it wasn't a good plan. It was, I guess. But it depended on might-have-beens, and might-have-beens ain't things to grieve for unless you want to roll in pity of yourself."

He didn't have an answer to that. He had to admit it was partly true. He looked at her small earnest face and saw how determined she looked, and he began to feel better. She seemed to see his feeling change, for she grinned at him, a wide grin, showing her teeth.

"Maybe you'll get to buy that barn yet, Tom. The man who has the place wouldn't want that barn, old and all as it is. I wouldn't think he would, anyway."

Tom grinned a little ruefully. "Maybe he won't," he said. "But he won't let me have it as cheap as if I could have bought the place for taxes."

"Maybe not," she told him, smiling back at him but with some of the old fierce earnestness still in her. "But I've got the idea you're going to buy it all the same."

He wanted to ask her who was dreaming now, but thought he better not.

33

It wasn't until near Christmastime that Tom found out who the real buyer of the Breen place was, and he didn't find out through Billy-Bob Baxter, though the old lawyer had been right about Ab Lambert's fronting for somebody else. Bancel Moucheaud told him that Ab Lambert had been acting for Mr. Armond, whose land bordered on three sides of the Breen place. Armond wanted to fill out his boundary there. He had a great deal more land, more than a thousand acres, than he could ever farm, but he liked the idea of squaring up his property. By all accounts he could afford to.

The Armonds came up from New York City every spring with a chambermaid, a waitress, a cook, and a laundress, and last summer with a coachman too, and Bancel Moucheaud had been paying attention to the chambermaid all summer. He had found her especially pretty, and easy to talk to as well, and had hoped to per-suade her to give up returning to the city and to marry him instead. The hopes had dimmed, but he had stopped by the Armond place the other night to find out her ad-dress with the idea of putting in a final plea on paper.

The Armonds, of course, had long since left for the win-ter; but Bancel thought Parker Munsey, who ran the Armond farm with its big dairy herd, might tell him how to get in touch with his girl. Parker Munsey didn't turn out to be much help. He had no idea whether Prill, the chambermaid, was still with the Armonds. The best he could do for Bancel was to give him the Armonds' address. Parker Munsey indicated he was no longer interested in the subject, but when Mrs. Munsey brought in coffee and chocolate cake, he got a little more talkative.

Parker wasn't friendly, Bancel said. He was a big, bony, stubborn man, and inclined to be sour with other people. But he told Bancel about Mr. Armond's getting hold of the Breen place. "No idea what he paid for it. It's not worth anything, so he paid too much, that's sure. You get to be a lawyer in New York City and what you spend up in this country don't mean anything to you."

Mrs. Munsey said he oughtn't to talk that way about Mr. Armond, and Parker told her to shut up.

"I like him well enough," he said, "but that don't mean I got to bow down. That Breen place wouldn't be good for anything except to grow potatoes, and it ain't flat enough for more than a dinky little patch of them, being mostly on that hill. The house is all tore apart, too, by people hunting money. That's one thing I'm going to put a stop to."

Bancel said he'd heard that the Flanchers were doing most of the money digging, and they were people it was dangerous to get on the wrong side of.

"I don't care who they are," Parker Munsey told him. "They'll get off and stay off."

Bancel said that Parker Munsey himself appeared a man who could act mean if he wanted to, and with people like him and the Flanchers both hanging around Breen's it would be a good place for ordinary people to stay away from. He himself wasn't going to go up there, money or no money. He wondered if Tom could lend him the price of a two-cent stamp. What he wanted to write to his Prill wasn't the kind of message you would like to put onto a postal card.

Tom happened to have a five-cent piece in his pocket that day and he gave it to Bancel, who promised to give him back the change. Bancel Moucheaud was always happy-go-lucky in his money dealings. You couldn't get annoyed with him, though, because he would as soon lend Tom a two-bit piece as borrow a nickel. The trouble was he never seemed to have any money himself, not in his pockets at any rate.

Like most such people, he was always glad to give away a piece of news, and within two days practically everybody in town had heard about Armond's buying the Breen place. When Tom next went to see Billy-Bob Baxter the old lawyer said he ought to have guessed it, first off.

"Butting on his property that way," he said. "And he's picked up other land like that through Ab Lambert. Anyway I found out what he paid for it. A hundred dollars. Five dollars an acre. That's twice what it's worth and no doubt why the County was willing to let him have it."

Tom said gloomily, "I guess he ain't likely to let me buy it. And if he was, he'd want more'n I could pay him."

"I don't know. I don't see what he'd want the barn for. Way back there at the end of his place. How much could you pay?"

"I've got a little over fifty dollars saved," Tom said. "In spring I ought to have about eighty."

"He might take that. I don't know. These big city lawyers, they're different from people living up here. I'd go see him and ask whether he would take it," Billy-Bob said.

"I couldn't afford to go to New York City."

"I didn't mean that. Of course you can't. I meant, see

him next spring. With a man of his sort it's much better if you make your offer in person," Billy-Bob said shrewdly, looking at Tom across his desk. "Yes, I'd go next spring, a little after he's got up here. And I think I'd offer him fifty dollars down, and fifty dollars after the barn is up on your place."

"I'm going to have to buy some new siding and roof boards," Tom said. "And shingles. That is if he'll let me have it."

"Don't worry about that," Billy-Bob told him. "You'll have thirty dollars towards that the first year. If you need more money, I'll go to the bank with you and help you arrange a loan."

34

It meant waiting through a third winter. The early part was easier. There was Christmas to think about. He bought presents again for Polly Ann and the girls and Birdy Morris because he didn't see how he could avoid doing so, having already given them presents two years in a row. One thing always seemed to lead to another, the way his dreaming of the barn made him paint the house.

Mr. Hook came by Christmas Day as he had the year before, and this time he brought candy for the girls and Polly Ann as well as a set of carpenter's tools for Tom. He said they had belonged to an uncle and they showed they had seen use. But Birdy Morris said that tools that had been used and kept well were always worth more than brand-new ones. He admired them and nothing was said about his having given Tom a saw the year before.

This year Polly Ann persuaded the old man to stay, and before long he and Mr. Hook were sharing recollections of older times until Birdy suddenly burst out with, "Why, George! When that happened you wasn't knee high to a calf, hardly."

George Hook had to admit that must have been so. It must have been he recollected what his father had told him of the event, which Birdy accepted as a possible thing. They had a great deal to talk about, and when Polly Ann, who had disappeared for a while with the twins, came back into the parlor to say supper was on the table, neither Birdy nor Mr. Hook mentioned having to go home. They sat down to the platter of cold ham she had sliced off the Christmas roast, with pickles and potato salad, and cider to drink, and went right on talking about fishing trips and horse trades and the old-time hermits who lived way back in the woods with no friends except the garter snakes and toads around their shacks. Then, all of a sudden, it was half past eight, which *was* time to go home. Tom could see that Mr. Hook was enjoying himself. And Polly Ann's cheeks and eyes were bright. She listened to the men, breaking in now and then with some recollection of something her father, Chick Hannaberry, had told her when she was a little girl. The men listened to her and laughed at some of the things she said. Tom never recalled seeing her look livelier or prettier.

It was along in the end of February that doubt began to gnaw at his mind. Buying the Breen barn, taking it apart, moving the timbers down, and putting them up again had seemed simple. A thing that was bound to happen. Like one or two of the Arabian fairy stories in the girls' readers. Now he had learned a lot about what work meant. He had learned a good deal about carpentry and had done a bit himself on the house, and the more he knew about doing things the more difficult moving that barn and putting it up again appeared to be. He became gloomy and discouraged, until Polly Ann took notice of his state of mind and got him to talk about it.

"You hadn't ought to get discouraged, Tom. Sure, it seems bigger than you thought, now you've learned what it takes to get a thing done. But, Tom, you got this idea about the Breen barn three years ago. You've never let go of it. You were a dreamy young boy then, and it seemed as long as you wished something it would surely be. Now you're sixteen. You've changed. You're big as some men are. Strong, too. And you've been growing up inside. But, Tom, that idea was *good*. It would be a sin to give it up because it looks some harder. That idea was what started you doing things, like working for Ackerman and Hook, like fixing up our house. It's not only been good for you, it's been so for the girls and me, and we are proud of you. You go and make Mr. Armond an offer, come spring."

She looked at him earnestly, searchingly, as she always did when she felt strongly about anything. He hoped suddenly that when he got married it might be to a girl who felt as earnest as Polly Ann did about things. It made him feel a good deal better about the barn then. And he thought back to what she had said once more the Sunday morning he made up his mind to drive over to see Armond. When he told Polly Ann where he was going, she took it as a matter of course. She smiled and wished him luck.

He was wearing his ordinary clothes. Polly Ann had thought he ought to buy a new jacket to wear when he went to see Mr. Armond, but he had decided against it, mainly because he didn't want to spend the money. Mr. Hook had agreed with him. "Don't try to look different than you are," he said. "It will only make you uneasy."

George Hook had stopped by to visit several times in the course of the winter. Polly Ann would give him a cup of tea and he seemed to enjoy having it with the family in the kitchen. It occurred to Tom that he must lead a lonely life, and he liked the chatter of the girls. Tom could see also that Mr. Hook was taken with Polly Ann, which wasn't surprising. With her pretty looks she had a sturdy practical common sense.

"You mustn't feel bashful when you talk with Mr. Armond, Tom," she told him when he had harnessed Drew to the spring wagon and was ready to go. She was looking up at him from beside the wheel — she wasn't a lot higher than it was — and he could see the dust of freckles on her nose. "You're as good as he is, Tom, and you've come to make him an offer. If he don't want to sell the barn, that's that. Tell him good-bye and come home."

He said, "Yes." But the farther he got along the road the harder, he knew, it was going to be for him to feel offhand like that. He didn't know how he ought to behave with a man with Mr. Armond's fine city ways. He wasn't sure now that Polly Ann had been wrong in suggesting he buy a new jacket. But then he realized it was too late for that kind of second thought. In for a penny, in for a pound, as Birdy Morris was fond of saying, and that was how it was for him. He clucked at Drew and shook the lines on his rump, and the old horse shuffled into a trot as they turned up the river road beyond Hawkinsville Bridge.

The forks where one branch led up the hill to the sand flats and the Breen place seemed to come in half the usual time, so he slowed Drew down to a walk once more and took the river road. He had never been that way before. In about three quarters of a mile the spruce woods on his left opened out and presently he came to the driveway of the

Armond place. As he turned Drew into it, he felt as if a gaping void had opened in the pit of his stomach. He couldn't think how he was going to talk to Mr. Armond, what he could say to him.

A short distance from the road a gateway had been put up of two-foot spruce logs, with the bark left on, and angled braces supporting the crosspiece. Within this frame a wide gray gate stood open. Tom was impressed by the size of the timber. He had never seen anything like it. He thought it handsome, and it occurred to him, also, that Mr. Armond liked things on a large scale. No doubt his idea of what the barn was worth would be the same.

The drive curved gently through some trees, then the meadows opened out, and he could see the place itself: a group of gray painted buildings, almost enough of them, it seemed to Tom, to make a village. The main house, with wings going this way and that, was separated from the others by a fast-running creek. There were two large barns; one especially, which he took to be the dairy barn, must have been over a hundred and twenty feet long. Coming up the driveway he could not tell how wide it was, but it looked to him like thirty feet or so; and the gable end was at least fifty feet above the ground. He had heard there was a barn down at Lyons Falls two hundred and fifty feet long, but he had never seen it. This one looked big enough to him.

Besides the two barns he could see two houses, much smaller than the main one, and seven or eight other buildings. There was more to it than any farm place he had seen. Being Sunday no work was going on in the fields, but it seemed to him a place this big must need two or three teams of horses and he wondered how many milking cows would be in the herd. It made the Breen barn and his plans for it seem sadly small. You could have put the Breen barn three times over in that big one.

There was a slight upgrade towards the house and Drew took his time covering it. He surely didn't look like much. Just an old and nearly worn-out horse hauling a ditto spring wagon, as Billy-Bob Baxter might have put it. The contrast they made to the place they were approaching became more painfully apparent the closer they drew near. Tom noticed now that the driveway had been raked. Not with a highway rake to shape a road, but with a garden rake, and he felt it must be somehow wrong for him and Drew to leave their tracks on it. There was a close-cut lawn all around the house, and around the two other houses across the creek as well. It must take a lot of help to keep a place looking like that.

Then he saw that a man was sitting on the front piazza. He wore a dark, pointed beard and mustache, and he had on a white felt hat, a near-white coat and knickerbocker trousers, with stockings that had fancy patterned cuffs, and shoes of a greenish-white leather. He had high-colored cheeks and eyes so bright that Tom could see the blue from a hundred feet away. He saw that the man was watching him, and he guessed he must be Mr. Armond himself. When he got opposite he pulled up Drew and started to get down over the wheel.

The man called sharply, "Do you want to see me?"

Tom asked, "You Mr. Armond?"

"Yes," he said.

"I'd like to talk to you a minute," Tom said.

"Then take your horse around to the carriage barn," Mr. Armond said. "You can leave him and your wagon inside and come back here. I wouldn't want your horse wandering over the lawn, you know. He would leave tracks in the grass."

Tom flushed a little, not having thought of that himself. He drove around the corner of the lawn and over a bridge across the creek. He didn't need to be told which was the carriage barn. Through the open doors of the first he could see wagons lined up with their tailgates to each side wall. An old man came from the back as Drew's hoofs stomped on the wooden floor. He showed Tom a ring on the back wall to which he could fasten his horse. There was another sliding door there and beyond Tom heard horses moving in their stalls.

The carriage part had walls and ceiling of varnished birch. Down one side were ranked a fringed surrey and a strange-looking carriage which the old man said was a wagonette, made by Brewster of Long Island. It had a flat top and windows that could be pulled up out of the sides and a door at the back with two steps mounting up to it; the sides were decorated with panels of basketwork; and the driver's seat was outside the main passenger part, but covered by the same roof. It looked like a heavy thing to drag.

Along the opposite wall were an open buckboard as highly varnished as the surrey and wagonette, a buggy with red wheels, and a cutter. For a single space, Tom thought, that made a lot of rollingstock, and he felt mighty insignificant as he walked back across the bridge to talk to Mr. Armond.

35

Mr. Armond was still in his chair on the piazza.

"Come up, my boy," he invited. "What did you want to see me about?"

Tom went up the steps and stopped in front of Mr. Armond. "They say you've bought the Breen place, Mr. Armond."

"Yes, I have. But I don't see what that has to do with you."

"I've been figuring for a long time on getting hold of that barn," Tom said. "I want to take it down and move it down to our place."

Mr. Armond's intense blue eyes stared into his. The funny thing about them, Tom thought, was that you couldn't see into them the way you could see into other people's eyes if they were blue. But Mr. Armond didn't act unkind.

He said, "I see. You better sit down and tell me your name, if we're going to talk business."

Tom sat down in the next chair and remembered to take his cap off and put it on his knee. He said he was Tom Dolan.

Mr. Armond kept his white hat on his head.

"Well, Tom, I've not given any thought about what I'd do with the Breen barn. So you better tell me why you want it."

So Tom told him a little about how they were fixed, his father, Nob Dolan, gone for all these years, and how their shacky barn was hardly fit for critters any more. He explained that his mother worked out and told how he had got a job to make more money when the idea had come to him he might save enough to buy a standing barn, but particularly Breen's, after he had seen it and visited a couple of times with the Widow Breen.

"Did you try to buy it from her?" Mr. Armond asked.

Tom said he hadn't. "I didn't have no money then," he explained. "I don't think she'd even have listened to an offer. She didn't want anything changed on the place."

"I never saw her," Mr. Armond said. "What kind of a person was she, Tom?"

Tom tried to describe her the best way he could. He told how she had come out on her front porch the first time he went there with Birdy Morris and had pointed her scatter-gun at his wishbone. He didn't tell anything about her reading the cards for him, but he told how she lived alone. And finally he told Mr. Armond about the last time he visited her in the winter, before she died, sitting in her nest of blankets on the settee in her kitchen, without any stove wood left, hardly. Mr. Armond asked him a question then, so he told about getting some wood up from her barn, and when he was done Mr. Armond didn't make any remarks for a few minutes. Then he surprised Tom by asking, "What's that barn worth to you, Tom?"

"I figure I can pay a hundred dollars," Tom said. "Not all at once, though. I can pay fifty dollars right now, but it would take a year for me to pay the rest. Maybe two, if I have to buy a lot of lumber to replace roof boards and siding we break taking it off."

"I should think you'd have to replace the best part of them," Mr. Armond said slowly.

"I don't know," Tom replied. "Side boards, maybe. But with the roof boards, I calculate we can piece out. Use some of the siding up top, too."

[143]

"You've put quite a lot of thought into this, haven't you, Tom?" asked Mr. Armond.

"I've been thinking about it quite a while," Tom admitted. "Three years, I guess."

He didn't say how near he thought he had come to buying the whole place for a quarter of what he felt obliged to offer now. Looking around Armond's buildings, he realized that a hundred dollars would hardly mean a thing to a man like him. But again Mr. Armond surprised him.

"I think a hundred dollars is too high a price, Tom. I'll take your fifty down, but twenty-five will be enough next year," Mr. Armond said. "However, just so you won't think I am being charitable, I'd like you to leave as little mess as possible and I'd like the old house torn down. I guess it's pretty near just a shell, anyway, from what my man here, Parker, tells me."

"It ain't much more'n a husk," Tom agreed.

"Well," Mr. Armond said, "I don't like the idea of people trespassing on my property, and destroying some of it, even if I don't want it myself. You can take the old house down and leave what's left after you've taken any timber out of it you want. Leave it in the cellar hole."

"All right," Tom said. "We'll do that."

"We?" Mr. Armond asked sharply.

"Yes. Birdy Morris and me. He knowed my grandpa and Bert Breen and helped Bert build the barn. He said he'd help me take it down and put it up again."

"That sounds fine," Mr. Armond said, smiling thinly. "I thought for a moment you might be fronting for someone else."

"No," Tom said. "And you'll be welcome to come down to our place and see it when I get it up."

"I'll do that," Mr. Armond said.

Tom got up and hauled his wallet out of his back pocket. He took the bills out of it and counted them into Mr. Armond's hand. Mr. Armond took a wallet out of the inside pocket of his coat and stowed the bills away.

"Wait just a minute, Tom," he said. "I'll write you out a receipt. You ought never to pay over money in cash without getting a receipt in writing."

He went into the house and looking through the window Tom could see him writing at a maple desk. Then he came out.

"I think we'll just go across the brook so I can introduce you to my man, Parker Munsey. So he'll know your taking the barn down is all right."

They walked across the bridge side by side. Parker Munsey must have been watching from a window in his house, for he came out to meet them.

"Parker," Mr. Armond said, "I want you to meet Tom Dolan, here. I've just sold him the Breen barn. He's going to take it down and put it up on his own place. And he's agreed to take the old house down as well."

Parker Munsey was a lean tall man, maybe six feet three or four inches, with unfriendly eyes and muscle-lumped along his jaw. When he said he was pleased to meet Tom, he made it plain he couldn't care less, and when he took Tom's hand, Tom had to set his own jaw to keep from yelling. He knew Parker Munsey wanted it plain who was boss.

"When do you calculate to start on taking it down?" Munsey asked.

Tom's eyes were still smarting with the pain in his hand but he managed to control his voice. "When I can get to it," he said.

He saw Munsey didn't like that either. "Don't drag the

job out. I don't like strangers hanging around on Armond property."

"Now, Parker," Mr. Armond remonstrated. "Tom will be way off at the back of the place."

Parker Munsey nodded. "I know," he said. "That's what I don't like about it."

PART FOUR

36

Tom took Drew by the headstall and backed him and the spring wagon out of the barn and when he climbed in he saw Parker Munsey still in front of his house watching him. But he didn't give any thought to him as he went down the drive and turned right on the river road for Hawkinsville. He kept thinking that there was no way for him to turn back now from putting up the Breen barn on their place, not after handing over that money to Mr. Armond. Any time he got doubts about *that*, he only had to take Mr. Armond's receipt out of his shirt pocket. He did it now, and he began feeling better. It was his barn for sure, and nobody could say different. Then for the first time he noticed it had some writing on the back. He read it to himself slowly. It authorized Tom Dolan to take down the Breen house in addition to the barn, saving what timber he wanted for himself and disposing of the rest in the house cellar. It seemed to him there was no way, with that paper to show, anybody could interfere with his taking possession of the barn.

He got back home a little after dinnertime, still turning over in his mind how it would be best to begin the job and thinking he had better go up and talk to Birdy Morris in the afternoon. The girls had gone off looking for wild strawberries, but Polly Ann was waiting for him in the kitchen. She looked at him when he came through the door and smiled, not asking about how things had gone.

"You must be hungry, Tom," she said. "I've saved you some dinner."

She brought him a plate with two patties of fresh sausage meat, fried sliced apples, and mashed potatoes with gravy.

Then she fetched two cups and the teapot off the stove and sat down across from him.

"Did you see Mr. Armond?" she asked.

He nodded. He had his mouth full, so he passed over the receipt for her to read. It seemed a better way to tell her, anyway, not yet being sure inside himself how he really felt about the whole business. But Polly Ann hadn't any doubts.

"Oh, Tom," she cried. "It's fine! It's just fine! And getting it twenty-five dollars cheaper."

"I know," he said. "That's because I agreed to tear the house down for him too. But he said I could keep any timbers and boards out of it I could use. Turn the paper over. He put it in writing on the back."

She read it out loud. "Will it be a lot of extra work?"

"Oh, I don't know. Not so much. We won't be trying to save every piece we can. And I figure we ought to get enough boards to fill out for any we break taking off the roof."

She kept turning the paper over, reading first one side and then the other, her smile widening every minute.

"To think of you paying him fifty dollars cash!" she said. "And think the way we were three years ago when you first got this idea about the barn. It's fine, Tom. It really is."

He felt embarrassed, but then she switched off on another track.

"Hasn't he got funny writing. Slanting all back this way. What's Mr. Armond like, Tom?"

He described him as close as he could, and she was mainly interested in the clothes Mr. Armond had been wearing. Then he told her about the buildings, and she nodded, and all of a sudden he remembered the way she had peddled berries for her father at the back door of the big house. It made him fall silent, and a minute later he said he thought he ought to go talk things over with Birdy Morris.

Polly Ann agreed, and a half hour after lunch he had harnessed Drew and hitched him to the spring wagon and once more turned up the Moose River road. The old horse was obviously disgruntled over having to leave home a second time in one day, so they made slow time. He walked the whole way to Buck's Corners, and for some reason became even more resentful when they didn't turn off on the road to Hawkinsville but kept straight on for Ketchum's Brook. He went up the sand hill beyond the bridge a step at a time, uttering sad groans. Tom humored him and when they got to the flat going beyond the hill Drew apparently became bored with his own behavior and broke into a trot without being asked. So they came to Birdy's place in reasonable style.

Except for being on a through road, Birdy's place was about as lonely as the Widow Breen's. On the Black River side the nearest neighbor was a mile away. In the other direction there wasn't a house till you reached the Moose River, which was eight miles off. The house and Birdy's small barn were weathered. If there had ever been paint on them, it didn't show enough so a person could tell what color they had been. The shingle roofs were patched here and there, sometimes with newer shingles, sometimes with pieces of tin. The buildings stood between two open fields where Birdy raised just enough crops and mowed just enough hay to keep his animals and himself alive. The critters were like himself — wiry, old, and tough. The only difference was that none of them were crooked in the shoulder.

The first to give notice of Tom's arrival were Birdy's

geese. They always put out an alarm before his dogs caught on; but the dogs now, as they always did, chimed in, adding their barking to the honks of the old gander and his nervous, babbling wives. In the rising clamor Tom saw the heads of the two horses crane around the corner of the barn. The only animals missing were the cows. They were some place off in the woods, no doubt eating wild onion, which gave the spring-made Limburger from the Hawkinsville cheese factory a special flavor. There wasn't anything in the world you could do to stop cows from doing that in spring if they pastured any in the wood lots.

Birdy Morris was the last to put in an appearance. He came out on the porch, shuffling in a pair of old fleece slippers, and stared up the road over his humped shoulder. He recognized Tom and Drew right away, and even from as far as he still was Tom could see the grin come on Birdy's face.

"Get down and visit a while," he invited.

Tom said that was what he had come for. So Birdy suggested he unhitch Drew, unharness him in fact, and turn him into the barnyard with his own team. "They know each other good," he said. "And Drew ain't looking as perky as he should."

Tom allowed that was a fact. He had had the old horse out on the road most of the morning.

"That so?" Birdy asked. "Where you been?"

Tom said he would tell when he got back from fixing Drew.

37

Birdy was still on the porch and he said he thought they
had better go inside. "It's kind of chilly out here, even in
the sun," he said. "You could get an ager setting out here,
and a spring ager is liable to last you the whole entire
summer if you get one."

He led the way into his kitchen, offered Tom a chair at
the table, took the second himself, and poured tea from a
gray enameled kettle into two white mugs. He apologized
for not having white sugar, only maple that he had made
earlier in the year. It gave the tea a different flavor, just
the way wild onion in the milk changed the taste of Limburger. It wasn't too bad, Tom thought.

"Well," Birdy said, with his tea mug hooked on his
blunt forefinger, "you look as if you had news."

"I bought the Breen barn this morning," Tom said. He
went on to tell Birdy about his visit with Mr. Armond.
Birdy heard him all through without interrupting.

"I think you got a good enough deal," he said at the end.
"Knocking that house down ain't going to amount to
much after taking down the barn. It's half destructed already what with the Flanchers and such people."

They spent pretty near the whole afternoon working
out how they were going to do the job. Birdy suggested
that the afternoons when Polly Ann was using Drew to get
to and from her house jobs Tom should set out walking to
Hawkinsville as soon as the mill closed. He, Birdy, would
come along with his team about the time Tom would get
across the bridge and ride him up to the Breen place from
there. It would save the time waiting to pick Tom up
beyond Fisk Bridge. Through most of the summer they

ought to get two or more working hours every evening. Sundays they would plan to work all day. It was going to be quite a job, but Birdy saw no reason they could not get it done.

"Do you think the Flanchers will try to stop us?" Tom asked.

Birdy thought it over.

"I don't think they'll bother us taking down the barn," he said. "But they won't like us working in the house."

"Well, I've got a piece of paper Mr. Armond wrote out that says for me to take it down," Tom told him.

"That won't make no difference to those boys. Yantis is the only one can read, anyways. We'll just have to see how it goes. One thing it means, though. Every time we quit we'll have to load our turkey and take it home with us."

"Tools?" Tom asked.

"Tools, and ladders, everything. They'd think it was a joke to saw the rungs out of our ladders."

It would be a nuisance, but Tom saw that Birdy was most likely right.

"There's another thing," he said. And he told about being introduced to Parker Munsey.

Again Birdy thought things over, rubbing the side of his nose slowly.

"Parker was born mean," he said. "Them Flanchers are rough and bad-acting and like to smash around. But Parker Munsey's meaner than a weasel squeezing under a henhouse door."

Still and all it was hard to see how Parker could stop them as long as Tom had that paper from Mr. Armond. They talked things over some more and agreed to make a start next evening, when Tom could have the use of Drew and the spring wagon. He would bring his ladders, but

after that Birdy would take them back and forth on his
lumber wagon. He said that when the time came he would
make a special reach to lengthen the space between the
axles so as to accommodate the longer timbers. But for a
while they would be hauling smaller stuff.

They decided to meet at the Hawkinsville bridge so
both wagons could keep together going to the Breen place.

38

Ox Hubbard and Mr. Hook were out on the loading platform next morning when Tom drove down from the depot
and obviously surprised to see him arriving that way. He
had his three ladders fastened to a frame he had made back
of the wagon seat so the ends of the ladders projected forward over his head at an angle. It looked enough like a
housepainter's rig to prompt Ox to ask if he was coming to
paint the mill.

"Not unless I get a contract," Tom said. Then he asked
if it would be all right for him to keep Drew in the shed
back of the mill all day.

"I don't know why not," Mr. Hook answered. "But
what are you planning to do?"

"Mr. Armond's let me buy the Breen barn, and Birdy's
meeting me at Hawkinsville this evening after work and
we're going to start taking it down."

"Well, of course, you can keep your horse and rig here
anytime, Tom." Mr. Hook came along as Tom led Drew
down to the shed and watched him unhitch the horse and
take his harness off and tie him to one of the shed mangers.
"I hope Mr. Armond named a fair price."

Tom told him.

"That sounds fair enough," Mr. Hook said. "Tearing down the house is a lot of extra work, though."

"Birdy Morris don't think so," Tom said. "It's the barn, Mr. Hook. I never really figured how big a job it's going to be — taking it down and putting it up again."

"Don't run scared, Tom. Most jobs seem a lot bigger than they are until you've got into them. Then they look a lot more possible."

It seemed to Tom that was easy to say when you weren't tackling the job yourself, but he couldn't tell Mr. Hook that. Luckily Ox called for him to fill an order, and from then on he was kept busy for the rest of the day.

He couldn't make up his mind if the time went fast or slow. It depended on whether he was thinking about the barn or listening to what a customer was talking about. It made no difference, because six-thirty came around at six-thirty on the office clock just the minute it always did, and ten minutes after that he was driving up to the depot and then out on the road to White Lake Corners. Before he knew it Drew was stomping up the incline of the canal bridge at Hawkinsville and then down the hill he saw the bridge over the Black River and Birdy Morris waiting for him at the other end. In three minutes he had pulled up beside Birdy's rig. Birdy nodded and said hello and something about not wasting their time and they started up the river road, with Birdy in the lead.

The sun was level with them when they drove in to the Breen place. It looked as if it rested on the far edge of the sand flats, as if when it went down it was going into the river valley. But of course it was farther away, beyond Jackson Hill, which was the far side of Boonville.

It seemed to Tom as if there couldn't be much point in

starting on their job so late in the day. But Birdy Morris wouldn't listen to him. "We'll get off as many shingles as we can before black dark," he said.

They unhitched the three horses and stalled them inside the barn. Then they put up the two extension ladders and Birdy handed Tom an old spade. He himself was carrying a short flat piece of iron about ten inches wide.

"All right," he said. "Up we get, Tom. Those shingles ought to come off easy, old as they be. No need to worry about keeping any. They ain't worth a thing except you want some kindling wood."

It seemed to Tom that it was getting darker with every ladder rung he climbed; but when he got to the eaves the light was brighter. He watched Birdy prying off the bottom course of shingles and followed suit. When Birdy had cleared a patch maybe four feet up the roof, he swarmed over the top of the ladder and stood up. The roof boards were spaced out, so the cracks gave him foot holds anywhere.

"You go easy to begin with," he told Tom, "until you get accustomed to being up here. Then you won't have no more bother. The ground won't get any closer for you, but then it won't get farther down, either."

Tom found it was so. He had never been so high on a roof before, but after the first few minutes it didn't bother him at all, and where he had stripped the roof boards of shingles and could hook his toe in the cracks between them, he felt as solid as he would have on the ground. But he never could move the same as Birdy. The old man scrambled all over the roof, as quick and nimble-footed as a boar raccoon. He looked like one too, with his humped shoulder, now the twilight was cutting down the size of things, and later on, when they began taking down the frame, he would swarm across a tie beam the same way from one post to the other.

The last thread of light on the horizon had faded out before Birdy allowed it was time to quit working.

"If it hadn't clouded we'd have had the moon," he said. "Maybe it will stay clear tomorrow and we can work till after nine."

The land under them was inky dark. Looking down into it, Tom wondered whether the Flanchers had been around. He mentioned it to Birdy, but the old man wasn't disturbed.

"Reckon maybe," he said. "But they won't bother us none while we're working on the top part of the barn. We'd better get down now. Know where to find your ladder?"

Tom suddenly found that it had vanished in the dark. He had stripped swaths of shingles up the roof well to each side and now he had no idea just where he was in relation to the ladder. He could vaguely see Birdy humped over walking down the roof as if it was the natural way to go, but he couldn't do that himself. He had to sit down, dragging the old spade as he went, hunching himself gingerly down towards the eaves. When his foot got to them and reached into space, he froze up for a minute. Then he swung his foot, but the ladder wasn't anywhere in reach.

He sat still, trying to think exactly where he was. His last stripping had been going up farthest to the right from the ladder, so now as he sat at the eaves facing down, the ladder should be to the right of him. He hunched along in that direction and after a couple of yards his foot met the sidepiece. When he got his hand on it, it was simple to turn facing the roof and find the rung with his foot. He went down then with no trouble and found Birdy beside him on the ground.

"Maybe you'd ought to have brought a compass," Birdy said.

Tom had an idea the old man was grinning at him in the dark and he had to grin back.

They let the ladders down, got the horses from the barn, and loaded the ladders on Birdy's wagon, after lighting the two barn lanterns. Birdy led off. An hour and a quarter later they were at Buck's Corners, saying good night.

It was after nine when Tom got home, but Polly Ann was waiting up to give him supper.

"How did it go?" she asked, and Tom told her it had gone all right. He could hardly stay awake to say any more.

39

Polly Ann drove him up to the depot next morning on her way to her own job, and from there he stumbled down to the mill. It was a dragging day. He found it hard to keep his mind on what he was doing until the time they took off to eat lunch. Then things began coming easier; but even so, after the mill closed, the walk to Hawkinsville seemed the longest three miles he had ever done and the sight of Birdy waiting with his team beyond the river bridge was the best thing he had seen all day.

He climbed over the wheel and Birdy started the horses at once.

"Feeling a mite tuckered after last night?" he asked. And when Tom admitted it, he observed, "You'll get used to it. We can work a lot later when the moon comes right. I been looking in my almanac. Two weeks from now, if it don't rain or cloud, we'll have moonlight as late as we can keep working. My pa used to call it traveling time. If you had a long ways to go in hot weather, you went between the first quarter of the moon and the third one. That way you have light enough, and you travel when it's cool. It'll be the same with us taking Bert's barn down this summer, I guess."

As far as Tom could tell, the sun was just where it had been the day before, ready to roll off the edge of the flat land; but a rig stood in front of the house and Birdy said it was Flanchers'. The three brothers were sitting on the porch steps. They didn't answer Birdy's "Hello, boys," but watched in silence while he and Tom unloaded the ladders and put the team and wagon in the barn. They didn't move or say anything even when Birdy and Tom had put up the ladders. They sat as they were, just watching, while Tom and Birdy climbed to the roof and took up lifting the shingles where they had left off. Tom felt a kind of chill to his back. He tried to keep his mind off their presence by stripping the shingles as fast as Birdy. After a while, though, he had to look over the roof edge towards the house. The Flanchers and their rig had gone.

Their departure if anything increased his uneasiness. He asked Birdy if he had seen them leave.

"I saw them after they'd got to the road," Birdy said.

Tom didn't know what to make of them, but there wasn't anything he could do, so he turned back to stripping the shingles. The sun had long since gone down, but a young moon hung in the sky and tonight the stars were out. Though it was near dark, you could see what you were doing, and they worked till close to nine. By then they had pretty nearly finished stripping the first side of the roof.

Again they loaded the ladders on Birdy's wagon and had

the long drive home. When they reached Buck's Corners, Tom insisted on getting down and walking the rest of the way to his own house. It would save Birdy almost another hour on the road. He said he wasn't tired, the way he had been the night before, and he'd be home in half an hour.

The girls had gone to bed so Polly Ann and he had the kitchen to themselves while he ate supper. He told her about the Flanchers being at Breen's, the wordless way they had watched him and Birdy start to work, and how they had gone off without any commotion at all. Polly Ann couldn't see that it meant anything, one way or the other, but he worried over it until he dropped off to sleep.

For the rest of the week, the Flanchers didn't appear at the Breen place. Tom and Birdy stripped the shingles from the other side of the roof and began the work of taking off the roof boards. A good many broke at the ends when Tom started prying them off the rafters. Birdy had a coaxing way of loosening them, hammering the board back down, and drawing the exposed nails. Watching the way the old man worked, Tom got better at it himself, though he never became as skillful.

"Never mind," Birdy told him. "There'll be plenty with what we get off your old barn."

Every night when they quit now, they loaded the lumber wagon with as many roof boards as it could carry and took them down to the Dolan place, so Tom no longer had to walk. On the days he had the use of Drew and the spring wagon they were able to bring down nearly half again as many boards. In two weeks they had the ground beside their own small barn stacked like a lumberyard, the boards piled on spacer sticks which it was Cissie-Mae and Ellie's job to collect each day.

Tuesday of the third week they had a first-quarter moon

in a clear sky and it stayed with them till after nine o'clock. They began taking down the rafters that evening. They were pole rafters of spruce, hard and dry and light with age, fastened to the plates and purlins with wooden pegs. They pried up fairly easily and Birdy told Tom that was one reason you ought to close mow doors whenever a storm was coming. If the wind got inside it might lift the roof entire. But with the weight of snow they set solid and staunch. A queen-post roof like this one, he said, could carry just about whatever the sky dumped on it.

That week and the next, through the full of the moon, they got more work done than they had in all the time before, and Tom found himself beginning to believe that they might after all get the barn taken down and moved to his place and even, somehow, put it up again. It was the way Mr. Hook had said: when you got into a job it began to seem easier.

By the next Sunday they had the rafters all off. Birdy had installed a long reach in his lumber wagon, letting back the rear axle five feet, so the twenty-foot rafters fitted comfortably on the bolsters. They made up another load and Birdy climbed on top of it and started the horses. There was still another load left which they would take down the end of the day. No reason for Tom to go along, so they had decided he would stay and begin taking off the siding boards. Birdy had shown him how to do the work: pry the bottoms loose and then the tops. After the first two were off, forget about the ladder and work from the plate. A good day like today with no wind he could loosen the bottoms all along one side and then get up on the beam. It took him a couple of hours to pry off the bottoms with his pinch bar, and it was close to noon when he put his ladder up and got onto the plate.

Before this he hadn't worked up there by himself. Straddling the wide timber of the plate, and looking out across the flatland beyond Breen's Hill, he felt the way a sailor must, high above the ship's deck, alone in the emptiness between sky and sea. Only he wasn't alone. On the road this side of Cold Brook a rig was moving along the flats and in a minute he saw it was the Flanchers, two of the brothers on the seat and the third lying on his back on a horse blanket in the bed of the wagon. Tom guessed that one would be Enders. Birdy said he was always going to sleep unless it was time to eat or it looked as if trouble might be coming. He liked both, according to Birdy, but probably eating best.

Tom decided not to let on he had seen them, so he went to work prying loose the third siding board, letting it down as far as he could before losing hold of it. Now and then he glanced up to see where the Flanchers had got to. Pretty soon it was obvious that they were coming all the way into Breen's.

Of course, he couldn't go on pretending not to know they had arrived, so he laid his pinch bar and hammer on the plate in front of him and looked down. Yantis was getting off the wagon, but Newman stayed, holding the lines and looking up. Enders didn't move. He had his hat over his face. He must really be asleep.

Yantis came to the foot of Tom's ladder and looked up. "How's it going, Dolan?"

Tom said it was going all right.

"Where's your partner today?" Yantis asked. The sun caught the dull gray in his eyes and suddenly they looked piercing.

Tom told him. Birdy ought to be coming back pretty soon, now. But when he looked along the road he could see nothing moving. He heard the ladder jouncing a little on the plate and when he looked down again, he saw Yantis coming up. He picked up the pinch bar, trying to look casual, and then began to pry on the next board. He heard Yantis climb up onto the plate behind him.

"You come onto anything yet, Dolan?"

"What do you mean?" Tom asked.

"You know what I mean. Old Breen's money."

"I told you before. I ain't looking for it," Tom said.

"I know you said it." Tom could hear the sneer in Yantis's voice. "You're just taking down this barn."

"That's right," Tom said.

Yantis had no comment. After a moment he said, "Let me get on by you."

Tom leaned to one side and Yantis stepped over him. He was as sure-footed as Birdy was, walking along the plate. He went out to the end and stared out at the Breen house.

"You look down from up here," he said, almost to himself, "and it looks different. Maybe I ought to have done it before we done all that digging. Can't see nothing now."

He walked back to where Tom was loosening his next board.

"Dolan," he said, "We keep watching you. You don't see us, but we are doing it just the same."

"Suit yourself," Tom told him. "It don't matter to me and Birdy what you do."

"Just so you know," Yantis said, stepping past him to get to the ladder.

He went down it and walked to the wagon, saying something before he climbed over the wheel. Newman looked up at Tom for a minute and then turned the horses. They drove back to the road and turned towards Hawkinsville.

[163]

As far as Tom could make out, Enders hadn't waked up at all. Tom felt himself begin to shake. He didn't know what he'd been afraid might happen. Like meeting an adder on a narrow path and having it after a long moment turn away.

Then, far along the road, coming up from Cold Brook, he saw Birdy's wagon.

Birdy turned out to let the Flanchers by and five minutes later was pulling up at Breen's. Tom went down his ladder to meet him and they put a second load of rafters on the wagon. Then they took their lunch up on the house porch, a basket with some sandwiches Polly Ann had given them and the bottle of cold tea Birdy always drank. Tom told him about the Flanchers coming, especially the visit Yantis had had with him up on the plate.

"They ain't stopped looking for old Bert's money," Birdy said.

"Well, we're not looking for it," Tom said. "So I don't see it matters what they do."

"I guess not." Birdy had a suck at his bottle of tea. "It seems queer though, with all the digging and tearing down that's been going on, nobody's got hold of it."

"How do we know nobody found it?" Tom asked.

"We don't know. But it would be hard for somebody who did to keep it secret."

"Then maybe it's still here." Tom said.

"It must be," Birdy agreed.

40

It started Tom thinking about the money again, mostly nights or during daytime when business slacked off at the mill. It seemed obvious that Breen hadn't kept his money in the house or in the ground anywhere near it. It would have been uncovered by now with all the tearing out of walls and digging that had gone on. Or, of course, somebody might have found it and said nothing about it. But that didn't seem likely to Tom. As far as he could see the barn was the only place where it might have been hidden. The question was where it could have been kept. The only likely places were the feed bins and mangers and they had been torn out and broken up long ago. He puzzled about it for the next week. Then he forgot it in the excitement of taking down the frame.

The job was harder than anything they had tackled so far. The pegs locking the mortise joints had to be driven out and the timbers lowered to the ground carefully so as not to break the tenons. If that happened, Birdy cautioned, they would have to make a whole new timber. As each reached the ground he painted numbers on it showing which bent and which part of the bent it belonged to. So the tie beam between the queen posts that carried the purlins was marked 1–T. The two queen posts became 1–Q N, and 1–Q S from being on the north or south half of the barn. The barn site on the Dolan place faced east and west the same as at Breen's, so there would be nothing to confuse them.

They worked on the frame only on Sundays. Birdy said handling heavy timbers was too risky unless you could see exactly what you were doing. During the weekday evenings between they kept busy at the Dolan place, putting up a shed for the cows and Drew from boards and beams of the old barn, as they took it down. It was a much easier job than the Breen barn, not only because it was smaller, but because they didn't care about saving timbers and siding. What might be usable they stacked to one side. The rest they hauled to a dump in the woods. Then Birdy had to stop to do his haying and the Dolans', which they put in a stack. It seemed to Tom that they would never get started on putting up the Breen barn. He hadn't had the faintest notion when they started in of how many complications would turn up. It was the fourth Sunday of July before they set out for Breen's to take down the final timbers.

There was only the front bent left. Birdy was up on the tie beam driving out the pegs where the tenons entered the corner posts, which he had stay-lathed from two angles. Tom was taking down the timbers that framed the entrance and carried the track for the door trolleys when he noticed something for the first time. This was the hand-wrought iron hook that connected with an iron U-bolt on the door to keep it shut. He had seen it dozens of times before without paying attention; but now something about it struck him as queer. He raised his head to tell Birdy about it, but suddenly decided not to, though there wasn't anybody in sight when he looked around. He waited till Birdy had the tie beam loosened and had come down the ladder.

"You ever noticed this hook?"

"Why sure," Birdy answered. "I seen Bert put it there myself."

"Does something about it seem queer to you?"

Birdy stared at it and scratched his head. "Looks like a regular door hook to me. Made a mite heavy, maybe, on account of it's for a barn door," he said. "Come to think of it, I remember Bert had Parschall Moody make it up special. In his forge over to Forestport."

He turned back to Tom. "What's on your mind, anyways?"

Tom started to tell him, but suddenly he changed his mind. He got embarrassed trying to think of some way to distract Birdy; but then he didn't have to. The old man had lifted his head, as far as he could raise it off his humped shoulder.

"Hear that?" he asked.

"Hear what?"

"Rig's coming up the road. Coming at a real good clip, too."

Tom heard it then, and a moment later it came into view beyond the line of chokecherries. You couldn't mistake who it was, either. The gray horse beyond the bushes at his slashing trot, the red wheels of the buggy fanning sand: he knew it was Mr. Hook before the horse swung through the gap and raced up to them.

Mr. Hook socketed the whip and gave the reins a turn around it. He looked tall and cool in his dust coat and panama hat, and Polly Ann on the seat beside him, made him seem still taller. The color was high in her cheeks — from the fast driving, Tom supposed — and both of them were smiling.

"We've brought along our lunch," he said. "We thought we'd picnic with you if you didn't mind."

At the notion of their minding that, Birdy grinned, showing his stained teeth.

"Why," he said, "we was just going to knock off and eat, ourselves. Wasn't we, Tom?"

Tom nodded. They hadn't discussed it, but he could see

how pleased and excited Birdy was at having company. He went to fetch their own lunch pails.

Polly Ann was handing down her lunch basket when he came back and Mr. Hook was holding up his hand to help her down over the wheel. She took it, though she needed steadying about as much as a bird on the limb of a tree. As soon as she was on the ground, Mr. Hook reached under the buggy seat for a lap robe and gave his opinion that it was too hot out in the sun. It would be more comfortable up on the porch.

He spread the robe on the porch floor and Polly Ann sat on it, her eyes for a moment on Tom's. He couldn't make out what she was thinking but it was a little as if she had thought of a joke and decided not to tell it after all.

Anybody could see that she was enjoying herself. She had always loved taking a picnic lunch somewhere, and she said so now as she laid out the sandwiches she had brought for herself and Mr. Hook.

"When we were little we were always taking our lunch out into the woods. Generally Pa went along, especially if we were picking berries. We always even took Prinny, though she was a lot younger than the rest of us. Ma died when she was born, and when she was five years old *she* died of diphtheria. Leastways that's what Dr. Grover said it must have been when Pa took her in to his office." She paused, looking about at them. "She must have died in the wagon going into town — but I didn't mean to talk about that. Just about taking picnics. It was fun. All of us always wanted to go."

Tom thought that perhaps the reason they liked going was because it took them away from the tumbledown houses they always lived in. But he didn't say so; he could tell that she didn't want Mr. Hook to realize how dirt-poor they had been. Poorer than most critters, tame and wild.

Mr. Hook asked how many sisters they had been, and she told him five, until Prinny died. Prinny'd been the prettiest, with hair silver-yellow, like ripe June grass, a baby princess for a fact. Then for a moment she seemed to withdraw from them, her face veiled in memory, and her eyes staring out over the open meadow to the line of trees that marked the swamp. Looking with her, Tom was surprised to see how different things looked without the barn. The swamp seemed an endless place with no feature but the unbroken line of bordering woods.

"Looly and I got lost in there once for most of half a day," Polly Ann said, breaking the silence, the brightness returning to her voice. "There was a five-acre burnt piece way in the middle of it where the best wild raspberries growed of anywheres around. Pa took the two of us in there to pick. He said he could sell any amount to Armond's because Mr. Armond liked red raspberries the best of any. So he took us in along an old lumber road, mostly growed over, and told us to come back out along it when we'd filled our pails. I guess we started back the wrong direction, because when we were nearly tuckered out, Looly said if it was past noon as we knew it must be, the sun ought to be shining against us, the way it had when we went in. So we turned around, walking as fast as we could and come out of the swamp just as it was getting dark, down there beside that big pine. That's where the road come out. With the barn gone I can see the place. That must be what reminded me of getting lost."

She laughed and reached into her basket for four plates and forks.

"I made a lemon pie," she said, cutting it into fours, with the largest piece for Birdy, knowing it was the old man's favorite, and something he could not make for himself.

"But it wasn't getting lost and getting out that I recollect the most about that day," she went on. "It was getting the strap from Mrs. Breen."

She paused to look at Birdy shoving the lemon pie into his mouth, and he grinned and lifted his fork in salute, leaving a small daub of white on his forehead.

Mr. Hook said, "What did Mrs. Breen want to whip you for, Polly Ann?"

"It seems funny now, with the barn gone, I guess," she answered. "But it really scared me then. When Looly and me came out of the woods it was so near dark we headed up to the Breen house because there was a lighted window. We figured it would be easier to go there and out along their road to the main road than cut across lots. But when we got pretty close to the barn we seen the front door open on the porch," and she turned to glance behind her, but it was open anyway, showing the broken plaster of the downstairs hall.

"Mr. Breen came down the steps, carrying a lantern. He came across to the barn, and of course we lost sight of him. But we heard the door roll open, and then it rolled shut. By then we were up beside the barn and went around in front of it, passing through the light from the house window. But when we got to the dark on the other side of the barn, I said to Looly I was going to see what Mr. Breen was a-doing in the barn that time of night with the door shut tight and all. Looly said we had no business doing that and tried to get me to come along with her. She went on towards the road, but I went down the dark side of the barn to where there was a big stone beside the foundation underneath a window. I figured if I stood on it I could look inside. So I set my berries down and got up on it. The window was so dirty, though, I couldn't see much of anything at all, even when I spit on my hand and smeared it on the glass. But then I seen a light coming along between the stanchels and I made out it must be Mr. Breen. He was carrying his lantern and he had something in his hand that looked as if it might have been a pinch bar. Though what he wanted a pinch bar for in the barn, what he wanted to pry off, wasn't anything I could think of.

"Then Looly gave a kind of squeak, like a meadow mouse in front of a fox, and the next I knew something hit the back of my legs that stung almighty bad, and Mrs. Breen was saying, 'Spying, are you? It ain't decent to spy. I'll learn you,' and before I could get off the stone she gave me another godawful lick with the strap, and I tell you she meant it to hurt."

Polly Ann paused again, and then she started to laugh.

"It was awful funny. I started to run off, and she come after me the fastest she could, lashing with that strap. Then I remembered my berries and I didn't want for her to get them. So I commenced circling around with her behind me, all the time yelling how she was going to learn me for sure. When I got back to the pail, I just grabbed it and even carrying it I could get out of her reach. I lost some of my berries, and Looly made me take some out of her pail so they was both alike. But that didn't do any good because Pa acted weasel-mean all evening on account of both our pails wasn't heaping full. We didn't care, though, because we'd got clear of Breen's with only the two welts on the back of my legs. And the funny thing was, the next time we went back there, Mrs. Breen didn't say anything about it. She never did, after, for that matter."

She laughed again.

"So we never found out what Mr. Breen was doing in the barn."

Birdy recalled that Bert used to go into his barn some nights, but he'd never troubled to inquire why. Bert Breen did things his own way and didn't favor anyone who asked questions. Mr. Hook said it seemed strange to him, but old people who lived way off by themselves like the Breens often got into ways of doing things other people wouldn't think of.

He looked at Tom when he said it, but Tom didn't have any comment to make. It seemed to him Polly Ann's story fitted in, in some way, with what was queer about the door hook, and he felt a notion beginning to take shape in the back of his mind. He wanted to get Polly Ann talking some more about what she had seen, however dimly, but this didn't seem like a good time to do it.

41

Not long after they had finished eating, Mr. Hook told Polly Ann they should pack up and leave Tom and Birdy to get on with their work. He handed her up into the buggy. The gray horse was eager to get going and took them towards the road at what looked to Tom like a dancing kind of single-footing; but the minute he turned the corner behind the chokecherries he broke into his reaching trot. The ends of the scarf Polly Ann wore round her head whipped out. She sat bolt upright with her hands folded in her lap and Mr. Hook turned to tell her something.

"Them two look to me as though they was getting pretty partial," Birdy observed and went to get his horses from where they had been left standing, with old Drew, on the shady side of the house. He was cheerful when he brought them back, and he and Tom started loading the timbers of the final bent because after this he could shorten the reach again, put back the wagon box, and ride with a proper seat.

"You want me to stay and help you with your load?" he asked.

Tom said he didn't need help. A pile of boards from the siding were still left; he would load as many as the spring wagon could take and come along in a few minutes. So Birdy climbed up on his load of timbers and the team took up the slack in their traces and headed for the road.

When they had turned the corner Tom got Drew and loaded the spring wagon but he didn't leave right away. He was thinking about the hook and Polly Ann's story about Bert Breen carrying his lantern in the barn and what might have been a pinch bar. It explained what had seemed queer to Tom about the door hook, which was that Bert had it on the inside. That was where he would put it if he wanted to make sure people wouldn't come in on him while he was inside the barn, and the only reason Tom could see for that must be the fact Bert didn't want people to find out where he kept his money. And you only wanted a pinch bar to pull a spike with, or pry up a board.

But now there was almost nothing left of the barn; it had all moved down to their own farm. There was nothing left but the flooring of the run between the stanchions. It lay there, squared six-inch timbers, laid close and snug, making a roadway eight feet wide and fifty feet from one end to the other. Nothing else that anybody could see.

[173]

Tom felt his heart begin to race. He was sure he knew where Bert Breen's money was. He wanted to look for it now, but he knew he shouldn't. And while he stood at the end a man's shadow came up beside his.

He didn't turn or say anything till Parker Munsey asked, "You got something on your mind, Dolan?"

"Yes," Tom said. "I was wishing I didn't have to use this timber floor. I'd like to put down a cement one instead, like the one Massey's got in his barn, but I won't have money for it."

"Your agreement with Mr. Armond is to take away the barn. That means all of it, Dolan."

"Mr. Armond said he wanted things left neat."

"And the house torn down, too," Parker Munsey said. "When do you figure to take away this floor and tear the house down, Dolan?"

"As soon as I can find the time," Tom answered.

He felt his arm taken just above the elbow and the iron tightening of Parker Munsey's fingers, until he wanted to gasp for breath. But he managed to control himself, and in a moment Munsey took his hand away.

"That's not the way to talk to me," Munsey said. "You clear up the house and get that house torn down. As long as it stays there those Flanchers will be hanging around as well as you, and Mr. Armond and I want to be rid of this whole rigging."

"I can't help the Flanchers coming," Tom said.

"As long as that house is standing, they'll be sniffing around for Breen's money like a bunch of wormy dogs. You get it *down*."

"I got to get my foundation built," Tom said, "and get the frame up and roofed. After that, me and Birdy will take care of the house."

"It better be quick," Munsey said. He moved away as noiselessly as he had come.

Tom waited till he had disappeared around the hill. He was tempted again to look for Breen's money, but Parker Munsey might just as well have turned back and be watching now from the edge of the woods. There was nothing to do but start for home with his wagonload of boards.

42

All his life Drew had objected to having to pull anything more than the lightest load and several times while Tom was piling on the boards he had craned his head around and stared with a bald accusing eye. Now, when Tom climbed onto the seat and took up the lines, Drew closed his eyes, leaned tenderly into the collar, and groaned. The wagon did not move.

Tom flicked his rump with the whip, sharp enough to make the horse toss his head and snort rebukingly, but he did lurch forward, the wheels turned slowly, and they started home. By and by, perhaps remembering that Birdy's team was on the road ahead, he made a little better time. But it was obvious that he was tired of this whole barn business, and Tom himself thought of the relief it would be when they traveled over this road for the last time.

Polly Ann was bringing the milk pails down from the kitchen porch when they turned into the yard. Birdy had unloaded the last timbers and left. Where their old barn had stood it now looked like a lumberyard, the timbers of each bent stacked in a separate pile and the siding and roof boards in high stacks wherever there was room. It looked like an awful lot of lumber to sort out and put into the shape of a barn, and Tom wondered if old Noah hadn't felt much the same when he was ready to start building the Ark.

He unhitched Drew, led him to his place at one end of the milking shed, and gave him a small measure of oats. He fetched a pail and sat down to milk. Polly Ann got up from her stool and came beside him, saying, "Molly's drying up, I guess."

"It's about time for her to," he said, looking up at his mother. She was warm from milking, little curls stuck damply to her forehead. He could see she was still full of the day she'd had.

"I been thinking about that time looking in at Mr. Breen, Tom."

"Let's talk about it after supper. I wouldn't want anybody maybe overhearing us," he said. "I'll take care of Susie."

"All right, Tom. I'll start supper, then."

She flashed a conspirator's smile at him, half-secret, half-gay, and went back to the house. Only a minute later Cissie-Mae and Ellie came out of the woods, looking cross and hot. They'd been after raspberries but had found hardly any. They didn't have any time for Tom, but hurried straight on to the house behind Polly Ann. Their coming out of the woods so suddenly made him think of Parker Munsey, slipping up on him just when he'd thought to try finding exactly where the money was. He wondered if he ought to tell anyone what he thought he knew, anyone at all. Yet he would need someone to help get the money away — if it was there — and he could think of no one better for the job than Polly Ann.

They sat out on the front porch after supper, where it was cooler, but the girls were fractious and wouldn't go to bed till long after their usual time. It was after eleven by the time they'd settled down and Polly Ann asked, "You were going to tell me something about Breen's, Tom?"

"Yes," Tom said. "But not out here."

So they went into the house, which was still hot from the day, closing and locking the door behind them. Tom did the same to the kitchen door and Polly Ann made a pitcher of raspberry vinegar with a chunk of ice in it from the bin they had in the cellar. Its cool, sweet-and-sour taste refreshed them. Tom looked at his mother across the table.

"I'd got a notion where old Bert Breen might have hid his money," he said. "Then when you told us this afternoon about that time you looked through the barn window and seen him walking along with his lantern and a pinch bar, I felt pretty sure."

"Where?" she asked with a catching breath. "*Where*, Tom?"

"Everything seemed to pull together when you told about it," he said. "The hook on the inside of the door and then that box that had the sand and chaft in it. I kept wondering about what he would want that for, but now it's plain as a duck's foot."

"Tom!" she said, just above a whisper. "Tell me!"

He kind of enjoyed keeping her on the stretch that way. Her face was so eager. But then he had to tell her, and as he did, small doubts began crawling back in his mind.

"What I came to figure all along was that he kept his money in the barn. Then we tore it down and brought it down here and didn't find the money. So that left one place where he could have put it."

"Where?" she said again.

"Underneath the floor."

"The floor, Tom? I'd think it would get spoiled. Wet."

"Not underneath the cow stalls. Under the runway." He paused. "I figure some of the timbers ain't spiked down. All Bert Breen needed to do was to pry up one end of one of them. Then take up the other two or three. When he put them back they'd wedge in tight enough. He had that sand and chaff to scatter over them and down the run far enough so it all looked natural."

Polly Ann kept looking at him. She seemed hushed.

"I think you've guessed it," she said softly. "I think that must be where he put it. You're smart, Tom, to figure it out that way."

"Well, if it ain't there, I don't know where else it could be."

"When are you going to go look for it?" she asked. "You ought to go quick, before somebody else gets the idea."

Tom shook his head.

"I don't think anybody will, now," he said. "Not till after the house gets torn down. What I figure is, Birdy and me will tear it down. Then the night after we finish, we'll go and get the money. If it's there."

"You mean, you and Birdy?"

He shook his head.

"You and me, Ma. Birdy and me will finish tearing down the house on a day when the moon's going to be dark that night. I figure by that time, most likely in November, the Flanchers will have got tired of keeping watch up there. Especially a night that's black-dark and cold like November. I don't know about Parker Munsey, though. He's liable to show up just when you figure he won't."

He told her about Parker Munsey joining him so suddenly.

"We'll have to get there some way they won't none of them be watching."

"We could come in from Forestport," she said, and he could see how excited she had become. "We could go up to Forestport along the towpath. There won't be no boats towing by night that late in the season. We'll come down to the bridge by Dutch Hill and drive through the town along towards Miller's hatchery and then turn up on the Irish Settlement road to Kehoe's pond. There's a bridge below it over Crystal Creek. Then we'll turn back towards the river and Breen's and come back of Wingert's old place. There's nobody lives there except Nelson Farr. The road's going back to brush."

"Do you think you could find the way in the dark?" Tom asked.

"Oh, yes," she said. "If we could get through with the wagon, we could turn along the town-line road. But it's too growed up, I'm sure. Best we come down onto the back of Breen's and leave Drew and the wagon by Cold Brook. There's a ford there, but it would make noise, him splashing through the water. We could leave him in the brush and wade over ourselves and bring the money back to the wagon."

Her eyes were shining. She looked at him a long moment, but he wasn't sure she saw him at all. She was seeing something way beyond him.

"You wouldn't be scared coming with me?" he asked.

"Oh, no," she answered, so soft he could hardly hear her. "Tom, how much do you think it might amount to?"

Tom knew she meant Bert Breen's money. The funny thing was, he hadn't ever thought of it that way. Now he began to wonder.

"Birdy said once he'd bet it would be two thousand dollars. Or maybe more."

"So much as that?" Polly Ann breathed. "I don't think

we ever had as much as ten dollars in our family in all our lives. All at one time, I mean."

"Did you talk to Mr. Hook about it?" Tom asked her.

"I thought of it," she said. "But then I thought I wouldn't." Color came up in her cheeks and she glanced away.

"You think a lot of Mr. Hook, don't you?" he asked.

"I don't know what you mean," she said. And then she swung back and looked straight at him. "Yes, Tom," she said. "Yes, I do."

"Birdy said he could see it. He said Mr. Hook thought a lot of you, too." He hesitated, and then he said, "Mr. Hook is a lonesome man, I think. Maybe he might ask you to marry him."

She flushed darkly.

"Don't talk silly, Tom," she admonished him. "And if Mr. Hook should ask me, I'd say no. A person from as poor as we are has no right to marry a wealthy man like him."

PART FIVE

43

Tom had supposed building the barn back up would be a long sight slower than tearing it down had been. But it didn't seem to be that way once they had got through laying the stone foundation. The low front part went fast enough, but it took time to build the wall at the rear end, seven feet high, where the barn was dug back into the knoll. Birdy said it would have been a lot more difficult if it had been a free-standing wall, and Tom could see how that was so.

Laying stone didn't come easy to him, but it was something Birdy liked to do more than most, and some days he came and worked on the walls while Tom was still at Ackerman and Hook's. Birdy had a natural eye for stone. He seldom had to turn a stone more than once to have the face come smooth and even with the ones already placed. Every now and then as the wall gained height, he would put a stone off to one side. When the wall was nearly to height, Birdy reached for these stones, one after another, and in a way Tom found it impossible to divine, they fitted in the place Birdy had chosen, maybe with a half turn or a turn, or after a couple of taps with his stone hammer to remove a knob or a sharp corner. And as he went along, the top of the wall smoothed out, right on a level with his marking cord. Tom's job was to hand Birdy stones not readily in reach, to lift the heavier ones to the top of the wall, and to mix the mortar as it was needed. Otherwise the wall was Birdy's work and nobody else's. Time came later, when, remembering those afternoons, Tom thought they must have been about the happiest time in Birdy's life.

He kept whistling all the time he was putting up the foundation wall. It really wasn't proper whistling. It came out through his teeth, half a tune, half the kind of hiss a man makes currying a horse whose hide is clogged with mud. But now and then, if he listened close, Tom could make out the underneath side of a tune, like "We're traveling home to Heaven. Will you go? Will you go?" Or something quite different, like "Sparking Sunday Night":

> *One two three sweet kisses*
> *Four five six you hook*
> *But thinking you have robbed her*
> *Give back those you took.*

Birdy's eye would roll around at Tom, looking over his humped shoulder, as if daring anybody to make a remark. Then he would draw a snorty breath, reach his trowel into the mortar bucket, and slap a dose on the top stone, starting his whispered whistle again as he spread it out. Generally by that time he would have got some of the mortar into his mustache, turning the hairs into a gray bristle, so that when he snorted he made Tom think of an old otter telling the young ones to get out of his way.

By the end of August the foundations were done and they started putting down the sills. When they had the bottom sills in, reaching to the rise in the foundation wall, Birdy brought down the two posts of spruce he had cut and shaped on his place. He had decided to make them fourteen by ten, he said, because the logs were plenty big. They would amount to a couple of corner posts halfway down the barn, and he had brought, besides, a heavy girt to tie them crossways. It would make the heaviest cross member in the barn and would help stiffen the whole building.

[183]

"Just like a bridge," Tom agreed. Then he grinned. "We'll call it Birdy's Bridge."

Birdy didn't say anything, but he looked pleased, which was well, because getting the timbers into place was heavy work. Tenons had to be made on the butt ends of the posts, and chiseling mortises in the iron-hard old sills was laborious and slow, especially as Birdy would not allow himself to be hurried in any way. Fitting the corner braces took time, too, but in the end it was done, and the posts stood solid.

Then they had the job of raising the girt. Tom couldn't see how two people could possibly get a timber that heavy seven feet up in the air. But it didn't faze Birdy. He managed the job simply, by levering one end up at a time enough to let Tom slide under it ten-inch blocks cut out of timbers from the old Dolan barn. It was slow work, but finally the girt got to its height. The wedged ends fitted into the notches Birdy had sawed in the inner third of the posts and his "bridge" was as solid as any road bridge Tom might ever hope to cross.

After that, putting up the corner posts was simple. Their tenons slipped into mortises originally cut in the sills and they stood there on their own. But Birdy stay-lathed them to make sure they stayed absolutely plumb. Then they put the second sill in place, reaching from the corner posts to the girt and beyond that lying on the new stone wall. The front, back, and side sills were joined by dovetail tenons, needing no joins. As the weight of the upper barn came on them, they just held that much tighter.

They put in the summer beams joining the side sills. These carried the floor joists and were lighter than the great girt. Once they were in, the joists could be placed

[184]

quickly, thanks to the careful numbers Birdy had insisted on painting on each one. The next evening they began putting down the floor planks, piecing out the broken ones from the Breen barn with planks from the old Dolan barn. In two evenings all were in. The mow floor was complete, and Birdy said it was time to make plans for putting up the frame. By then it was the end of August.

"A barn raising has to be on Sunday," Birdy said. "Or else you can't get enough people to come to it."

Tom said how about the first or second Sunday in September.

"Hell, no," Birdy said. "We got to get the bents put together first. That's why we had to have the mow floor laid. So we could put them together and then we raise them."

"Then how about the third Sunday?" Tom asked. "That would be the sixteenth. We don't want to leave it too late."

"Well," Birdy said, rubbing on his nose. "I guess that would be all right."

"How many men do you think we ought to get here?"

"We could use a couple of dozen," Birdy answered. "But I guess we could make out with maybe eighteen."

"That's a lot of people to get to come all the way here," Tom said.

"Oh, no. Folks always like to come to a barn raising. It's exciting, and if something goes wrong a person might get hurt. And they look to free victuals."

"I'll ask Ox Hubbard," Tom said. "He'd know people. And I guess the Moucheaud brothers would come."

"Bancel and Louis?" Birdy said. "They'd know people in Forestport. Loggers are handy at this kind of thing."

44

Next day as they were eating lunch Tom asked **Ox** Hubbard and the Moucheaud brothers if they would come and help him raise his barn on the sixteenth.

"It's a Sunday," he pointed out.

"Why, yes," Ox said with his slow smile.

Bancel said, "Sure," and Louis asked excitedly how many other men Tom intended to ask.

"Birdy thinks we ought to have eighteen or twenty," Tom said. "But I don't know that many people. I could maybe get Massey's four hired men to come. That would make nine including you and me and Birdy. We'd need to find maybe a dozen others."

"I get them," Louis said. "Nothing to it. The loggeurs will be coming back into the woods. They stop over Sunday in Forestport."

Tom was puzzled. "Loggeurs?" he asked.

Bancel said with some scorn, "My brother has not learned English too good, even yet. He means the lumberjacks."

Louis nodded, not at all put out.

"The jacks," he agreed. "They will come. They will work at anything. But they are always hongry. You tell your mamma to have plenty of food."

Tom said he would do that. It hadn't occurred to him it would be so simple to find a barn-raising crew. Ox explained that the lumbermen started coming back into the woods in September. By that time they were always out of money. Any that might be hanging around Forestport on that Sunday would be only too glad to come to Dolan's barn raising in exchange for a big feed. They were tough men. They talked rough and sometimes they acted rough. Some people called them timber beasts. But on the whole they were pretty good-natured and they could put their hand to just about any kind of work there was to be done.

News of Tom's barn raising got around. Before closing, Mr. Hook came out of the office to talk to him. He said he would like to help any way he could. Perhaps he could best do it by helping Polly Ann collect food enough. Barn-raising crowds ate more food than it took to stock a grocery store. Once the word spread, people would come from all over to watch. Nobody ever dreamed of bringing food for themselves. They all horned in on the spread laid out for the barn raisers. You had to be prepared to feed a small army.

People came, he explained, because it wasn't often anybody put up a hay barn. It was exciting to see men get the tall bents upright and hold them in place till the plates joined them solid. A sudden windstorm, anything, could happen. It wasn't exactly because they wanted to see anybody hurt — people weren't really that mean. He supposed it was because people were fascinated by seeing something done that might go one way or the other. Like Blondin walking his tightrope across Niagara. He'd done it three different years, but each time it got people just as excited. And it was much the same when it came to a barn raising. People were just as pleased when the timbers were up and solid as they were when Blondin made it to the other end of his tightrope.

Tom figured that the way Mr. Hook described Blondin wasn't exactly true. It seemed to him most people went to the performance expecting, even if they didn't exactly hope, to see Blondin lose his balance somewhere well out on the down curve of the rope. They would see his figure, made small in the distance, fall one way and his great balancing pole the other, and he would go down and down until he hit the raging rapids; and all their lives they would be able to say how awful it had been. He couldn't see how a barn raising would be in the same class, and before he got home he had put it out of his mind. What was important was to get the men to raise the timbers and to feed them and the crowd that Mr. Hook said was bound to turn up.

Birdy Morris had already arrived. He was putting together the bent at the front of the barn. He had the timbers lying on the mow floor and already the shape of the frame showed. At the moment Tom came up on the floor, he was fitting the tenon of the tie beam into the mortise of a side post and finding it a bit balky.

"Must have swelled being out in the weather," he said, as Tom stepped up onto the floor. "Hand me my old commander."

Tom had no idea what a commander might be, but Birdy was pointing at a beetle. It was like a vastly oversized hammer with a wooden head. When Tom picked it up, the weight of it almost dragged him off his feet. Birdy chuckled.

"Kind of heavy, ain't it? Lead-weighted in the head, that beetle is. Forty-fifty pounds. My old pa made it. He used to build barns for folks in his time. Sometimes bridges."

He took it from Tom and swung it sideways, as he might have swung a monstrous croquet mallet. The thump it made on the beam was rock-solid; and the beam's tenon slid home.

"Don't many sticks say no to this old hammer," Birdy remarked. "Reckon that's why it's called a commander."

The work of assembling the four bents went slowly, for

Birdy refused to be hurried. Tom's chief contribution was to whittle the pins or trunnels with which the beams and posts were pegged together. Quite a few of the original ones had been damaged when they were driven out or had been mislaid or lost in moving the timbers down from the Breen place. The wood was hard and dry from curing for years in the loft over Birdy's woodshed and each pin had to fit the hole it went into as tight as could be. Once in, Birdy pointed out, it would swell some in the damper air, even inside the barn. It would make an absolute bind. "A durn sight tighter than a marriage vow," Birdy said. A proper wooden pin would never give way. It wouldn't rust out like a spike.

They had the bents assembled more than a week before the barn-raising date. By then Polly Ann and the girls were already planning for the food they would provide. Mr. Hook had driven down from Boonville a couple of times and they had discussed the amounts of one kind of food or another that would be needed. Polly Ann had never been to a barn raising. In the sand-flat country during her lifetime, buildings weren't being built, and she and her family had lived in a house as long as it provided some sort of shelter, then moved on to the next best thing they could find. The idea of maybe a hundred people turning up and all expecting food appalled her.

Besides, as she pointed out to Mr. Hook, she had to keep on with her days of doing housework for her regular employers, as well as the one day doing washing for the men who worked at Massey's. And the girls' school had begun so they wouldn't have as much time to help out. Still, somehow she would have to get enough food together, though she had no idea where she would find the money to buy it all. Her brow puckered with dismay and Mr. Hook, watching her, said he thought the best thing would be for him to consult his housekeeper, Mrs. Conroy.

The next time he came he brought Mrs. Conroy with him. She wasn't at all the way Tom had imagined her from Ox Hubbard's description of an elderly and respectable person. She did have gray hair, but she was a big, raw-boned woman, as tall as Mr. Hook, with a voice you could hear from one end of the yard to the other. It was plain that she liked Polly Ann as soon as she laid eyes on her and right away she took charge of all the planning.

"You've fixed your kitchen real nice," she said. "But you couldn't bake the amount of pies you'll need in a month of Sundays — not in your small stove. No. We'll have to get two or three women in Boonville making pies for you. Not to mention getting meat roasted for your sandwiches. Now I think we'd better allow five sandwiches to a person. Say five hundred of them. That will take a lot of meat, but if you cut the bread pretty thick, sandwiches fill the people faster. Bread. We've got to get enough bread baked. I'll have to go home and figure out the amount of meat and loaves we got to have. Don't you fret, dearie."

"But we can't pay for all that food!" cried Polly Ann. "We are poor."

"Your boy's putting up a barn, isn't he? Then he'll have to do his raising proper. Don't worry, dearie. Mr. Hook will help out." She pressed her lip thoughtfully with her forefinger. "I think I'll go see Mrs. Ackerman. She likes getting into a thing like this. Only she has to be the boss. I'll go ask for her advice, Polly Ann, and in ten minutes she'll figure she's running the whole party. She'll be ready to do anything to make it go. She's that way always with dinners at the Temple."

Polly Ann felt as if she had been swept up by a great

wind, and she could only let herself go along with it. She looked up to see George Hook watching them from the door. He looked amused and winked. To her embarrassment she felt herself flushing.

"I'll be thankful for your help, Mrs. Conroy," she said in a muffled voice, and shortly afterwards Mr. Hook drove his housekeeper away. He'd hardly said a thing to her.

"I don't know how we're ever going to pay them back," she said to Tom that evening.

He was troubled too.

"Me neither," he said. "But I don't know no other way we'll get the barn raised."

Then, seeing she wasn't reassured at all, he added, "We'll pay them some way."

But he could hardly believe it himself.

45

That last week before the raising was so full of women coming and going that Tom always spoke of it, even long afterwards, as the most mixed-up time in his life. He didn't see how anything would come out of so much commotion. Polly Ann got only the most skimpy kind of scratch suppers, after which she would whirl into making bread or baking pies. By Saturday she had what seemed to Tom a pretty good stock of loaves and pies laid up in the cold pantry off the kitchen; but when he remarked so, she said, "Goodness, those aren't only a drop in the bucket."

She had him put a hook on the door so the cats couldn't get in and make trouble. That last Saturday she cooked the biggest jar of doughnuts Tom or his sisters ever saw. It was hard to believe.

Late in the afternoon, after the mill closed down, Mr.

Hook drove Mrs. Conroy down from town in a buck-board he had rented from Joe Hemphill's livery because she had more food to bring than his buggy could accommodate. There were three roasts of beef and the biggest turkey bird Tom had ever seen, and two large fresh hams, racks of pies, and loaves of bread as well. When it was all stacked up in the pantry it looked big enough, with what Polly Ann had already cooked, to feed an army. Mrs. Conroy shook her head, but she said Mrs. Ackerman was coming in the morning with additional supplies, and with those she thought they might get by.

She then wanted to see what Polly Ann had done about providing serving tables. Birdy had brought four sawhorses from his own place. With the two Tom had and planks from the old barn there would be three tables which they had supposed would be enough, but Mrs. Conroy wanted a fourth. So Tom said he would see if he could borrow two more sawhorses from Massey, down the road. He walked down after supper and Massey was agreeable. He led Tom into the barn to get them, and Tom looked enviously at the two lines of big Holstein cows in their iron stanchions, standing on the concrete floor. He wouldn't be able to afford anything like that for a long time. But when Massey said, "I hear you've got a real good barn," he agreed.

"Just the timbers, really, though," he told Massey.

He picked up the horses, one to each shoulder and Massey said, "See you tomorrow, Tom. I'm coming up with the boys. There's nothing makes a man feel better than seeing a barn raised."

It made Tom feel better. It was a nice thing for Mr. Massey to say, considering what a great lot larger his own barn was than Tom's. And Mr. Massey added, "We'll bring up the pike poles we used raising this barn, Tom.

You can't ever have too many if you've got the men on hand to use them."

Tom said his thanks. And walking home he thought how he had first seen the barn at Widow Breen's and remembered the old lady standing on her porch, pointing her shotgun at him. That was when he had got the notion of moving the barn, but it didn't seem likely then that it would ever get as far along as this.

Birdy had stayed for supper, but he had gone by the time Tom got home, leaving word with Polly Ann that he would be down early next morning, to make sure that everything was how it should be, and for Tom not to worry.

But, of course, Tom did. He and Polly Ann sat in the kitchen to have a cup of tea together and he could see she was as worried as he was. It was the money they were going to owe that bothered both of them. Birdy wasn't worried that way. It wasn't him getting into debt, naturally; but then he never worried about money anyway.

Cissie-Mae and Ellie came into the kitchen, but seeing their Ma and Tom so silent took themselves off to bed after a minute or two. After that there wasn't anything to hear but the late crickets fiddling in the meadow beyond the barnyard. So pretty soon they, too, went up to bed.

For a long time, however, bed wasn't a place for going to sleep. Tom got too hot and threw the covers off, and then after a while he got too cold. No matter what he kept on top of him, he couldn't get things right. When he dozed off, at last, a mouse gnawing inside the wall woke him, and then that changed into a dream of a great mouse chewing off the bottoms of the bents as fast as they could get them upright, so they never had two of them raised at one time long enough to join. That woke him right up and he was sweating again, but this time he felt cold. He pulled the quilt up and curled up under it, and suddenly he felt himself sliding off to sleep, but at the last instant it came into his mind how awful it would be should it come on to rain next day.

46

When he woke, he kept his eyes closed for a minute; but there was no sound of rain. So he opened them to a brilliant sunrise and at once got up. He had barely finished washing on the kitchen stoop when he heard the sound of a wagon coming along their road, and a minute later Birdy Morris drove into the yard. Birdy waved as he drove by to a place behind the milking shed. At the same time Polly Ann rattled wood into the kitchen stove and upstairs he heard Ellie's voice complaining querulously that it was too early. Over at the edge of the yard one of the hens announced the arrival of an egg as if it were a wonder of the world. The brightening sunlight touched the mow floor where the assembled bents lay flat and Tom tried to remember just how they had looked, standing bare as bones up at the Widow Breen's place, before he and Birdy took them down.

After unhitching his horses, Birdy came back to the house and admitted he could drink a cup of coffee, and then he confessed that he had left home without eating anything. He had been troubled that they might not have enough pike poles, so Tom was able to ease his mind by saying that Massey had said he would bring the ones he had used raising his own barn.

It was warm enough for them to eat breakfast with the kitchen door open. Birdy even unbuttoned the collar of his shirt and Tom noticed for the first time that it was brand-new gray flannel with a thin green stripe. He wondered if Birdy had bought it just for the barn raising. Cissie-Mae and Ellie clattered down the stairs and came sleepily into the kitchen. Polly Ann told them to be quick: there was more than plenty of things for them to do. As they went over to the stove, drumming hoofs sounded down the road with a whir of wheels, and Mr. Hook swung the big gray into the yard, stopping his buggy by the kitchen steps. Mrs. Conroy got down lugging a monumental coffee kettle; and Tom realized that his barn-raising day was really under way.

Afterwards it seemed to him that he hadn't had much of anything to do with the program. For a time Mrs. Conroy monopolized almost everybody — getting the tables set up on the sawhorses; showing just where she wanted them placed, as much in the shade as possible, since the sun promised to be hot and the sandwiches might dry out. Then she had Polly Ann and the girls go to work slicing bread in the kitchen for the sandwiches. They worked in a fine smell of coffee, which drifted out across the yard all the way to the barn. About nine-thirty they began coming out with platters stacked with the sandwiches and six huge pans of cold baked white beans, each with its own cruet of vinegar and an arrangement of separate plates and forks. When these were all positioned, they placed pies at intervals, each with a pie knife beside it.

By then the men were starting to show up. Massey came with his four hired hands, carrying pike poles on their shoulders as they walked up the road.

"Thought there'd be rigs enough around the place without ours," Massey said.

All the others arrived in wagons. First came the Mou-cheauds, riding together with Louis's wife and children, not to mention some relations. There were fourteen of them, and the moment the children got their feet on the ground they took off on the run, going all over the place, this way and that, like small chickens. It was impossible to keep track of them. Tom figured they would have had half the sandwiches eaten in no time if Mrs. Conroy hadn't taken up a guard post with a buggy whip which she wasn't at all afraid to use.

All of a sudden the Moucheaud children were distracted by a clamor on the road. Not exactly a hullabaloo, not exactly yelling, just a good-humored uproar; it prompted Louis to declare they must be the loggeurs from Forest-port.

"He means the lumberjacks," Bancel said scornfully, as he had before.

They wheeled into the yard in two buckboards, one a three-seater, the other a four-seater. There were thirteen men dressed in heavy shirts like coats with cotton shirts underneath and wearing every kind of hat you could imagine. They shouted greetings at the Moucheauds, who brought them over to Tom to be introduced, and they expressed astonishment that a boy like him should be putting up a barn for himself.

"Don't worry," they said. "We'll put them bents up. Even if we have to toss them up with our hands."

"How about tapping one of those barr'ls?" another suggested, and Tom saw that each buckboard had a keg lashed on the tailboard. But the one who had first talked to Tom said, "Not until we have these timbers up." He turned to Tom. "The boys brought along the drink because it was Sunday. No offense intended to you or your mamma."

Tom said all he wanted was to get the frame raised. He hoped they would like the lunch that had been laid out.

Mr. Hook came off the kitchen porch just then with a couple of pails of switchel, which he put down near the barn.

"Mrs. Dolan thought this would help keep your thirst down, for now," he said. Each bucket had a dipper floating in it, and the lumberjacks took turns drinking from them with the hired men from Massey's. There was considerable talk about how hot the day was likely to be, mostly to justify this early assault on the switchel. By the time Birdy and Mr. Massey came over to join them, everybody was feeling amiable.

Mr. Massey introduced Birdy to them.

"Birdy Morris is the man who built this barn in the first place. For Bert Breen, up on the sand flats by the Forestport line. He's helped Tom Dolan take it down and bring it here. I'd say he was the man to be caller for us."

Lumberjacks didn't step to one side for anybody, but they recognized boss material when they met it, and though Birdy didn't look like much, with his humped shoulder and all, they agreed he ought to be their man.

Birdy nodded soberly.

"Well," he said, "I guess we might as well commence."

As they moved towards the barn, three more wagons drove in. Two were from Port Leyden, with three men, three wives, and seven children between them. The other was from Potato Hill and brought three single men. All six men had brought pike poles with them, so Birdy's anxieties on this matter were quieted for good. They all introduced themselves and joined the men moving towards the barn. The whole group filed up the stairs to the mow floor or climbed the ladders leaning against it.

Birdy's first move was to have the pike poles laid out in some sort of order, the short ones in one rank and the twelve-footers in another. He suggested that Ox Hubbard and one of the men from Port Leyden take charge of the planting of each post of the first bent. There were heavy blocks to keep it from slipping off as it went up. Ox and the Port Leyden man, whose name was Hennessy, had stay laths ready to fix the bent as soon as it stood plumb and each had a couple of helpers with hammers and spikes. After it was in position, the braces would be put in and pinned.

The first step of the raising was done with the men's hands. They had to get the bent head high before the short pikes could be used. Those first feet upwards were the hardest part of the whole job. Half the men hooked their hands under the tie beam and braced their feet, their eyes on Birdy Morris, who stood at the center of the mow floor underneath where the tie beam would be once it was full up. He gave his mustache a wipe with his forefinger. Then his voice sounded, much bigger than you would expect.

"Hee-yo — HEAVE!"

At the word, the men lifted all together and the bent rose slowly with the butts of its posts against the end blocks. The men held it just over their heads and Tom, at his place in the line, felt a tremor in the bent. It didn't surprise him. His own arms were trembling with the strain. But then the men with the short poles sank their pike picks in the tie beam, taking up the weight, while Tom and his team stepped back. Already a lot of them were showing sweat marks on their shirts.

Birdy's voice came again.

"Hee-yo — HEAVE!"

The bent rose higher. The first group grabbed up the

twelve-foot poles and sank their pike picks into the beam between those of the short-pole crew.

At Birdy's call, they heaved again. Ox's voice sounded calmly over their labored breathing. "She's up."

Hennessy from Port Leyden echoed him. Seven men on the ground outside the barn, waiting with still longer poles, sank the picks into the beam and held it steady against those of the men on the mow floor. Ox and Hennessy raised the end of the stay laths which had already been single-spiked on the outside of the second sill with enough overlap to give a bite head-high on the post. They put their levels against the post and called for a little more pressure from the outside pike poles, and suddenly their hammers sounded together. They drove two more spikes into the post, and then, at the other end of the laths, into the second sills.

The first bent stood properly erect.

47

The beams to connect the bents were next to put in place. Men raised them until their tenons entered the mortises in the posts. A rope from the end of each was passed over the tie beam and two men on the ground took hold of the end, keeping the beam horizontal to meet the next bent when it was raised. The pike-pole crews were still around the switchel pails. Birdy shouted for them to come back to the job. It was time to raise the second bent. At that moment the fringed surrey from Hemphill's livery wheeled into the yard. Joe Hemphill himself was driving; it was less than a year old and he was choosy about renting it out for anyone else to drive. He was wearing his derby hat, which he only did on occasions of importance and Tom at once saw why. On the back seat were Erlo and Mrs. Ackerman.

Mrs. Ackerman was built as solid as Erlo and looked more so on account of the hat she was wearing — stiff with a multitude of ribbons. As they got out, first one and then the other, the surrey rocked from side to side like a boat in the trough of a wave. Erlo made for the kitchen porch and settled himself in a rocker right at the top of the steps, where he would have an uninterrupted view. Polly Ann brought him a glass of switchel but he asked for coffee so she brought him a cup and small side table from the parlor to put it on. Mrs. Ackerman meanwhile was going down the tables checking on everything there was under the cheesecloth with Mrs. Conroy accompanying her. The Moucheaud children, now joined by a dozen others, considered this a good time to stage a raid at the far end of the farthest table; but they hadn't counted on Mrs. Conroy's agility. She caught them with their hands under the cloth and got in a couple of licks with the buggy whip that sent them off yelping like puppies.

The commotion temporarily put a stop to the raising. Nobody seemed to mind, except the men on the ropes holding up the connecting beams, who made jokes about staying as they were till the barn got shingled or what would they do if a couple of them died of old age. Tom came down to make his manners to Mrs. Ackerman, who took no notice of him, and then he said hello to Erlo.

"You got things going good," Erlo told him. "I'm sorry we're late, but don't pay attention to us. The barn's what's important, Tom."

Things got going quickly then. The second bent went up as smoothly as the first. The tenons of the connecting beams found their mortises with very little difficulty. It was plain that Ox and the men working with him knew

what they were about. The work went on well. They had
the third bent up and locked in place a little after noon
and decided to knock off and eat.

This was not only the moment Polly Ann, Mrs. Conroy,
and the other women had been preparing for, it was the
one the children had been waiting for almost to the point
of desperation. All in an instant twenty or thirty small
hands were grabbing and the sandwiches melted away like
feasts in dreams. As soon as they had snatched their food
the children would rush off somewhere out of sight, but in
a few minutes they came tearing back, all in a bunch, like
swarming bees.

The men helped themselves to stacks of the sandwiches,
to hunks of cheese, to cherry or blueberry or apple pie, and
drank quantities of coffee and switchel. They ignored the
gyrations of the mob of children or tolerated them good-
humoredly, perhaps remembering other barn raisings
when they themselves had been small. They kept in separate groups, the lumberjacks sitting by themselves in the
shade of the house, the farmers under the mow floor. The
Moucheaud brothers circulated from one group to the
other. Working at the feed mill and living in Forestport
made them parties of both worlds. Tom, feeling himself
the host, tried to do the same, but he felt shy among the
lumberjacks and found little to say to them.

Mr. Massey came up to him and said that the raising
seemed to have gone well. "Looks like you have a good
sound barn, there," he said. "We'll be glad to come another Sunday and help put the roof on."

Tom said he would appreciate the help and led Mr.
Massey up on the porch to where Erlo Ackerman was sitting. Massey was, naturally, one of Erlo's biggest customers
and was welcomed accordingly. Suddenly, in the windless,

warm noon, the party seemed as peaceful as a church sociable. Tom took some sandwiches from Cissie-Mae and sat down on the steps near Mr. Hook.

"It looks as if everything's going well, Tom," Mr. Hook said.

"Yes," Tom said. "But there's going to be an awful lot to do after we get the frame up."

"Erlo and I were talking about that. We thought maybe you would like to take a week off from the mill. Maybe two. Of course," Mr. Hook added, "that would be without pay. Erlo wanted to make that plain."

"It might be a good idea," Tom said. "Only I've got to make money anyways I can. I've got to find money for the shingles and the siding somehow."

"I'd be glad to make you a loan, Tom. If you want one."

Tom thought about it. He had an uneasy feeling that Polly Ann wouldn't like him to take money from Mr. Hook. Even loan money. He said, "Thanks," because he had to. But he didn't know what was right. He said, "I'll let you know, Mr. Hook, if I have to have it."

"Think about it, anyway, Tom."

They sat silent, watching the people moving around the yard. The children suddenly appeared from the far side of the house, still running bunched up. They were after pie or cake and it took some active work on the part of Mrs. Conroy, Polly Ann, and Cissie-Mae to cut them all pieces before they made grabs for an entire pie. Mrs. Ackerman didn't approve of giving them any. She said the manners of children had got worse ever since she was a girl.

Mr. Hook smiled lazily, and then he said, "Who's that man under the barn floor with Ox, Tom? I saw him a couple of minutes ago talking to Massey. But I didn't see him here at all before then."

There wasn't any mistaking who it was.

"That's Yantis Flancher," Tom told him. "He's got two brothers. They generally always go together."

"He looks like a rough character."

"I guess he is. Him and his brothers have been up at Breen's most of the time this summer. Looking for Mr. Breen's money."

"Did they make any trouble for you?" Mr. Hook asked.

Tom shook his head. "Just told me not to go hunting for the money myself."

Tom told him how Yantis and his brothers, Newman and Enders, had ripped the walls of the house apart and dug trenches all over the place.

"I don't see what he wants to come here for," Mr. Hook said.

Tom grinned thinly. "Checking up on me, I guess. Wondering if maybe I have found that money."

"You'd think," Mr. Hook said, "somebody'd have found the money by now, if it was there."

"Yes, you would," Tom said.

He got up. Birdy Morris was climbing up on the mow floor and Tom wanted to talk to Ox before they started work again.

Ox said, "Yantis was asking me why you and Birdy hadn't put the cattle floor down yet. I told him I didn't know. You was doing the job your own way."

Mr. Massey came up to them. "He asked me the same thing. Did I know why? Said it seemed a queer way to put up a barn. I told him maybe you were figuring to lay a cement floor, like my barn."

"What did he say?"

"He wanted to know where you were going to find the money to pay for a cement floor. I didn't know. I said that was your business." Massey smiled. "He didn't like me saying that. I could see he didn't like me. But then I didn't like him, either."

Birdy called them then. The men trooped back. Tom looked past the house to the road. He saw the Flanchers' wagon driving off, heading downriver towards Port Leyden. Yantis's brothers, Newman and Enders, were with him. He figured they must be going back home to Highmarket.

48

The last bent went up quickly, without a hitch. The job was made simpler by the knoll into which the barn had been dug. The men raising the bent were standing on ground level with the mow floor.

After it was standing, the farmers started leaving. They had their own evening chores coming up. But the Moucheauds and the lumberjacks stayed on, helping to put up the plates, the beams joining the top corners of the bents, on which the rafters would rest. The lumbermen were like cats running back and forth along the beams and with Ox Hubbard and Birdy supervising, the plates were fixed in short order. The frame was raised and the shape of the barn stood there for anyone to see. It looked bigger to Tom than it had up on the Breen place.

Louis Moucheaud put the longest ladder up to one of the top posts of the bent facing the house and climbed it, carrying a small balsam tree. He fastened it there with a length of twine, the "brush" to bring luck to the barn.

The men raised a cheer and came tumbling down off the frame. They got their kegs off the buckboards, drove the bungs, and in no time every man had a dipper, glass, or mug of frothing beer. Erlo Ackerman came down the steps of the kitchen porch and joined them.

They drank to the barn's future and to Tom, who was tasting beer for the first time in his life and not liking it at all. After the second or third round, one of them began to sing, a sad haunting kind of tune in which the Moucheauds joined. It was a song from Canada, somebody said, and the reason Tom and most of the others couldn't make out the words was because they were French. It was another half hour before they were ready to leave, and even then it took a while to round up the Moucheaud children. But at last they were gone.

Mrs. Conroy helped Polly Ann and the girls to clear up while Mrs. Ackerman offered advice. But then she came over to Erlo and said it was time for them to leave, too. They had to hunt up Joe Hemphill, who had gone to sleep on the old settee at the end of the front porch. Tom had some difficulty rousing him. His breath was strong, but not with beer, so Tom guessed that he must have brought something stronger with him as a precaution. Livery men were known to have precautious instincts. He got Joe up on his feet, which showed a reluctance to move in the same direction, but by the time they had reached the fringed surrey he was navigating to some purpose, and when the Ackermans climbed on board, Tom felt no anxiety about their getting back to Boonville. Joe Hemphill's horses knew the way home better than he did.

He returned to the back of the house to find that the tables had been stripped. Mr. Hook was carrying the planks back to the pile they had come from. Tom put his own sawhorses away and took the four Birdy had brought to Birdy's wagon. The old man had gone back to the mow floor. He stood in the middle of it looking up at the timbers, back together in their proper shape, the way he had helped fix them in the first place. A long time, that was. He wondered what Bert Breen would think to see them down here. Or Amelie, either.

Then he saw Tom and Mr. Hook approaching him, and he came down the ladder.

"I got to get back home, Tom," he said. "But the raising went good, didn't it?"

"It did," Tom said. "Thanks mostly to you, Birdy."

Birdy looked embarrassed, especially when George Hook put in his word of agreement.

"Pshaw," he said. "Raising a barn ought to go good, when it's the second time around."

He got into his wagon and drove the team slowly through the yard. He took his hat off when he passed Mrs. Conroy and Polly Ann.

"Been a good day," he told them.

"Yes," Polly Ann said. "Thank you, Birdy, for all the things you've done for Tom. For us all."

"Pshaw," he said again. "We've got to roof it yet, and put the siding on."

He drove out on to the road. One of his wheels started to squeak. Tom said to Mr. Hook that he had never known Birdy to let an axle go dry. Then he realized that he hadn't looked at his own wagon either for too long. That was something he couldn't leave a minute longer. But he had to wait till Mrs. Conroy was ready to go and Mr. Hook drove his gray back out of the yard.

Polly Ann drew a deep breath.

"We got just about enough left over for our supper,"

she said. "We'll milk, and eat, and go to bed. It's been a long day. A wonderful day, though. I never thought to see so good a barn standing here."

But when they had milked, Tom said he had to grease the wheels on the spring wagon. Polly Ann stared at him.

"Why tonight?" she asked. "After all there's been to do."

"I'll tell you when we've ate supper," Tom said.

They were sitting at the kitchen table when he came in, to find four sandwiches on his plate. He couldn't see any more, but Polly Ann said they had had theirs and if anyone was still hungry there was bread and some meat left in the pantry. He ate and took a cup of coffee. All the pies were used up.

He looked from his mother's face to his twin sisters.

"I want to go up to the Breen place tonight," he said.

"*Tonight!*" Polly Ann exclaimed. "*That's* why you greased the wagon wheels?"

He nodded. Ellie and Cissie-Mae just looked bewildered. Polly Ann explained to them that Tom thought he had figured out where Bert and Mrs. Breen had kept their money and she was going to go with him to look for it.

"But I don't see why tonight," she protested. "When we are practically wore out."

"That's why," he answered. "The Flanchers were here nosing around. Yantis begun asking Ox and Mr. Massey why we hadn't brought down the floor for the stable. Yantis may get a notion why I left it. But he wouldn't think of our going up there tonight any more than you did."

He paused a minute.

"It ought to be a good night for us to go. Moon's already set. We won't get more than starlight. And it looks as if it might cloud over too. You think you'd feel able to come with me?" he asked. "After all the work you've been doing all day?"

"Yes, I will," Polly Ann said. "You couldn't keep me from going, no matter if you tried. Besides, you wouldn't ever find your way in from the Irish Settlement road by yourself."

"Then we'll go," Tom said. "We'll wait until half past six, to let it get a little darker."

49

Twilight was beginning to give way to darkness as they topped the long slope up to the canal. He turned Drew to the left, onto the towpath, and glanced at his mother. He could see her profile against the last streak of light along the top of Tug Hill, but only as a silhouette. She had on a thick sweater with a collar that rolled up around her neck under her small, determined chin. He was glad she was coming with him.

Cissie-Mae and Ellie had come out of the house to see them off. He had told them that if anybody came asking for him and Polly Ann they were to say she had been taken sick and he was driving her up to Boonville to see the doctor. No telling when they'd be home. Tom could have hung one of the lanterns he had brought on the dashboard hook, but the light might be seen from a canalside farm, and he didn't want people speculating who might be traveling the towpath that night.

Now he looked back down the valley. It was too dark to see the road from Port Leyden. No lights shone in all the valley except the windows on the Quarry place, and a hundred feet farther along a fold in the ground shut them away. From then on, the wagon moved through the dark with only the reflections of a few early stars on the water of the canal beside the towpath to mark their course. Once, the clank of a cowbell told them a pasture was nearby, and a little later they heard a cow breathe out a heavy sigh, as if she carried the world's sorrow.

Drew paid no attention to such sounds. He plodded on at his own pace, halfway between a trot and a walk, and Tom let him have his head. The old horse had always been clever at finding his way along a road in the dark.

They made very little sound. The fellies of the wheels hardly whispered as they tracked along the double path beaten by the canal teams. It came as a shock when the thump of Drew's hoofs and the grating of the wheels over sandy gravel echoed suddenly from planking overhead. They had not seen the shadow of the bridge ahead of them. Now for a moment the stars were blotted out. Then they left the bridge behind and were again moving in almost total silence.

There were three more bridges to pass under before they reached the one that carried the Dutch Hill road down into Forestport. The first of these, at Hawkinsville, was the only one that troubled Tom. Unlike the first bridge, it showed up well ahead as they approached, its white timbers picked out against the sky by the dim glow from the village windows on the hill below it. Anyone crossing it was bound to see the spring wagon coming along underneath on the towpath. It all depended on luck; but luck was with them, and not a rig passed over. Drew hauled the wagon underneath and out on the other side. They passed the village without hearing anything at all, not even a dog's bark.

There was small chance of their meeting a canalboat.

Boaters didn't like navigating the winding stretch from Forestport to Boonville, with its four-mile current, at night. After Hawkinsville, he and Polly Ann and Drew ought to have the towpath all to themselves. They met no one, and the only lights they saw came from the windows of two small houses, about a quarter mile apart, where the Barton brothers lived. Both the Bartons were over seventy. They lived by themselves, never having worked up enough nerve to get married. They never spoke to each other, either. But at the same time neither one of them had thought of moving somewhere else.

Tom got to thinking how queer some men could get to be. Now the Flanchers had none of them married, but they lived together in the same house, and they made a lot of trouble for other people. But the Bartons never made trouble for anybody else, beyond one brother telling stories about the other one's meanness.

A heavy mist was lifting off the water. It thickened and kept rising as they went on. By the time they reached Forestport about an hour later, it had risen high enough to blot out the towpath and canal.

They crept ahead in a silence broken only by the sound of the river rapids forty feet below and occasional anxious snorts from the old horse. He seemed to push his way into the mist, going cautious and very slow, his forefeet feeling for the towpath. Tom felt they must be getting close to the Dutch Hill bridge. He put a little pressure on the left rein to warn Drew to look for the turn off the towpath down to the river. The horse seemed able to make it out in some way a human would not comprehend. The wagon pitched downhill, and they went on a step at a time with the mist much heavier against their faces, carrying the cold of river water. Suddenly the wheels rumbled out onto bridge planking. They heard the rush of water underneath. Then the road sloped up and presently the mist began to thin out.

They were moving along a street with houses on each side. Beyond the lighted windows they could see people: three old men sat in front of a stove in a harness shop, which Polly Ann said was Mr. Utley's; in the next house a woman and a small girl were clearing up supper plates. They passed a couple of saloons and a church with a house beside it. Inside a man in a black cassock was talking to a woman who appeared to be crying. After that there was another house standing separate, and then they were in open country, with the mist behind them.

"The road forks a piece ahead," Polly Ann said. "The one to the left goes down to the Armond place, but we take the one straight ahead. It's the Irish Settlement road."

It began with a steep hill. At times the wheels grated on gravel and then bumped with the roughness of the road. Drew heaved against the tugs, uttering grunts of self-pity, but eventually the road leveled off and though they were traveling through woodland, Tom judged they had reached the beginning of the sand-flat country. They passed house lights here and there. As near as he could make out, the houses were mere shanties, all of them one-story, with one or two rooms, built close to the road. Even though there were quite a lot of them, it seemed a lonely place. On the damp, still night air, he could smell poorly tended privies. It wasn't the kind of place he would ever want to live in.

Polly Ann said, "There were a lot of Irish people came over and worked digging the canal. When it was finished they didn't want to go back to the city, so they settled up here. They get what work they can and hunt and fish. I guess they are as poor as us Hannaberrys used to be."

Her saying that made Tom realize that in her mind the Dolan family was better off now. They had the frame of a good barn standing on their place. The determination to get the roof and siding on came back to him again. He slapped the reins on Drew's rump, persuading the old horse into a shuffling trot. The road cleared the settlement and went on across a natural meadow. The sky was speckled bright with stars, framed by the outlines of trees on either side. He could dimly make out the wheel tracks leading on with the path beaten by a single horse between them.

"There's nobody but Nelson Farr uses it," Polly Ann said.

Tom had heard about Farr, a thin, middle-aged, silent man who lived by himself in a weathered house above Wingert's pond. He got paid wages by the Wingerts and the Kehoes for keeping other people from poaching their trout ponds, one above the other, on Crystal Creek. Lower down, Crystal Creek ran into the Armond pond and past their buildings into the Black River; and it was said Farr would take the young Wingerts and Kehoes fishing down it and even fish the Armond pond at night. Parker Munsey had gone up after them more than once, but he had never got close to Farr and the boys. It seemed queer, Tom thought, how wealthy people tried to fish each other's property; same as stealing, some people said. You expected it of poor folks like the Hannaberrys, but not of such as Wingerts and Kehoes.

In the fall Nelson Farr took parties out shooting, first for birds and later on for deer. He always had at least one bird dog living with him in his house, and a hound for running deer. It was the hound, mainly, Tom had on his mind now. The dog slept outside in an old kerosene barrel, Polly Ann said, and if he noticed the wagon going by he would bark. He had a voice, running deer, you could hear half across the township.

Polly Ann said in a low voice, "Nob used to come here once in a while to fetch Farr whiskey. The hound was a pup then, but he might recognize Drew if he smells him, so long as he's not roused."

50

A faint stir of air came out of the southwest, moving from the house towards the road. They went along with no more sound than the faint plop of Drew's hoofs on the dusty track. Imperceptibly the roof of Farr's house took shape against the stars. Then they could see the corner of one wall against a yellow glow so dim it hardly showed. Farr's kitchen window faced out towards the pond and the lamplight showed he must still be up. As they moved softly along, the glow vanished, and with it the shape of the house. They heard the faint clink of the hound's chain and a low whimpering whine. Whether he had heard them or caught their scent there was no way of knowing. But they were now by and the flat land that marked the end of the Breen place began to open out ahead. The track turned right for fifty feet and then left.

"That's the corner of Armond's land," Polly Ann said. "There used to be good blackberries in there."

What made her think of blackberries now was more than Tom could figure out. He was trying to get his bearings. He thought that Breen's Hill ought to show up just ahead, but he couldn't make it out. And he knew they would have to get across Cold Brook yet, to reach the barn.

He felt Polly Ann's hand on his arm.

"We better get down and lead Drew."

She pointed to a line of scattered trees barely visible against the stars.

"We want to get near them, Tom. There's a farm track goes along them to Cold Brook. That's where the ford is."

They led Drew ahead. He didn't like it much now he was off the road, poor as it had been, but as they were walking beside him he made no objection, and he turned instinctively as his hoofs felt the track she had mentioned, before they themselves were aware of it. They followed it towards the brook until the land began to slope down.

"This ought to be Cold Brook," Polly Ann said just above a whisper; and sure enough, now they were stopped Tom could hear the gurgle of moving water.

He looked around for something to tie Drew to. The old horse wouldn't wander far, but Tom didn't want him moving at all if it could be helped. A little way off a dark shadow stood on the land about eight feet high. It was a young white pine. He led Drew over to it and tied him to it with a hitching rope. His silhouette and that of the pine would make one shape, supposing anybody would be able to see that far from where the house was. Then he felt in the wagon for one of the lanterns he had brought and his pinch bar. He didn't intend to light the lantern unless he had to.

"I'm going over there now," he said in a low voice. "You stay here, Ma."

"I will not. I'm coming with you, Tom."

Her voice was so determined it was as good as seeing her

cocked chin and set jaw. When she sounded that way, there wasn't much use trying to change her mind.

The wheel tracks deepened as they generally did on each bank at a brook crossing and Tom felt his way down, trying to keep between them. When he stepped into the water, it was so cold he was glad he hadn't put off coming until the black part of November. His legs were numbed from the knee down, even though the brook was less than eight feet across. He heard Polly Ann draw her breath sharply just behind him. Then they were both going up the other bank.

The floor of the barn was no more than two hundred feet ahead. They approached it slowly, finding their way by the wagon track until what was left of the Breen house showed up on their left, a black and gloomy smudge against the stars. There was no light, no sign of a person anywhere, but they stood still together, straining to hear any sound. Behind them a barred owl started hooting in the Armond woods. The bird repeated itself twice and then fell silent. Presently from the big swamp east of the Breen place, another answered. Then they began a dialogue, punctuated by silences of varying lengths as if what each said in turn was of variable importance.

Listening, Tom fell into a sort of trance until Polly Ann took his arm.

"Just two fool birds calling," she said. "We hadn't ought to waste more time."

Tom gave himself a shake. He didn't know what had got into him, but his head came clear. He led the way to where the barn had stood and all at once they felt the floor timbers of the cow run under their feet.

Tom set the lantern down close to where the sill had been.

"I don't want to light it unless I've got to," he said quietly. "Anyways until I've found where the money is. If it's there."

"It's there, Tom," Polly Ann said, almost in a murmur. "Don't you doubt it."

But now that he was about really to look for it all his confidence seemed to have gone. His idea had been that Bert Breen would not have had his loose flooring too near his box of sand and chaff, maybe halfway down the length of the barn. But it seemed best to begin at one end and work straight on until he did or didn't find something loose. He was sure that they wouldn't be right inside the door, but he began there anyway.

He was right. All the timbers were spiked solid to the three stringers underneath them. He kept on giving one after another a pry with his pinch bar until he was well past where the box was. They continued to be spiked fast all the way past the middle and a cold doubt about his being dead wrong in his ideas took hold of his mind. Then he thought maybe the natural place to look would have been the far end. He was tempted to go down and try. But it seemed better to keep on the way he was going. If the money wasn't at the far end, he'd have wasted that much more time.

He heard the sound of Polly Ann's feet moving quietly down the run behind him. She said, very softly, "Tom."

But he had the pinch bar prying against the end of the next timber, and it lifted.

"What is it, Ma?"

"The owls have stopped hollering," she said. "If they *was* owls."

"They're owls all right, Ma. They've just said everything they had to say."

"Perhaps. But the second one has flew up out of the swamp and now he's near the road, opposite us," she said. "He was the one quit first."

"Well, I've got a loose piece here," Tom said. "I better try the next."

He lifted the loose timber out and laid it to one side. He took hold of the next one with his hand, and it was loose also. Then the next and a fourth. He put them down in order so he could put them back the way they'd been. Polly Ann was kneeling at the edge of the uncovered space.

"Tom," she whispered. "They made a hole here, and there's a couple of trunks in it."

He touched her arm and felt her trembling. Or maybe it was himself. He listened against the dark, but heard only the crickets.

He had to struggle to control his voice, even to whisper. "Are they heavy, Ma?"

She tugged. "Yes. Kind of. But I guess we can carry them all right."

He moved over to kneel beside her and felt for the first trunk. It was small, maybe three feet by two on top, he judged. It oughtn't to be too heavy.

He got a grip on the handles and heaved it up. It was a good deal heavier than he'd expected, but he got it out without much trouble. The second was a bit smaller but seemed to weigh even more. He heaved it out also.

"We've got to get them over to the wagon," he said.

She whispered, "Yes."

Each of them took hold of a handle of the second trunk and started back towards Cold Brook. It was harder to make their way in the dark carrying the trunk. The weight interfered with their balance and it was necessary to move very slowly. They made a good deal more noise, also, crossing the brook. But finally they got the trunk up the far bank and located Drew and the spring wagon and heaved the trunk onto the wagon bed.

Polly Ann was breathing quite hard, but she wouldn't hear of resting and they went straight back for the other trunk. Its larger size made it clumsier to handle, but it wasn't quite so heavy, and made the second trip seem easier. They got it onto the wagon with no trouble and Tom said, "I want you to take Drew back to the corner of the Armond land. If anybody shows up they won't see you that far off, and if there's any kind of a commotion here you better start going home. I'll walk back."

"What do you aim to do, Tom?"

"I want to get those floor timbers back where they were," he told her. "And scatter some of that sand and chaft over them."

"All right. I'll go over to the corner, but I won't start home till you get there too, Tom."

She watched him turn back towards the barn.

"Tom," she said quietly. "Don't forget to bring the lantern."

Tom had forgotten all about it, never having had to use it. He raised his hand, not thinking that she couldn't see him at all. After he crossed the brook, he could hear her taking Drew away across the open land towards Armond's corner.

51

He had no trouble finding the loose timbers and it didn't take long to fit them back in place, even in the dark, for he had laid them down in proper order. He felt his way back then along the flooring to the box where the chaff and sand was, and it was then he realized he hadn't brought anything to carry it in. He tried to remember if there was an old shovel lying about. But he couldn't recall having seen any such thing. There would probably be a saucepan or something in the house. But to find one he would have to light his lantern, and he didn't want to do that. He scratched his head, wondering what to do. His hat tilted over his eyes and suddenly it came to him that it would do as well as a saucepan. He set it down in the box, filled it with handfuls of sand, and carried it back to the loose timbers. He would have liked some lantern light now. Scattering sand evenly in the dark wasn't easy. Besides, from having been out in the weather, it was damp. He had to hope that a night's dew would make it appear more natural. But that was only a guess. He went back for another hatful, wondering how long they had spent at Breen's. Too long, he thought. And all at once he felt a trickle of sweat between his shoulders run down to the small of his back. He went back to the loose timbers and scattered the second hatful as well as he could.

He was going to get a third, but before he reached the box a light appeared on the road. It came along smoothly, so he knew it was on a wagon. A lantern carried by hand always has a kind of bob to it. Whoever it was could be coming only to Breen's.

There wasn't time for any more sand. He felt around for

his own lantern, which he had put in one corner of the box of sand, and picked it up. It was time to vamoose. He went down to Cold Brook and waded through just as the wagon lantern turned the corner to come into the Breen place. He moved up the bank to where they had left the wagon and stood close beside the pine tree. He could see the wagon come up to the barn floor. A man got down; then two more. To his mind they couldn't be anybody but Flanchers.

He drew back behind the pine and when it was between him and the men, set off across the open land to find Drew and Polly Ann. He kept himself from hurrying. Rapid motion could attract attention no matter how dark it was. He moved evenly and slowly, making as little noise and disturbance as he knew how, his legs brushing easily through blueberry bushes. And in about five minutes he was nearing the corner of Armond's back line.

With the woods and underbrush beyond, Tom could see absolutely nothing of the wagon or Polly Ann, but presently he heard Drew blowing deep, soft breaths in his direction and when he reached out his hand it met the felly of a rear wheel.

"Ma," he said quietly. "It's me."

"I know," she said. "Drew heard you first and then I did. Coming so quiet I knowed it was you."

He said, "There's three men back at the barn. It's the Flanchers, probably. I'm going to lead Drew until we get around the bend and up past Farr's."

He felt his way along the wagon and stroked Drew's shoulder. The old horse blubbered his lips on the back of Tom's hand as he reached for the chin strap, and the wagon started forward with hardly a sound. Tom was glad, now, he had greased the wheels.

They moved on, feeling for the track, turned the corner, and in a minute or two were behind Farr's house once more. Tom couldn't see any light from the kitchen window this time. The hound was quiet, too. There was no sound of his chain. Tom continued leading Drew, though, till they reached the foot of Kehoe's pond and crossed the bridge over Crystal Creek. He felt it was safe to stop for a few minutes then, and he went back along the wagon, telling Polly Ann to hold the lines.

"I want to tie those trunks down," he told her.

He had brought a length of light rope which he passed through the trunk handles, securing the ends to rings on the sides of the wagon bed. And then at last he lit a lantern.

"You think it's safe going with a light?" Polly Ann asked.

"I want to make better time," he said. He hung the lantern on the dashboard hook and for a minute it blinded them, as if the night had suddenly become a room with solid walls around them. But in a moment their eyes became accustomed to the light and then they could see a bit of the road reaching forward from Drew's front hoofs. Drew plainly liked the change, for he started ahead without a word from Tom or a hitch of the lines. They could see each other, too.

"Why don't you put your hat on?" Polly Ann asked him.

"I used it to carry sand and chaft in," he told her. "I shook it, but there's still some left in it."

She gave a sniff. "I'd have thought a boy your age would have sense to turn his hat inside out if he was going to put dirt into it."

"I know, Ma," he said sheepishly. "But there wasn't anything else to carry it in, and I wanted to get away from there."

"Yes," she said, and he could see she was smiling a little. Then she asked what was in both their minds. "Why do you suppose those Flanchers came up to Breen's tonight, Tom?"

"I don't know. I thought they'd started back home. They'd think after the raising we was too tired to do anything but go to bed."

"Maybe they came back just to check up. And when they saw the spring wagon and Drew was gone, they asked the girls."

"We told them to say I'd taken you to the doctor," Tom said.

Polly Ann nodded. "But they didn't believe it. They came up to Breen's instead. Likely, when they don't find anything, they'll go back to our place."

"I was thinking that too," Tom said. "I don't think we should take the money back home."

Polly Ann agreed. "But where could we take it?"

"I was wondering if Billy-Bob Baxter would be up still."

"I don't know," Polly Ann said. "But I've heard he sits up most of the night sometimes."

They were passing through the Irish Settlement. There were no lights at all now, except their own traveling the edge of the road as Drew pulled the wagon in a steady trot. Once a door opened — they could hear the hinge squeak — but whoever looked out didn't have anything to say. Then they were rolling down the steep hill and five minutes later, passing through Forestport.

There were lights in the saloons and Utley's harness shop, but the rest of the buildings were dark. Tom caught sight of a wall clock through the saloon window; he thought it said half past eleven.

"It'll be way past midnight when we get to Boonville," he said.

"Never mind," Polly Ann said. "We'll go to Mr. Baxter's, and if it shows no lights, we'll knock until he comes to his door."

Tom had to agree, for he couldn't think of anything else for them to do.

The mist had left the river. After they crossed the bridge he turned Drew into the Dutch Hill road, and they went up the steep pitch to the canal. They got past the house beside the towpath before anybody came out. But a man yelled after them, wanting to know where they thought they were going this late.

Tom didn't answer. He hoped they had got far enough away so they could not be recognized.

PART SIX

52

Misgivings seized Tom as Drew turned the corner into Leyden Street, his hoofs thumping a loud tattoo on the packed dry dirt. Boonville had gone to bed. The only lighted window they had seen since coming off the towpath opposite the depot was in the front of Dr. Grover's house, no doubt left on for his return from some protracted child-birth on a back farm.

Calling on anybody so late at night didn't seem a proper thing to do, but as they rolled up the street he was reassured to see a light reach out towards the street from a window of the lawyer's little house. Billy-Bob Baxter was undoubtedly still up, working his mind over whatever case he had in hand at the moment. Tom turned Drew into the drive beside the house, so that the wagon was hardly noticeable from the street, and gave Polly Ann the lines to hold while he went up on the front porch and knocked gently on a pane of the office window. He couldn't see Billy-Bob from where he stood, but he heard the scrape of his desk chair being shoved back and presently the lawyer came into view, looking just the way he had before in his worn, shiny jacket and a trail of cigar ash down his waistcoat. He had taken his watch from its pocket and now he was putting it back. When he saw Tom standing outside the window, he nodded and a moment later opened the front door.

"Well, Tom," he said, "must be something on your mind to bring you here this late. I heard you had a barn raising on your place today."

Tom said, yes, they had had one.

"Should have thought that would be enough for one day, even for a strapper like you. But come in and tell me what you want."

Tom didn't go in. He told how he and Polly Ann had decided to go up to the Breen place, and why. And then how the Flanchers had showed up. They'd been lucky to get away.

Billy-Bob looked at him a minute.

"You mean you found something, Tom?"

Tom told him. "Two trunks, not big ones."

"With money into them?"

"We didn't want to stop to look."

"You've got them outside in the wagon? Where anybody can see them?"

"Yes. But it's around the side of the house and Ma's sitting in it."

"Well," Billy-Bob said, almost fussily. "We can't have them out there. You go and lead your horse around to the back and we'll bring the trunks and Polly Ann in through the kitchen. Then put your horse in my barn and come inside yourself."

It took only a few minutes to get the trunks into the kitchen, where Billy-Bob made a jerky little bow towards Polly Ann and said he remembered her when she was no bigger than a shaving, "but mighty pretty you were. And still are, Mrs. Dolan."

Tom went out to lead Drew into the barn. Billy-Bob no longer kept a horse. Tom found some oats in a bin, but they smelled stale and sour, so the old horse would have to go hungry until he got home. Tom told him he was sorry and left him standing there, probably philosophizing on the unreasonableness of people.

Polly Ann and Billy-Bob had moved the trunks into his office and the shades had been pulled down over the windows.

"Let's get them up on my desk," Billy-Bob said.

They showed they had been in the ground. There was some mildew on the leather sides, but they still looked sturdy and the smaller one had wood slats reinforcing it. Both of them were locked.

"Seems a shame to break them," said the lawyer. He pulled open a drawer in his desk and took out a flat box filled with keys. "Ought to be something in this lot to open them up. Here. Try that one, Tom."

It didn't fit the lock of the first trunk at all. It entered the keyhole of the second lock, but Tom couldn't turn it.

"Put it to the side," Billy-Bob said, "and try this one."

None of the first eight keys worked. But with the ninth, Tom gave a twist and saw the hasp move a bit. He got out his jackknife and pried with the blade and the hasp came free. But he hesitated about lifting the lid.

"Open her up," Billy-Bob said impatiently.

Tom obeyed. A piece of muslin cloth covered the top and Polly Ann lifted it. Underneath were bundles and bundles of money, each tied with fine string. Polly Ann's face flushed scarlet, right to her hair, and then turned white, and Tom remembered what she had said about herself and Mr. Hook, and being poor. And then with a sinking feeling he wondered whether they would be entitled to keep any of it.

Billy-Bob Baxter broke the silence with a kind of chortling noise in the back of his nose and said, "Looks like there's quite a pile of money there, if old Bert Breen didn't keep his underwear underneath it."

Tom lifted out a bundle. It seemed to be all ten-dollar bills.

Polly Ann said, "I think we ought to open up the other trunk and then count all the money at once."

"I agree," Billy-Bob said. So they went to trying keys, and the eighteenth or twentieth fitted the second trunk. When Tom heaved up the lid, they saw it was loaded full of money like the first one.

"Well," Billy-Bob said, "let's start counting it."

He gave Polly Ann and Tom each a pad and pencil, telling them to put down the total of each bundle, and put the figure on a strip of paper to go under the string when they tied the money up again. That way none of the bundles could get counted a second time. Then they would put all the totals together and find out how much money the whole lot amounted to.

It took them quite a while. The square black clock with a brass horse on top of it, that stood on the shelf behind the small chunk stove, struck one and then it struck one again for the half hour before they had finished counting. The piles of counted bundles mounted up more than you would have thought from seeing them inside the two trunks. Billy-Bob drew a long breath and got out a big pad of yellow paper and asked Polly Ann to read off the totals of her bundles, putting each one aside as she read it. He jotted down the figures in a column. Then Tom read off the figures for his bundles, and Billy-Bob listed them in a second column. Finally he read off his own pile and made a third column.

After that he added up each column in turn, letting out a soft hissing sound between his teeth. When he was done, he added the three figures, still hissing, and for a long minute he just sat there looking at the complete total while Tom and Polly Ann sat wordlessly watching.

"Well, Tom. By this count you're eight thousand seven hundred seventy-nine dollars richer than you were yesterday when you and Polly Ann went up to Bert Breen's. That doesn't include the loose silver in the bottom of the little trunk, but I don't expect it will amount to any big amount more. The question is, what are you going to do with it?"

Tom couldn't find words to answer. In all the thinking he had done about Breen's money, he hadn't thought of what it might amount to. If he had, he would never have thought of it coming to anything as big as half that amount. He just didn't know how to answer Billy-Bob.

"Well," the lawyer said. "You can't keep it around here. I'm not going to sit on what will come to maybe nine thousand dollars cash money in my house. You've got to get it into the bank."

"I wouldn't want to take it home," Tom answered. "On account of Yantis Flancher."

"I agree. I'll keep it here for tonight. But tomorrow I'll take it down to the bank. I'll hire a rig from Joe Hemphill and aim to deliver it there at nine o'clock, sharp. You be there, too." He chuckled suddenly. "It's going to be worth the whole amount to see Oscar Lambert's face. We won't tell him it's Bert Breen's money. We'll just tell him you had a cash inheritance, Tom. He'll guess. No doubt about it. But he won't bring himself to ask."

"Couldn't we say Tom inherited it from his Great-Uncle Phister?" Polly Ann asked. "That's how I come to name him Tom. Uncle Phister was wealthy. He kept his own carriage, with a hired coachman, too."

"No," Billy-Bob said. "The less lies you tell about something like this, the better. As a matter of fact we won't say it was an inheritance at all. We'll just say Tom came into money." He looked from one to the other with his thin smile. "The less talk about it there is, the better. Now, I suggest we put the money back in the trunks and Tom locks them. And he keeps the keys. You'll unlock them tomorrow in front of Oscar Lambert and he and his teller will have to count it all over again. They can count the silver at the same time. After that, Tom, we can come back here and discuss what you're going to do with it."

They packed it back in the trunks. Tom locked them and put the keys in his pocket and helped Billy-Bob carry the trunks into a closet off the office, the door of which Billy-Bob locked also. Then Tom and Polly Ann went out, got Drew out of the barn, and started home. They hardly had a word to say all the way, except that Polly Ann drew a deep breath after they crossed Fisk Bridge and said, "Oh Tom, it's going to be so different for us now!"

53

Tom had never been in the bank before. While he was saving up his money to buy the barn, he had kept it in a box in the chest of drawers in his bedroom. It hadn't occurred to him to put it in the bank and maybe earn some interest. Neither Chick Hannaberry nor Nob Dolan had ever had money enough in hand to think of banking it. As Polly Ann had said, Chick Hannaberry hadn't ever made as much as ten dollars at one time, and as quick as Nob got a hold of any cash he went off and drank it up. It gave Tom a strange sensation to think he was entering the bank to do business there, the same almost as Erlo Ackerman might do.

Erlo Ackerman had grunted some before he told Tom he could take time off, and then only after Tom explained he had to meet his lawyer at the bank to transact business. Erlo's thick eyebrows had lifted up at that, but he didn't ask any questions. Luckily Mr. Hook had not been in the office at the time, for he would probably have guessed that only one thing could have happened to take Tom to the bank.

Inside the walnut doors with their long glass panels Tom found himself in a place like nothing he had seen before. A counter ran all down one wall but it wasn't like any counter in a store. It had a wall with sort of windows in it, only they had gratings over them like prison windows. Three of them there were, each one with a man behind it. Two said "Teller" across the top of the gratings; the third one had the word "Cashier." Tom couldn't see any real difference in the men behind them, though. They had palish faces and the hands that kept coming out through the openings at the bottom of the gratings were pale too. It wasn't the kind of place he could feel easy in, he thought, though that might be because he didn't know how you went about depositing or drawing money.

Then, to his relief, he saw Billy-Bob Baxter coming through a door at the far end of the room, and Oscar Lambert walked through after him. Even though he had never done any business in the bank, Tom knew who he was, just as everybody in the town of Boonville knew who the president of the bank was. Mr. Lambert always wore a hard black hat on the street and carried an umbrella no matter what the weather was like, and he looked as respectable and solemn as Mr. Vance, the undertaker. He had a pink face like Mr. Vance, too; and he looked as if maybe he fed even better.

Billy-Bob introduced Tom to Mr. Lambert, who said he was pleased to make Tom's acquaintance, which for some reason caused Billy-Bob to grin like a fox finding the henhouse door left open. That seemed to make Mr. Lambert embarrassed, so Tom said he was pleased to meet Mr. Lambert, and they shook hands.

"I think," Mr. Lambert said, "it would be a good idea if we adjourned down to the vault."

On the way to the back of the room he walked over to the cashier's window and said, "Mr. Wynn, will you come down to the vault with us?"

"Is it going to be for long?" Mr. Wynn asked.

"I should think maybe an hour," Oscar Lambert told him.

"Then I'll have a word with Murdock and be right with you."

As they went through the door at the back, Tom saw Mr. Wynn talking to the first teller. It began to seem as if keeping a bank going was a pretty intricate business. But he didn't have much time to think about that because they were going down a flight of stairs, and then Mr. Lambert was working at a complicated kind of knob in the middle of a heavy iron door. It opened after a minute and they went into a dark place with a smell that was strange to Tom, until he decided it might be the smell of money. Perhaps it seemed more noticeable because it was pitch-dark in there until Mr. Lambert had lit a candle and then a handsome kerosene lamp.

The light showed up the walls, which seemed to be made up entirely of metal drawers or boxes. They themselves were standing in a narrow little hall with a small room off to one side that had a table in it and a couple of chairs. On the floor stood his two trunks.

"There's not enough room for us here, Oscar," Billy-Bob said.

"I agree," said Mr. Lambert. "We'll take the trunks to the outside room."

The room at the foot of the stairs had space for a much larger table as well as four chairs. They brought out the trunks just as Mr. Wynn was coming down. He had brought another lamp and when its light joined the first one the place was bright enough for anybody.

The lawyer and the two bankers stood on the far side of the table watching Tom as he unlocked first one trunk and then the other.

"I've told Oscar here," Billy-Bob said, "that you came into this money just as it is."

"It seems a queer way to have money left to you," said Mr. Lambert, skeptically.

Tom didn't know what to say. They were all looking at the stacks of bills.

"I haven't touched none of it," he said. "It's just the way it was."

Oscar Lambert and Mr. Wynn glanced at each other and Tom had an idea they guessed pretty well where the money had come from. But it didn't seem likely that they would refuse to handle it for him. And Billy-Bob said, "Hadn't we better get it counted, Oscar?"

It didn't take anything like as long to count as it had the night before. Tom was filled with astonishment and admiration at the speed with which Mr. Wynn's thin fingers riffled through the bills. It seemed he hardly picked up a bundle before he had put it down again, neatly retied in its string, and jotted down the total on a pad at his side. Oscar worked slower, but he was still very much faster than any of them had been the night before. When they had finished the paper money, the two bankers turned their attention to the coins, which they sorted into piles of quarters and half-dollars and silver dollars. After they had counted these, they added up the combined totals and Mr. Wynn announced that the money came in all to eight thousand eight hundred and fifty dollars.

Then he looked back inside the smaller trunk. He reached a hand in and began poking and prying around the bottom. A moment later he shook the trunk back and forth on the table. They could all hear a faint sound like clinking. Mr. Wynn said, "I bet this has a bottom comes out."

He brought a penknife out of his pocket, opened a blade, and began poking and prying round the edge of the trunk bottom much as Polly Ann had described Dr. Lederer, the dentist, poking and prying around her sore tooth with his pick point.

"Ha," said Mr. Wynn. "I thought so."

He had got the bottom loose and now lifted it out. Underneath it had been placed two brown envelopes.

"Will you take them out, Mr. Dolan?" Oscar Lambert asked.

Tom lifted them out and put them on the table. They seemed heavy.

"You better open them, Tom," Billy-Bob Baxter told him.

So he did, and a number of gold-colored coins spilled out on the table top. What was strange about them was that Mr. Wynn when he had looked at a few of them said they *were* gold.

"That's a twenty-dollar piece," he said, and it was not the size of a twenty-five-cent piece. Not by a long shot.

There weren't a great many of them, but when he and

Oscar Lambert had finished counting them up, Tom's total money amounted to nine thousand, two hundred and forty dollars. Mr. Wynn wrote it out in his small neat writing and put the figures beside the sum: $9,240.00. In all his life Tom had never dreamed there could be as much money as that belonging to anybody.

It put his mind in a kind of blur. He couldn't think how he was going to handle it, and when Oscar Lambert said, "I expect you will want to open a savings account with this," he nodded.

But then when Billy-Bob Baxter said, "That's the best thing, but I think Tom's going to want to draw two or three considerable sums very soon," he nodded again, though at the moment he couldn't think what they might be for, except possibly Billy-Bob's fee, and he didn't have any idea of how considerable that was likely to be.

When Mr. Wynn had gone upstairs to get a bank book, Oscar Lambert repeated what he had said earlier, that it seemed a queer way to have money left to a person — just cash, and in a couple of trunks. Tom nodded a third time, as if words were things he had lost the use of entirely.

Billy-Bob Baxter looked at Tom over the tops of his glasses. He must have seen how things were with Tom, for he answered Oscar. It didn't seem to matter what way you got left a sum of money, he said, just that you got left it at all. Oscar couldn't argue with that and just then Mr. Wynn came back down with some papers and a bank book.

The papers had to be filled in and Tom had to sign his name and Mr. Wynn wrote in the bank book and handed it to Tom. He had never seen one before. It was small, very thin, and blue; and on the cover there was a number in red letters — 67881 — which Mr. Wynn explained was his account number. It was on the inside of the book, too, together with his name, Thomas Dolan, in Mr. Wynn's copperplate writing. The page was divided by red lines and at the top, underneath the account number and his name, Mr. Wynn had made the first entry with the date in the first column on the left. Next it were two columns headed "Interest" and "Withdrawal," which were blank, but in the last one, under "Transaction," Mr. Wynn had entered the sum $9,240.00.

"Be careful of that book, Mr. Dolan," Mr. Wynn said. "Inform us at once if it ever gets lost or is stolen. And it's a good idea to make a note of your account number."

"I've got it in my head," Tom answered to his own surprise, as he pocketed the book. "It's 67881."

Mr. Wynn smiled. Billy-Bob said it was time for him and Tom to be leaving. They shook hands and went up-stairs.

54

Outside on the sidewalk, Billy-Bob said he wanted to talk to Tom about a few things, but Tom said he had to get back to the mill. He had already spent more time than he had asked Erlo Ackerman for. But he said if it was all right he would come to Billy-Bob's office after the mill closed. Billy-Bob agreed to that, but he cautioned Tom not to tell anybody about getting the money.

"Above all, Tom, don't tell *anybody* outside of Polly Ann how much it comes to."

Tom said he wouldn't.

It was all he could do, though, to keep from taking the bank book out of his pocket to look at it, even when he felt certain he was by himself. But once in a while, to reassure himself, he would repeat his account number — 67881.

There were plenty of customers during the morning, but towards noon business slackened, as it generally did, and Tom got his lunch box and joined the Moucheauds and Ox in a sunny corner of the mill, for the day had turned too cool to eat outdoors. The Moucheauds talked mainly about the barn raising, reminding each other of this incident or that with a good deal of laughter. Ox had less to say about it but agreed, when Bancel asked him, that it had gone very well.

"It must have taken you and your ma a good long time to pick up all the mess we left," he said.

Tom said that it had, wondering if his face showed the small amount of sleep he'd had. Even after he and Polly Ann had reached home and gone to bed, it had been hard to fall asleep. The drive up the canal and through Forest-port and the Irish Settlement to Breen's, finding the trunks, the drive back to Boonville and counting the money in Billy-Bob's office went through his mind in order as they had happened in fact. And afterwards he started wondering if the Flanchers had found where Breen had kept his money hidden and whether Yantis had guessed who had been ahead of them, and what he would try to do about it if he had. By the time his mind darked up and shut off for good there was hardly more than an hour left for sleeping.

The girls had been in bed when he and Polly Ann got home, but next morning at breakfast they were full of how three men in a wagon had come to the house the night before and asked for Tom. That is, one of them had come up on the porch. He had light-gray eyes, "pickerel eyes" Ellie said, but Tom didn't trouble to put her straight about that, and she had been afraid to talk to the man through the door. But Cissie-Mae had gone out and told

him Tom had taken Ma to Dr. Grover's a good hour earlier. She didn't know when Tom would bring Ma home.
He had gone back to the wagon without saying anything
else and the three of them had driven off.

If they had gone to Boonville, they had undoubtedly
found out that Dr. Grover was away on a borning case.
That would account just about for the time they had used
up getting to Breen's. The question was what they might
have found there. Tom worried about it off and on all day.
The money was where they couldn't get at it now, but they
could work out ways of getting even with him. He remembered stories of barns burned that they were thought to
have set fire to or the people they had beaten. He didn't
want to think of either one.

Towards the end of the afternoon, though, Joe Hemphill drove down from the depot with an order for his livery
stable, and he had news that lifted quite a load of worry
from Tom's mind. There'd been trouble last night up at
the Widow Breen's, Joe Hemphill said; you might almost
say there had been something like a battle. What started it
was Sol Prichard seeing the Flanchers, all three of them in
their wagon, flogging along the river road from Hawkinsville. Old Sol had been on his way to Forestport, having
run out of gin, and the Flanchers damned near ran him
and his stump-hocked little black mare into the ditch.
They'd kept right on, taking the fork up to the sand flats,
and Sol was upset enough so he turned into Armond's
drive and stopped to tell Parker Munsey about it. He told
Joe later on at McGee's bar in Forestport he thought
everybody on the river road must have been crazy that
night. Parker grabbed a shotgun and went out of the house
like answering a fire and in five minutes him and the two
hands was driving full tilt up to the sand flats by the road

past Armond's pond. Well, Sol said, there wasn't nothing after that to keep him at Parker Munsey's house, so he went on to Forestport, where he told Joe Hemphill all about it.

What had happened up at the Breen place wasn't very clear, but it seemed as though Parker Munsey and the two farmhands must have found the Flanchers there. Joe Hemphill said there must have been some shooting because Enders had been brought to Dr. Grover's office to have some bird shot picked out of his back end. But there was likely some straight-out fighting, too, because later on Parker Munsey went into Doc's office with his wrist broken. He had it in a cast now and was in a holy rage. He had sent for the County Sheriff to arrest the Flanchers for trespass and assault. Sheriff Purley with some deputies was due up from Utica next day; and if they managed to make the arrest, it was figured the Flanchers would end up in jail. If the Sheriff failed to round them up, Mr. Hook pointed out that they'd hardly be likely to make themselves noticeable for quite some time. In any case, Tom decided, he needn't worry about the Flanchers at the moment.

After the mill closed down that evening, he walked up to Billy-Bob Baxter's and found the old man sitting alone in his office.

"Come in," he called, and when Tom entered the office, he told him to sit down. "I don't aim to keep you long."

He got a cigar out of his desk.

"Tom," he said, "perhaps I've got no business telling you what I'm going to say. But I hope to God you're not thinking of all the ways you can spend that money."

The idea that maybe he would start throwing money

around made Tom redden up. He said he had no intention of doing so.

"There's things I ought to get, though," he added.

"What's them?" the lawyer asked.

"Well, now I can pay for it, I want to put new siding on the barn. I've got to have shingles for the roof, anyway, but new siding is something I'd need in the long run, and better to put it on now as long as I can pay for it."

Billy-Bob nodded. "What else?" he asked.

"I always hoped some day I could have a concrete floor in the barn. It seems to me it would make sense to do that now instead of putting in the old wood floor and tearing it up later on."

Billy-Bob was a bit slower nodding than before. "I guess that's so," he said. "What else?"

"Well," Tom answered, "there's some things I'd like to buy for Ma and the girls. Clothes, and such."

"Don't they make their own clothes?" Billy-Bob asked.

"Yes, but they ain't the same thing as a store-bought dress," Tom pointed out. "I'd like for Ma to have one. And a hat and coat, too."

"All right," the lawyer said. "Some clothes for Polly Ann. Anything more?"

Tom couldn't see how it was really Billy-Bob's business what he was planning. But he remembered that the old lawyer had helped him several ways, and it helped him now to go over what he had had in mind to do. It had been in his mind for a long time, from the day he first drove their dinky little cows back to the old shacky barn and realized they weren't as good as other people's cows.

So he told Billy-Bob Baxter about it and how he hoped to buy a couple of Mr. Massey's heifers.

"They'll cost me the same as cows, I calculate," he said. "But when they've grown, I'll have two cows worth a good deal more than that."

"Tom. If you're going for that kind of farm you're going to need machinery."

"I know that. But I can wait a while to pick up some at auctions, and Birdy Morris will help me out with his old mowing machine and plow. There's another thing I'll need — a good young team and a proper lumber wagon."

"That's all going to come to quite a sum of money, Tom. I can't tell just how much, can you?"

"About three thousand dollars," Tom said, and was suddenly astonished at himself at being able to mention such an amount of money in his normal voice. "Of course, I won't spend it all at once."

"I should hope not. But, Tom, it seems to me you've left one item out."

Tom colored up a second time. "That's right, Mr. Baxter. I've got to pay you for what you've been doing for me."

Billy-Bob smiled, put his smoked-out cigar in the blue saucer, and shoved it away from him.

"Oh, I'm not going to charge you very much. I've enjoyed being in on it. And maybe as a man of means, later on, you'll have need for a lawyer. And after all, I'm not the only person's been helping you."

Tom sucked his breath in. "Birdy Morris," he said. He hadn't thought of him before. He'd always taken Birdy for granted, they being friends and all. But Birdy was hardly better off than the Dolans had been only two days ago.

"Exactly," said the lawyer.

"You think I should give him some money?"

"Yes, I do. Without him you wouldn't have been able to move your barn at all, Tom."

"I know. How much do you think I ought to give him?"

"I think that's for you to decide."

Tom drew another breath. "Would five hundred dollars be right, Mr. Baxter?"

"I think that would be fair, Tom."

But Tom had had another thought: "You know, Mr. Baxter. I've got an idea he won't want to take it from me."

"You may be right about that," Billy-Bob said. "So why don't you put it in a savings account for him. You don't need to tell him right away. In fact it might be better not to. He'd be bound to guess you'd found the Breen money, and the less people know about it right now, the better."

"Birdy wouldn't talk about it," Tom said.

"Even so, I'd wait a while. The money would be there in the bank for him anyway, if he got to need it."

Tom agreed, and in his noon hour next day Billy-Bob joined him at the bank to arrange the account for Birdy.

55

Knowing you have money in the bank makes all the difference in how a man feels and thinks, but only somebody like Tom, who had never had anything like that in his life, would know how much the difference amounted to. It wasn't that the work of building the barn up again had changed. He and Birdy worked just as hard. It was the fact that now he could see that certain definite things were going to be in reach in the time ahead. When they were poor, time had to go from one day to the next; the future was a cold gray curtain just ahead and frightening — not because of what might be going to happen beyond, but for what you knew could not happen.

During the first week Birdy came each evening to work at putting up the rafters. The job went quickly because the rafters were all numbered and there was no trouble getting them back in place. They had finished by the end of the week, which was well because of shortening daylight.

Sunday, Tom and Birdy began putting on the roof boards. They spaced them, as people did then, an inch or so apart so a man, working on a roof, had endless toe and finger holds. Again the work went fast. That night they had most of one side boarded over and before Birdy went home he raised the question of ordering shingles. Tom said he'd like to have Birdy join him in the noon hour at Garfield's lumber mill. They would order the shingles then and new undressed pine boards for the siding. Birdy looked thoughtful.

"Where you getting the money, Tom?"

"From the bank," Tom told him.

"In your account?" asked Birdy.

Tom said it was. Birdy looked down at the toes of his shoes for a long minute.

"That would be Bert Breen's money," he said, and Tom, in spite of Billy-Bob's warning, nodded.

After a minute Birdy asked, "Then you found it? In the barn?"

"Me and Polly Ann," Tom said. "The night after the barn raising."

Birdy's mouth curved into a smile. "I'm glad, Tom. It's right you should be the one to get it. I bet Amelie's glad it was you. Bert, too, if it comes to that."

Tom said, "I've put some of it in an account for you, Birdy."

"Pshaw!" Birdy said. "There's no call for you to give me any of it, Tom."

"Yes, there is," Tom said. "You know as well as I do I'd never have got that barn moved down here and set up as far as this without you. I'd never have got it finished, except you helped me. I can't let you do that unless I give you a share of Bert Breen's money."

Birdy looked increasingly embarrassed. But in the end he said, "All right, Tom. As long as it's not too much."

"It's five hundred dollars." Tom said. "Which isn't as much as it ought to be."

"It's as much and half over as I'd have got working for anybody else."

His eyes got a bit watery, but in the end he agreed to accept it, thanking Tom two or three times over, and they made a date to meet at noon next day at Garfield's mill.

56

It was amazing to Tom to watch how quickly the counter clerk at the lumber mill could calculate from the dimensions Birdy provided how many bundles of shingles were needed for the barn roof and the number of board feet of unfinished pine boards for the siding. Then he figured the price, which was high up in three figures, and asking Tom and Birdy to excuse him for a minute, went into the small inner office where Mr. Garfield was sitting in front of his rolltop desk. Birdy leaned on the counter and stared, hissing under his breath, and Tom filled in the time looking around the room, from the calendars on the wall to the corner where the typist, in a white shirtwaist and black skirt, was operating her typewriter. He would have liked to go over and watch the machine work, but it didn't seem to him as if that would be mannerly, so he stayed where he was until someone said, "Mr. Dolan?" close by. Mr. Garfield had come out of his office, followed by his counter clerk, and moved down behind the counter to where Tom and Birdy waited.

"Mr. Dolan," he said again. He seemed to have a little trouble with his throat and had to clear it. "I'm glad to have your order, Mr. Dolan. It's a worthwhile order, too. Very worthwhile, I should say. But it seems, well, kind of large for a man like you."

"What you mean, Joe Garfield," Birdy said in an amiable way, "is you wonder how Tom's going to pay for it."

"Well, er, yes. I suppose that's one way of putting it."

Tom said, "Mr. Lambert at the bank said I was to tell anybody to call him if they thought I might not be able to pay for what I order. Him or Mr. Wynn."

"We'd like to take the shingles with us, Joe," Birdy said. "We can be loading them on my wagon while you telephone the bank."

"Yes, of course," Mr. Garfield said and hustled back into his office where the telephone was on the wall at the corner of his desk.

The counter clerk gave them a slip for the shingles and said they were in Shed 3, and as they went out they could hear the bell of the telephone as Garfield cranked it. When they drove back across the yard with the shingle bundles stacked in the wagon behind them, Mr. Garfield was standing on the steps outside the office door, natty in his dark suit, but looking a bit fussed. He had put a wad of tobacco in his mouth and tried to speak around it but little brown springs bubbled at the corners.

"Your credit's good with me, Mr. Dolan," he called out. "Good as gold. I'm glad to have your business, anytime. When do you want those boards delivered?"

"We'd like them by the end of the week," Tom said, with a glance at Birdy, who nodded.

"They'll be down tomorrow afternoon," Mr. Garfield promised.

Tom said that would be fine. He had almost a friendly feeling for Mr. Garfield now. But Birdy gave a sniff as he drove the team out of the yard and muttered something about a dollar-chewing old goat. At the depot he stopped the horses to let Tom get off and then drove on with the load of shingles. Tom went down to the mill, where three wagons waited at the loading platform. There wasn't much business going on right then, though. People were all talking about Sheriff Purley and his deputies bringing the Flanchers into town and waiting in the baggage room at the depot for the afternoon down train to take them back to Utica. They were in there now. The Sheriff wouldn't let anyone so much as look in through the window, but somebody who had seen them getting off the buckboards said the Flanchers all had handcuffs on their wrists. Joe Hemphill was bound to know the whole story because Sheriff Purley had hired the two rigs from the livery stable. It would be good riddance for the whole region if the Flanchers got even four years.

Whatever time they got in jail, Tom realized, would give him time to finish fixing his barn without having to trouble his mind about them. When the mill closed up he went into the office and said he would like to take two weeks off, starting the next Monday. Erlo agreed it would be a good idea for him to get finished with the barn well before winter. He just wanted to be sure Tom understood that he would be working at the barn on his own time.

PART SEVEN

57

The shingling of the roof went a good deal faster than Tom had supposed it would, even when just he and Birdy were at it in the last hour of daylight. He had never had new lumber of any kind to work with before and it made the job seem a great deal easier. Then on Sunday as he had promised, Mr. Massey turned up with his men. Tom hadn't expected Massey to work himself, but one of his hands had taken sick and he came to fill the man's place.

Massey took his men back in time for milking and Tom and Birdy climbed back onto the roof and nailed on boards for the peak. When they came down at last, they brought the roof ladders with them and then took the other ladders down for the night. After that they had to sit out on the porch for a while to admire the spread of new shingles like red gold in the deepening sunset light — the most impressive sight, Tom thought, that he had ever seen. But it wasn't a patch on how the barn looked when they finished nailing on the new side boards two weeks later. From outside it looked completely new, but Birdy said it was better than a new barn would be, having the frame from Bert Breen's barn.

Two wagons from Garfield's mill had delivered the boards as promised and putting them up gave Tom more satisfaction and pleasure than any other single thing he did in building his barn. Looking at it now from outside, he no longer thought of it as Breen's. It was his, and he had built it where it stood — he and Birdy Morris, that is. Now and then he found himself forgetting the ways Birdy had helped him, as he had forgotten in Billy-Bob's office till the old lawyer reminded him, and the next day at noon he got

Birdy up to the bank so that his savings account could be put in order. When Birdy opened his bank book and put his finger where it said $500.00, he had very little to say beyond the fact that he had never expected to have so much money.

He and Tom discussed what Tom ought to do about flooring the stable. Tom wanted to lay down a cement floor, but Birdy persuaded him that that would take too long.

"You ought to get your critters out of that shed," he pointed out. "It's going to start getting winter cold before long, Tom."

Tom couldn't deny that.

"I think you ought to bring the old flooring down from Breen's," Birdy went on. "When you've got the stanchels up again and built a stall for Drew, then you ought to get that haystack inside the mow. You can work at making your cement floor all during the winter, laying a section at a time."

It made sense. They went up the next Sunday, taking an early start. It was one of those bright October days with ranks of clouds rolling out of the northwest on top of a steady wind. At Breen's nothing had changed as far as Tom could see. The floor timbers did not look as if they had been disturbed, but now Birdy would be bound to see old Bert's hide-hole, so Tom told him how he and Polly Ann had gone down the run in the dark, prying at the timbers with a pinch bar until they found four that hadn't been spiked down. After so many days even he could not tell which ones they were.

They started now methodically prying up the spiked timbers, beginning at the front end, and loading each timber after it came loose and the spikes had been driven back and pulled. When Birdy figured they had as much on the wagon as they ought to ask his old team to haul, they loaded the spring wagon. By then they were well over three quarters of the way down the run, just about to where he had begun that night to think he must be wrong about Bert's hiding place. When they came back for the next timber, Birdy's pinch bar moved it with no effort. So they lifted the next three, too, and looked down into the hole where Bert had kept his trunks of money. It was the first time, come to think, that Tom had seen it, either.

"The old skunk," Birdy said. "He was smarter than a weasel." He looked up at Tom. "I think it would be a good idea, maybe, if we filled up old Bert's hole."

Tom agreed. They had no shovel with them but they found pieces of board and shoved sand in from each edge and walked back and forth on the new sand so, though a depression remained, there was nothing to show anything had been buried there.

58

It took three trips to move down all the floorboards and timbers and the stringers on which the timbers had been spiked. By the end of the week the floor was all down in place in Tom's barn.

It worked out just right because he had hired the Moucheaud brothers to come on Sunday for as long as necessary to put his haystack into the mow. Birdy came with the rack on his wagon and Bancel and Louis worked on the stack. They were like terriers tearing out the hay. When Birdy had enough of a load they came into the barn with him to unload while Tom mowed the hay away. It did not look like so much spread over the mow floor, but it would have been enough to fill their old barn to the rafters. He could see that if he brought in more cows he would have to have a lot more meadowland.

He finished putting up the stanchions that night and the next night he got enough of the stall for Drew built so that he could bring the old horse in. Drew did enough snorting to show he knew that he was in a new place. He rolled his eyes at the low sides of his unfinished stall as Tom led him in. But once in front of the manger he lost no time in plunging his nose into the hay.

Introducing cows into a new barn at night would have been a great deal more difficult. A cow could find as much to scare herself with in nighttime shadows as half a dozen horses, and when you had a bunch of them together they worked on each others' imaginations until panic began to build up faster than compounding interest at a bank. So Tom got away from the mill an hour earlier than usual next evening. The girls had put the cows in the shed after bringing them from pasture and now joined Tom and Polly Ann in herding them into the barn.

It didn't prove as hard as Tom had feared. The cows put their heads through the door all together and then tried to back out. But suddenly Drew whickered from the far end of the barn reassuringly and it took only a switch or two on their backsides to convince them that if it was all right for a horse in that barn it would be all right for them. They trotted ahead and turned to their stanchions in their usual line-up as if they had been using the barn for all of their natural lives.

Polly Ann and the girls had put off milking till Tom could get home, so now they milked together in the lantern light in the new barn while Cissie-Mae went up into the mow and pitched hay down the chute and Ellie gently forked it in front of the cows. They mouthed it slowly and quietly. Behind him Tom heard Drew moving and grumbling in his stall. He felt the cows' heat slowly making warmth in the barn. His heart swelled with the knowledge that the barn stood here complete because of his idea of bringing it down from Breen's. Polly Ann came down behind the cows with her full pail and said softly, "It's nice, Tom. I never milked in any barn so nice." And then, still softly, she said she was going to get supper and called the girls. They went out. The trolleys rumbled on the track as they pulled the door open and closed. Even after he had wrung the teats dry he sat on for a minute, letting his satisfaction soak in, before he got up, blew out one lantern, and took the other from its nail and left, carrying it in one hand and his milk pail in the other.

Supper was ready when he got to the kitchen. Pork chops and hashed-brown potatoes and a pumpkin pie. As the girls took off the dishes and brought a fresh pot of tea, Polly Ann said, "Why don't you give up the notion of putting in the cement floor this winter, Tom? Why don't you wait till next summer to do that? The barn is fine for us, the way it is."

What she said made sense in one way. But he didn't want to give up his concrete floor. He had his barn, as good as a new one, as good as it had been when Bert Breen and Birdy Morris first put it up; but it seemed that when you had a thing you wanted, it always led you on to wanting one thing more. Polly Ann couldn't convince him. It took Birdy to do that.

"One thing you haven't thought about, Tom. You'll need water for mixing your cement. You'll need a lot and you won't want to carry it by the pail from the kitchen pump across the yard, one pail after another. You'd spend more of your time lugging water than you would mixing up cement."

That hadn't occurred to Tom. In winter it was enough of a chore to carry pails of water twice a day for the cows and Drew. Summers, of course, the cows drank from the spring that ran through the near end of their pasture.

"Where'll I get water?" he asked.

"Well," Birdy said. "I been thinking we could put in a box where that spring comes out of the hillside and run a pipe down to a trough inside the barn. Come to think, if the box is high enough we might carry the pipe on into the house so all Polly Ann would have to do would be to turn a faucet, instead of working the pump. But we can't do that in winter."

Tom saw that they couldn't. But it was exciting to think of having water running into the barn — and into the house, for that matter. So he gave up the idea of working on the barn until spring. As matters stood, there was only one thing he still had to do, which was to tear down the Breen house as he had promised Mr. Armond.

59

The sand flats were white and lonely the day he and Birdy drove up. Tom couldn't even see a crow crossing the sky. The Widow Breen's house when they came in sight of it stood gaunt and sad with its sightless windows.

They tied Birdy's team in the leafless brush alongside the road, where there would be a little shelter if a wind started blowing, and walked over to the house carrying their tools and kerosene.

The front door was open, swinging loose on its hinges when the handle of Tom's crowbar bumped against it.

Rain from the broken windows had streaked the walls and floor of the sitting room, and there wasn't a stick of furniture left in it. Somebody had made off with the few pieces that had still been in the house when Tom had come with Sheriff Purley, Joe Hemphill, Doc Considine, and Mr. Vance. It seemed a long time ago, now.

"She used to keep a proud house," Birdy remarked. "She was real choosey about the way things looked."

On the stairs were leavings of a porcupine, as if he had found the climb too steep and tried to ease himself from time to time. The second floor looked the same as downstairs. Everything had been carted off. Tom wondered if the Flanchers hadn't done it, and when he mentioned the idea, Birdy said it probably was them.

Breaking in the roof did not take long. Many of the rafters were half rotten. They smashed down, taking the broken roof boards with them, and as they settled, the smell of bats rose in clouds. Tom choked and Birdy said the attic must have been a summer tabernacle for them. By this time, though, they had all flown off for the winter. Tom wondered whether in the summer nights after Bert died, the Widow Breen had listened to their squeaking and the slither of their wings along the rafters up above.

He had a strange feeling that she knew, somehow, what they were doing, like the last time he had seen her, watching him from her cocoon of shawls and blankets as he came in through her back door. But he had no feeling of her being angry with them, just that she was still looking on. When Birdy said there was no sense in breaking down the floors of the two bedrooms, they had enough holes in them already, made by the money hunters to provide a draft, Tom went down ahead and stepped quickly into the kitchen.

For some reason nobody had taken the settee, perhaps because the mice had eaten into it to make themselves what one might call a hotel for the winter. The stove was still there, too, but so rusted from rain leaking down, it hardly seemed worth saving. Birdy, though, said they should take it out. You hadn't ever ought to throw away good iron. And anyway, some poor family would be glad to get hold of it. So they carried it out by the back door, but Birdy didn't think the pump would be worth trying to take because they had no wrenches to unfasten it from the pipe.

Tom recalled how he had pumped water from it the last time he had been to see the Widow Breen and taken tea with her, and he wanted now to get done with the burning as soon as they could do it.

Birdy said they ought to light two fires, one in the cellar and one in the front hall. The one in the cellar would draft up the stairs into the kitchen. The one in the hall would have the front stairs for its chimney. After a few minutes they would feed each other into a powerful fire.

It worked out exactly that way. They made a pile of laths and floorboards in the cellar and another over it on the ground floor and poured half the kerosene on each. Birdy lighted the one in the cellar and came scuttling up the cellar steps and as soon as he joined Tom, Tom dropped a match onto the kerosene-soaked wood and they went outside.

Both fires caught. In seconds they were roaring. The draft made a single flame come up above the second story like a giant burner flame. In fifteen minutes the walls were blazing; the clapboards, made flimsy by years and years of weathering, disappeared first, leaving the beams and studding like a skeleton of fire, and in a little while the frame started giving way. The burning second floor dropped down in a mass and broke through the ground floor and a cloud of sparks and flame exploded upwards in a roar. After that the fire burned in the cellar, which was like a huge stove of red-hot coals. Tom and Birdy only had to poke odd studs and timbers into the coals. The smaller pieces wriggled like snakes and turned suddenly into white ash that disappeared on the upward draft of red-hot air.

They stopped a while to eat their lunch. There wasn't much for them to do afterwards, but they stayed until all the timbers had turned to coals. They went back to Birdy's wagon then, turned the horses onto the road, and started home. Halfway to the hill over the river valley, it began to snow, not hard, just scattered flakes floating down in the still air.

60

The snow that began softly the day Tom and Birdy burned down the Widow Breen's house during the night became a heavy storm. Ten inches of snow covered the ground next morning. They were forerunners of another deep-snow winter.

Christmas came again, and it was like old times, sitting in the parlor, with the stove muttering at one side of the room as it felt its draft, and the balsam tree decked out with paper chains and cones and snowflakes that had gone on from year to year. Birdy and Tom reminded each other of things that had happened when they were taking down the barn, like their meetings with the Flanchers, now temporarily in jail. It was like old times, but it was different, too.

For one thing there were more presents than there used

to be. The girls were wearing new dresses and each of them had bought a necktie to give Birdy. He had never worn one and had no idea how to tie it, so the girls had to show him, Cissie-Mae making the knot with her arms around his neck while Ellie held a mirror in front so he could see how it was done, both the girls giggling and taking on and Birdy flushing up because of the attention.

Then he tried tying it himself, and that made the girls laugh more and tease him. Even Polly Ann, coming in to see what the commotion was about, had to smile. But in spite of all, he managed to get the knack and looked at himself in the mirror with a bashful kind of grin. The tie was from Ellie, so Cissie-Mae said he must try hers on and see how it looked. But he wouldn't do it, and Polly Ann told the girls not to pester any more. It was about then Mr. Hook drove into the yard in his cutter.

Tom put the gray horse in the barn, and the men went back into the house to find dinner being carried to the table. Polly Ann had bought a turkey bird. She put it down on the table in front of Tom with the kitchen fork and Chick Hannaberry's butcher knife, which he had used in cutting up deer and carving off the venison steaks long ago. It was so old that it had worn down almost to razor shape with an edge near as thin. Tom picked it up with the fork and then stood face on to the big brown bird. He had never cut up anything like that and suddenly suggested maybe Mr. Hook would know how to do it right. But Polly Ann would not hear of it. She said Tom was in his own place and head of the family, with a fine new barn and all, and Mr. Hook agreed.

"It's just the same as carving a roasting chicken," he said. "Only bigger."

Tom felt his face heat up.

"All right," he said to Mr. Hook. "But if you see me going wrong, just tell me."

He made out pretty well and Mr. Hook said it was just a matter of getting accustomed to it. He stayed on into the afternoon till Polly Ann brought in tea in the pot Tom had given her a year ago. Birdy Morris had left for his own place by then and Mr. Hook said, "Most everybody knows you have come into money, Tom. It's no affair of mine where it came from or how much it is. But if you'll tell me, I'd like to know how you plan to use it."

Tom thought for a minute. He didn't like to go on leaving Mr. Hook with the wrong idea of where the money came from. Polly Ann might tell him when she wasn't thinking, and it seemed better for him to do so first. So he said the money had been in Bert Breen's barn and he told Mr. Hook what it amounted to and how he wanted to put a concrete floor in the barn, like Mr. Massey's. He said he wanted to start getting better cows than their little Swiss ones, and how he had to find a team of horses and a lumber wagon and some machinery.

"With more cows, you're going to need more land," Mr. Hook said.

There was a piece along the river, Tom told him, in front of their place, near eighteen acres. It belonged to Walt Sweeney, but he hadn't worked it for years. Tom figured to buy that to start with. He'd offer eight, maybe ten, dollars an acre, which was a good price.

Mr. Hook agreed. But he asked, "Are you sure you want to get into farming, Tom? You couldn't keep on at the mill and work a real farm at the same time."

Tom realized that. But he wanted to have a going farm.

"Grandpa never even had a house was his own. People around here didn't think anything of the Hannaberry family. They didn't think any better of my pa, when it comes to that. I want to make the Dolan place a paying farm. When it does pay, I'm going to put our name up on the barn. DOLAN FARM. Up to now nobody, Hannaberrys nor Dolans, ever did a lick of work if they could help it. Except Ma. I want people to start thinking different. Working in the mill they wouldn't see it."

"That isn't altogether true," Mr. Hook said mildly. "But I agree it would take longer for people to realize. If you've made your mind up, Tom, stick to it. Now, about a team of horses, I heard a couple of days ago about a handy pair coming on sale in Utica. About eleven hundred or twelve hundred pounds. Handy and quick. I have to go down tomorrow and I thought maybe you'd like to come with me."

It took Tom's breath to think of maybe buying a team of his own. He couldn't answer for a minute; but then he said he'd like to go if he could get the time off from the mill. Mr. Hook assured him it would be all right and told him to draw a hundred dollars from the bank for a down payment if he decided to get the horses.

61

They took the morning southbound train. Tom hadn't been on the railroad before. He sat beside the window at Mr. Hook's suggestion. It was astonishing the way the land flashed back. When woods came close to the tracks, he could hardly see the trees. They made a blur in his eyes. Up ahead he could hear the engine, whistling at each farm road crossing the tracks. It didn't seem possible the train could stop itself. But it slowed down, all right, and came to a halt right at Alder Creek Station. By the time they reached Utica, he could see that there was really nothing to it.

They walked four blocks to where the horse dealer had his barn. Inside the door there were a couple of rooms built in, one of them for the handlers and the other was the dealer's office, with a stove burning in it and a desk where a man in a brown coat and a black derby hat was sitting. Mr. Hook walked in and said, "Al, I've brought my friend who might be interested in buying that team."

Al turned around and got out of his chair. He shook hands with Mr. Hook, who said, "This is Tom Dolan, Al Rathbun."

They shook hands, too.

"You want a farm team, George tells me."

Tom said he was thinking of buying one.

"Well," said Mr. Rathbun. "I've got just the pair for you. They are Vermont-bred, eleven-eighty and twelve-ten pounds, own sister and brother. I'll bet you fancy them."

It turned out that Tom did.

The minute the horse handler led them from their stalls Tom saw they were a perfect match. Dark bay, both, with black manes and tails and black feet, the fetlocks neat, with none of the shagginess some workhorses showed. The mare had a small white star on her forehead, the horse a sliver of white between his nostrils. They stood just over sixteen hands, he judged. They looked sound, as far as he could see, and Al Rathbun assured him this was so. Mr. Hook nodded.

Tom asked their names.

"Dan and Molly," Al Rathbun said. "They're four and six."

"What's the price, Mr. Rathbun?"

"Four hundred dollars," the dealer said. "But for a friend of George's here, I'll make it three seventy-five."

"I'll buy them," Tom said. "I can give you a hundred dollars down."

"That's fine with me," the dealer said. "Any friend of George's."

He said he was taking several horses north by rail on Saturday. If Tom could meet the late afternoon freight he would unload them there and take the balance of the money. He asked if Tom would be interested in buying a set of harness that had come with them.

"It ain't brand-new but sound. It would black up handsome."

Tom agreed to his price. It was a good deal less than a new harness would cost, and he wouldn't have to fuss with breaking in new collars.

As he and Mr. Hook were leaving, Al Rathbun had a final word. "They go better hitched with the mare as the nigh horse. She's the steady one."

Tom could see this was so when the horses were being led down out of the boxcar Saturday evening. Molly managed it without any fuss where Dan, even though he had seen her go down ahead, had to be coaxed down step by step. He didn't act mean, but you could see that he felt nervy.

Tom had brought Ellie with him to sit in the back of the sleigh and keep an eye on the horses as they were led home. She had a calmer way with animals than Cissie-Mae did. She sat facing backwards and when she talked to them, both horses pointed their ears. She spoke as the sleigh turned into the yard so Dan and Molly trotted in behind with their ears up, and Tom doubted if there was a better-looking team in the county. Polly Ann and Cissie-Mae came out to admire them and the girls led them into the barn.

"I can't hardly wait till we get a wagon," Polly Ann said at supper, "so we can drive up to town and show the team off."

62

It was Ox Hubbard who put Tom in the way of buying his wagon. One day at noon, he gave Tom a catalogue from Sears and Roebuck. Tom had seen the thick catalogues before, once in a while, but they were too old to bother reading from and not kept where the light was good, anyway. But that night at the kitchen table, he opened up the one Ox had given him, with Polly Ann and the girls looking over his shoulder. Where he opened it there happened to be a picture of a lumber wagon. Three other wagons were pictured, but right away he knew the first was the one he had to have. He pointed it out to the girls and they agreed it would be just the thing. Cissie-Mae read the description printed underneath: green sideboards with yellow striping, and red wheels.

He marked the page by turning down the corner. There was no hurry about ordering, though the catalogue said to allow three weeks for delivery. Two, maybe three more months of snow were due, so he didn't send in the order for the wagon until the end of February. It took longer than three weeks to arrive. Then one morning at the end of March Mr. Hook called him into the mill office to take a telephone call. It was the freight office at the depot, telling him a lumber wagon had arrived addressed to him and would he call for it as soon as possible.

He brought the team up next morning in their harness with a yoke fastened to their neck straps, riding Molly. The horses seemed to enjoy going up the road abreast with no wagon to haul. For horses of their weight they moved very quickly. It was only quarter after seven when they reached the freight office, and there was the wagon beside the loading platform looking just as the catalogue had described it.

The freight agent came out of his office with receipt slips for Tom to sign. He had a monkey wrench in his free hand.

"Reckon you'll need this," he said, "to put the pole and eveners on. Most folks don't think to bring a wrench when they're getting a wagon by freight. Not anyways if it's the first time. That's a likely pair of horses you got there."

Tom said he had bought them in Utica after Christmas. He paid the freight charge and drove the team down to the mill. They would have to stand in the shed till closing time, but before he could unhitch them from the wagon, Ox Hubbard, the Moucheaud brothers, Mr. Hook, and even Erlo Ackerman came out to look them over. There was a long discussion as there always is when anybody shows up with a new team but general agreement that Tom had done well for himself. Ox declared he didn't think there was another pair of horses in Boonville to match them.

63

All that was left for Tom to do to complete his deal for the Breen barn was taking Mr. Armond the balance of his money. He waited till he learned from Parker Munsey at the mill that the Armonds had returned from the city. He drew twenty-five dollars out of the bank and on Sunday afternoon, about an hour after they had finished lunch, he hitched Molly and Dan to the lumber wagon.

Polly Ann went with him. The girls had wanted to come, too, but he had vetoed that. They would be coming only out of curiosity. He would have preferred it if his mother had stayed home, for that matter. As he saw it, this was a business call which concerned nobody but himself and Mr. Armond. But when she told him she would like to drive up to Armond's with him, he couldn't refuse her. He remembered the way she had helped him keep up his nerve when moving the timbers and setting them up on their place had all of a sudden seemed too big a job for him ever to carry through. Thinking back, he could see how she had stood with him on the whole deal, all the way from the day he had first told her his notion to get the barn until the night they drove up to the Breen place and found the money.

"I won't get off the wagon, Tom," she told him, after they had got started. "It's just I'd like to drive in there for once without having to peddle something."

He had an idea the way her mind was going, recollecting the times she had told about Chick Hannaberry driving into the place with her sisters and herself and how she had had to go up on the kitchen porch to the back door with a five-gallon pail of red raspberries, or blackberries, or whatever kind of berry they had been picking — a little girl in a ragged dirty dress and bare legs still showing bloody scratches from the berry vines, looking up when the hired girl fetched Mrs. Armond but not able to say a thing. Well, he thought, glancing sideways at her sitting on the high wagon seat beside him, you'd hardly believe she had ever been that little shabby girl.

She had put on her best dress, dark green with rose-pink stripes that had little red and yellow flowers printed on them, and over it a short black coat. She wore a small black straw hat she had decorated herself with green ribbons and a green velvet rose, and a tiny fan of partridge feathers. It was cocked a little to the left side of her head, but she sat straight up on the seat, her hands folded in her lap. She looked ladylike, Tom thought, but that wasn't quite the word for her, either. Dainty, maybe. Yet he knew how strong she was. Tougher than whiteleather, as Birdy Morris would say, when she had to be. He turned suddenly hot, having a vision of her standing in front of Nob Dolan, his father, a big heavy-set man by what he had heard and vaguely remembered.

She turned her head just then, as if his thought had touched her, and smiled.

"You do look fine, Tom."

Tom was wearing a suit. They had ordered it long ago from Sears and Roebuck, about the time they had sent in the order for the lumber wagon. This was the first time he had had it on, except in the house. It was pepper-and-salt pattern and he also wore a shirt and necktie. The shirt was white with black stripes quite far apart and the necktie was dark blue. He had felt stiff and queer putting it on and going out to hitch up the team, but now they were away from home he felt more natural in it, especially after what Polly Ann had said.

Mr. Armond was sitting on the front piazza of the big house the way he had been sitting the first time Tom came. As soon as they got up to where the lawns started, his eyes showed bright, hard blue, the same as they had the first time, but there was a questioning look in them, so Tom realized that Mr. Armond didn't recognize who he was. That made Tom feel good inside. Having things happen bit by bit you didn't realize how big the changes were. He gave Polly Ann the lines to hold and got down off the wagon.

"I'm Tom Dolan," he said, starting across the lawn. "I've come to pay the balance I owe you for Breen's barn."

He could tell that Mr. Armond was really surprised, but then it was plain that he now recognized Tom after all; and he got up from his chair and held out his hand and shook Tom's.

"It's nice to see you again, Tom," he said. And Tom said he was glad to see Mr. Armond.

He reached into his pants pocket and brought the money out, five new five-dollar bills fresh out of the bank.

Mr. Armond took them and put them in his wallet, and then he looked out at the team and wagon, and Polly Ann on the seat, holding the lines.

"Is that your mother?" he asked.

Tom said it was.

"Won't she come in?" Mr. Armond said. "My wife's just going to have tea."

Polly Ann had overheard.

"Thank you, Mr. Armond," she said. "But we ought to

be getting back home. Working in the mill weekdays means Sunday is Tom's busy day on our farm."

"I see," Mr. Armond said. "If you wait a minute, Tom, I'll write out your receipt."

Tom waited on the piazza. Polly Ann smiled at him and drove the horses around the house, crossing the bridge and turning them in the yard in front of the carriage barn. By the time Mr. Armond came out of the house with Tom's receipt she was pulling them up in front of the walk, headed for home.

Mr. Armond walked out with Tom to the driveway. He looked the team over and said they were a smart-looking pair.

"I wouldn't mind having a team like them myself."

Then he looked up at Polly Ann on the wagon seat and asked if she and her family had had a good winter.

She colored up a little, for she had seen his eyes taking in not only Molly and Dan but the wagon and Tom's suit and herself, too.

"Why yes, Mr. Armond," she told him, and added straight out, "it was the best winter we ever had."

Mr. Armond looked as if he were going to ask something else, but he seemed to change his mind, shook hands with Tom, and wished them well.

"You've got a fine son, Mrs. Dolan," he said.

"Why yes, Mr. Armond," she said again, giving him her widest smile. "I believe I have."

Tom climbed over the wheel, his face reddening, and took the lines from his mother.

Later, when Tom pulled the team up in the yard, the late afternoon sun was on the barn. Looking up at the mow door, he remembered how he and Birdy had stood there while the Widow Breen stood opposite on her front porch, pointing her shotgun at his midriff. The recollection was so vivid that he turned quickly to their own kitchen porch to be sure she was not standing on it, but she wasn't. It wasn't her barn now. It was his — absolutely. He didn't have to go around like a low-down Dolan any more. It came suddenly into his mind that the Widow Breen had told that to him long ago.